BEYOND THE PALE

Also by William Trevor

William Trevor

BEYOND THE PALE

and other stories

The Viking Press   New York

Published in 1982 by The Viking Press
625 Madison Avenue, New York, N.Y. 10022

Library of Congress Cataloging in Publication Data
Trevor, William, 1928–
Beyond the pale, and other stories.
I. Title.
PR6070.R4B4   823′.914   81-52221
ISBN 0-670-16115-2   AACR2

Grateful acknowledgment is made to the following, who published these stories originally: *Antaeus:* "Being Stolen From"; *The Bodley Head:* "Mr Tennyson" (originally titled "The Real Thing" from *The Real Thing: Seven Stories of Love* edited by Peggy Woodford); *Encounter:* "The Blue Dress" and "The Teddy-bears' Picnic"; *London Magazine:* "Mulvihill's Memorial"; *The New Yorker:* "Beyond the Pale," "The Bedroom Eyes of Mrs Vansittart," "Downstairs at Fitzgerald's," and "Autumn Sunshine"; *Macmillan, London:* "The Time of Year" (from *Winter's Tales 26*, edited by A. D. Maclean); *The Observer (London):* "Sunday Drinks"; *The Times (London):* "The Paradise Lounge."

Printed in the United States of America

Set in Plantin

CONTENTS

The Bedroom Eyes of
Mrs Vansittart

'You couldn't trust those eyes,' people on Cap Ferrat say, for
they find it hard to be charitable where Mrs Vansittart is
concerned. 'The Wife Whom Nobody Cares For,' Joe-John
remarks, attaching a tinselly jangle to the statement, which
manages to suggest that Mrs Vansittart belongs in neon
lights.

At fifty-four, so Joe-John has remarked as well, she remains
a winner and a taker, for in St Jean and Monte Carlo young
men still glance a second time when the slim body passes
by, their attention lingering usually on the rhythmic hips.
Years ago in Sicily – so the story is told – a peasant woman
spat at her. Mrs Vansittart had gone to see the Roman ruins
at Segesta, but what outraged the peasant woman was to
observe Mrs Vansittart half undressed on the grass, permitting a local man to have his way with her. And then, as
though nothing untoward had happened, she waited at the
railway station for the next train to Catania. It was then that
the woman spat at her.

Mrs Vansittart is American, but when she divides her
perfect lips the voice that drawls is almost that of an English
duchess. Few intonations betray her origins as a dentist's
daughter from Holland Falls, Virginia; no phrase sounds
out of place. Her husband, Harry, shares with her that
polished Englishness – commanded to, so it is said on Cap
Ferrat, as he is commanded in so much else. Early in their
marriage the Vansittarts spent ten years in London, where
Mrs Vansittart is reported to have had three affairs and

sundry casual conjunctions. Harry, even then, was writing his cycle of songs.

The Vansittarts live now in the Villa Teresa just off the Avenue du Sémaphore, and they do not intend to move again. Their childless marriage has drifted all over Europe, from the hotels of Florence and Berlin to those of Château d'Oex and Paris and Seville. To the Villa Teresa the people from the other villas come to play tennis twice a week. In the evening there is bridge, in one villa or another.

Riches have brought these people to Cap Ferrat, riches maintain them. They have come from almost all the European countries, from America and other continents. They have come for the sun and the bougainvillaea, purchasing villas that were created to immortalise the personalities of previous owners – or building for themselves in the same whimsical manner. The varying styles of architecture have romance and nostalgia in common: a cluster of stone animals to remind their owners of somewhere else, a cupola added because a precious visitor once suggested it. Terracotta roofs slope decoratively, the eyes of emperors are sightless in their niches. Mimosa and pale wistaria add fairy-tale colour; cypresses cool the midday sun. Against the alien outside world a mesh of steel lurks within the boundary hedges; stern warnings abound, of a *Chien Méchant* and the ferocious *Sécurité du Cap*.

In her middle age Mrs Vansittart's life is one of swimming-pools that are bluer than the blue Mediterranean, and titles which recall forever a mistress or a lover, or someone else's road to success, or an obsession that remains mysterious: Villa Banana, Villa Magdalene, Morning Dew, Waikiki, Villa Glorietta, Villa Stephen, So What, My Way. The Daimlers and the Bentleys slide along the Boulevard Général de Gaulle, cocktails are taken on some special occa-

sion in the green bar of the Grand-Hotel. The Blochs and the
Cecils and the Borromeos, who play tennis on the court at
the Villa Teresa, have never quarrelled with Mrs Vansittart,
for quarrels would be a shame. Joe-John is her partner: her
husband plays neither tennis nor bridge. He cooks instead,
and helps old Pierre in the garden. Harry is originally of
Holland Falls also, the inheritor of a paper-mill.

The Villa Teresa is as the Vansittarts wish it to be now;
and as the years go by nothing much will change. In the
large room which they call the salon there is the timeless
sculptured wall, a variety of colours and ceramic shapes.
There are the great Italian urns, the flowers in their vases
changed every day; the Persian rugs, the Seurat, and the
paper-weights which Harry has collected on his travels.
Carola and Madame Spad come every day, to dust and clean
and take in groceries. The Villa Teresa, like the other villas,
is its own small island.

*

'Ruby, don't you think it's ridiculous?' Mrs Vansittart said a
month or so ago. 'Don't you, Joe-John?'

Mrs Cecil inclined her head. Joe-John said:

'I think that sign they've put up is temporary.'

'If they spell it incorrectly now they'll do it again.'

Two tables of bridge were going, Mrs Cecil and Signor
Borromeo with Joe-John and Mrs Vansittart at one, the
Blochs, Signora Borromeo and Mr Cecil at the other. In the
lull halfway through the evening, during which Harry
served tea and little pâtisseries which he made himself, the
conversation had turned to the honouring of Somerset
Maugham: an avenue was to be named after him, a sign
had gone up near the Villa Mauresque, on which, un-

fortunately, his surname had been incorrectly spelt.

'Then you must tell them, my dear,' urged Joe-John, who liked to make mischief when he could. 'You must go along and vigorously protest.'

'Oh, I have. I've talked to the most awful little prat.'

'Did he understand?'

'The stupid creature argued. Harry, that's a polished surface you've put your teapot on.'

Harry snatched up the offending teapot and at once looked apologetic, his eyes magnified behind his horn-rimmed spectacles. Harry isn't tall but has a certain bulkiness, especially around the waist. His hands and feet are tiny, his mouse-coloured hair neither greying nor receding. He has a ready smile, is nervous perhaps, so people think, not a great talker. Everyone who comes to the villa likes him, and sympathises because his wife humiliates him so. To strangers he seems like a servant about the place, grubbily on his knees in the garden, emerging from the kitchen regions with flour on his face. Insult is constantly added to injury, strangers notice, but the regular tennis-companions and bridge-players have long since accepted that it goes rather further, that Harry is the creature of his wife. A saint, someone once said, a Swedish lady who lived in the Villa Glorietta until her death. Mrs Cecil and Mrs Bloch have often said so since.

'Oh, Harry, look, it *has* marked it.'

How could she tell? Mrs Cecil thought. How could it be even remotely possible to see halfway across the huge salon, to ascertain through the duskiness – beyond the pools of light demanded by the bridge tables – that the teapot had marked the top of an escritoire? Mrs Cecil was sitting closer to the escritoire than Mrs Vansittart and couldn't see a thing.

'I think it's all right,' Harry quietly said.

'Well, thank God for that, old thing.'

'Delicious, Harry,' Mrs Cecil murmured quickly, commenting upon the pâtisseries.

'Bravo! Bravo!' added Signor Borromeo, in whom a generous nature and obesity are matched. He sampled a second cherry tart, saying he should not.

'We were talking, Harry,' Mrs Vansittart said, 'of the Avenue Somerset Maugham.'

'Ah, yes.'

He pressed the silver tray of pâtisseries on Signora Borromeo and the Blochs, a wiry couple from South Africa. '*Al limone?*' Signora Borromeo questioned, an index finger poised. Signora Borromeo, though not as stout as her husband, is generously covered. She wears bright dresses that Mrs Vansittart regards with despair; and she has a way of becoming excited. Yes, that one was lemon, Harry said.

'I mean,' Mrs Vansittart went on, 'it wouldn't be the nicest thing in the world if someone decided to call an avenue after Harry and then got *his* name wrong.'

'If somebody —' Mr Cecil began, abruptly ceasing when his wife shook her head and frowned at him.

'No, no one's going to,' Mrs Vansittart continued in a dogged way, which is a characteristic of hers when her husband features in a conversation. 'No, no one's going to, but naturally it could happen. Harry being a creative person too.'

'Yes, of course,' said Mrs Cecil and Mrs Bloch swiftly and simultaneously.

'It's not outside the bounds of possibility,' added Mrs Vansittart, 'that Harry should become well known. His cycle is really most remarkable.'

'Indeed,' said Joe-John.

No one except Mrs Vansittart had been permitted to hear

the cycle. It was through her, not its author, that the people of the villas knew what they did: that, for instance, the current composition concerned a Red Indian called Foontimo.

'No reason whatsoever,' said Joe-John, 'to suppose that there mightn't be an Avenue Harry Vansittart.'

He smiled encouragingly at Harry, as if urging him not to lose heart, or at least urging something. Joe-John wears a bangle with his name on it, and a toupé that most remarkably matches the remainder of his cleverly dyed hair. Sharply glancing at his lip-salve, Mrs Vansittart said:

'Don't be snide, Joe-John.'

'Someone's bought La Souco,' Mrs Cecil quickly intervened. 'Swiss, I hear.'

Harry gathered up the tea-cups, the bridge recommenced. While the cards at his table were being dealt, Joe-John placed a hand lightly on the back of one of Mrs Vansittart's. He had not meant to be snide, he protested, he was extremely sorry if he had sounded so. The apology was a formality, its effect that which Joe-John wished for: to make a little more of the incident. 'I wouldn't hurt poor Harry for the world,' he breathlessly whispered as he reached out for his cards.

It was then, as each hand of cards was being arranged and as Harry picked up his tray, that a bell sounded in the Villa Teresa. It was not the telephone; the ringing was caused by the agitating of a brass bell-pull, in the shape of a fish, by the gate of the villa.

'Good Lord!' said Mrs Vansittart, for unexpected visitors are not at all the thing at any of the villas.

'I would not answer,' advised Signor Borromeo. '*Un briccone!*'

The others laughed, as they always do when Signor Borromeo exaggerates. But when the bell sounded again, after only a pause of seconds, Signora Borromeo became excited. '*Un briccone!*' she cried. '*In nome di Dio! Un briccone!*'

Harry stood with his laden tray. His back was to the card-players. He did not move when the bell rang a third time, even though there was no servant to answer it. Old Pierre comes to the garden of the Villa Teresa every morning and leaves at midday. Carola and Madame Spad have gone by five.

'We'll go with you, Harry,' the wiry Mr Bloch suggested, already on his feet.

Mr Cecil stood up also, as did Joe-John. Signor Borromeo remained where he was.

Harry placed the tray on a table with a painted surface – beneath glass – of a hunting scene at the time of Louis XIV. Nervously, he shifted his spectacles on his nose. 'Yes, perhaps,' he said, accepting the offer of companionship on his way through the garden to the gate. Signora Borromeo fussily fanned her face with her splayed cards.

It was Joe-John who afterwards told of what happened next. Mr Bloch took charge. He said they should not talk in the garden just in case Signor Borromeo was right when he suggested that whoever sought entry was there with nefarious purpose. He'd had experience of intruders in South Africa. Each one caught was one less hazard to the whole community: the last thing they wanted was for a criminal to be frightened away, to bide his time for another attempt. So as the bell rang again in the villa the four marched stealthily, a hand occasionally raised to smack away a mosquito.

The man who stood at the gate was swarthy and very small. In the light that went on automatically when the gate was opened he looked from one face to the next, uncertain about which to address. His glance hovered longer on

Harry's than on the others, Joe-John reported afterwards, and Harry frowned, as if trying to place the man. Neither of them appeared to be in the least alarmed.

'It is arranged,' the man said eventually. 'I search for Madame.'

'Madame Spad is not here,' Harry replied.

'Not Madame Spad. The Madame of the villa.'

'Look here, my old chap,' Mr Cecil put in, 'I doubt that Madame Vansittart is expecting you.' Mr Cecil is not one to make concessions when the nature of an occasion bewilders him, but it was Joe-John's opinion that the swarthy visitor did not look like anyone's old chap. He thought of saying so, *sotto voce*, to Mr Bloch, but changed his mind.

'Better,' he advised the man instead, 'to telephone in the morning.'

'My wife is playing bridge tonight,' Harry explained. 'It's no time to come calling.'

'It is arranged,' the man repeated.

In a troop, as though conveying a prisoner, they made their way back through the garden. The man, although questioned further by Mr Bloch, only shrugged his shoulders. No one spoke after that, but similar thoughts gathered in each man's mind. It was known that old Pierre would shortly be beyond it: after tennis one evening Mrs Vansittart had relayed that information to her friends, enquiring if any of them knew of a younger gardener. What would seem to have happened was that this present individual had telephoned the villa and been told by Mrs Vansittart to report for an interview, and now arrived at ten o'clock in the evening instead of the morning. When they reached the villa Mr Cecil began to voice these conclusions, but the man did not appear to understand him.

He was placed in the hall, Joe-John and Mr Bloch guarding him just to be on the safe side. The others re-entered the salon and almost immediately Mrs Vansittart emerged. As she did so, Joe-John took advantage of the continuing interruption in order to go to the lavatory. Mr Bloch returned to the salon, where Harry picked up his tray of tea things and proceeded with it to the kitchen.

'I told you not to come here,' Mrs Vansittart furiously whispered. 'I had no idea it could possibly be you.'

'I tell a little lie, Madame. I say to the men there is arrangement.'

'My God!'

'This morning I wait, Madame, and you do not appear.'

'Will you kindly keep your voice down.'

'We go in your kitchen?'

'My husband is in the kitchen. I could not come this morning because I did not wake up.'

'I am by the lighthouse. It is time to fix the table-cloths but I stand by the lighthouse. How I know you ever come?'

'You could have telephoned, for God's sake,' whispered Mrs Vansittart, more furiously than before. 'All you had to do was to pick up the damn telephone. I was waiting in all day.'

'Yes, I pick up the damn telephone, Madame. You husband answer, I pick it down again. All the time Monsieur Jean watch me. "It is no good this time to fix the table-cloths!" he shout when I come running from the lighthouse. My hand make sweat on the table-cloths. I am no good, he shout, I am bad waiter, no good for Grand-Hotel –'

'I cannot talk to you here. I will meet you in the morning.'

'This at the lighthouse, Madame?'

'Of course at the lighthouse.'

All this Joe-John heard through the slightly open lavatory door. It was not, he recognised at once, a conversation that might normally occur between Mrs Vansittart and a prospective gardener. As he passed through the hall again his hostess was saying in a clenched voice that of course she would wake up. She would be at the lighthouse at half-past six.

'He's a waiter from the Grand-Hotel,' Joe-John reported softly in the salon, but not so softly that the information failed to reach anyone present. 'They're carrying on in the mornings at the lighthouse.'

*

Signor Borromeo won that night, and so did Mrs Cecil. At a quarter to twelve Harry carried in a tray with glasses on it, and another containing decanters of cognac and whisky, and bottles of Cointreau, cherry brandy and yellow Chartreuse. He drank some Cointreau himself, talking to Mrs Cecil and Mrs Bloch about azaleas.

'Harry dear, you've dribbled that stuff all over your jacket!' Mrs Vansittart cried. 'Oh, Harry, really!'

He went to the kitchen to wipe at the stain with a damp cloth. 'Hot water, Harry,' his wife called after him. 'Make sure it's really hot. And just a trace of soap.'

He'd had a bad day, she reported when he was out of earshot. In his Red Indian song Foontimo's child-wife – the wife who was not real but who appeared to Foontimo in dreams – continued to be elusive. Harry couldn't get her name right. He had written down upwards of four hundred names, but not one of them registered properly. For weeks poor Harry had been depressed over that.

While they listened they all of them in their different ways disliked Mrs Vansittart more than ever they had before. Even Joe-John, who had so enjoyed eavesdropping at the lavatory door, considered it extravagantly awful that Mrs Vansittart's seedy love life should have been displayed in front of everyone, while Harry washed up the dishes. Mrs Bloch several times tightened her lips during Mrs Vansittart's speech about the difficulties Harry was having with his creation of an Indian child-wife; her husband frowned and looked peppery. It was really too much, Mrs Cecil said to herself, and resolved that on the way home she'd suggest dropping the Vansittarts. There were all kinds of people in this world, Signor Borromeo said to himself, but found that this reflection caused him to like Mrs Vansittart no more. A *cornuto* was one thing, but a man humiliated *in pubblico* was an unforgivable shame. Harry was *buono*, Signora Borromeo said to herself, Harry was like a *bambino* sometimes. Mr Cecil did not say anything to himself, being confused.

At midnight the gathering broke up. The visitors remarked that the evening had been delightful. They smiled and thanked Mrs Vansittart.

'She has destroyed that man,' Mrs Cecil said with feeling as she and her husband entered their villa, the Villa Japhico.

Signora Borromeo wept in the Villa Good-Fun, and her husband, sustaining himself with a late-night sandwich and a glass of beer, sadly shook his head.

'She has destroyed that man,' Joe-John said to his friend in El Dorado, using the words precisely a minute after Mrs Cecil had used them in the Villa Japhico. In the Villa Hadrian the Blochs undressed in silence.

*

Mrs Vansittart lit a cigarette. She sat down at her dressing-table and removed her make-up, occasionally pausing to draw on her cigarette. Her mind contained few thoughts.

Her mind was tired, afflicted with the same fatigue that deadened, just a little, the eyes that people are rude about.

★

Harry sat at the piano in the snug little room he called his den. It was full of things he liked, ornaments and pictures he'd picked up in Europe, bric-à-brac that was priceless or had a sentimental value only. The main lights of the room were not switched on; an ornate lamp lit his piano and the sheets of music paper on the small table beside him. He wore a cotton dressing-gown that was mainly orange, a Javanese pattern.

The child-wife who visited the dreams of Foontimo said her name was Soaring Cloud. She prepared a heaven for Foontimo. She would never leave him, nor would she ever grow old.

Harry smiled over that, his even white teeth moist with excitement. He had known she could not elude him for ever.

★

The following morning Joe-John watched from the rocks near the lighthouse. He carried with him a small pair of binoculars, necessary because the lie of the land would prevent him from getting close enough to observe his quarry profitably. He had to wait for some minutes before Mrs Vansittart appeared. She looked around her before descending a path that led to a gap among the rocks from which, later in the day, people bathed. She sat down and lit a cigarette. A moment later the swarthy waiter from the Grand-Hotel hurried to where she was.

Joe-John moved cautiously. He was slightly above the

pair, but well obscured from their view. Unfortunately it would be impossible to overhear a word they said. Wedging himself uncomfortably, he raised his binoculars and adjusted them.

A conversation, apparently heated, took place. There were many gestures on the part of the swarthy man and at one point he began to go away but was recalled by Mrs Vansittart. She offered him a cigarette, which he accepted. Then Mrs Vansittart took a wallet from a pocket of her trousers and counted a large number of notes on the palm of her companion. 'My God,' said Joe-John, aloud, 'she pays for it!'

The couple parted, the waiter hurrying back towards the Grand-Hotel. Mrs Vansittart sat for a moment where he had left her and then clambered slowly back to the coastal path. She disappeared from Joe-John's view.

*

Privately, Mrs Vansittart keeps an account of her life. While Harry composes his songs she fills a number of hard-backed notebooks with the facts she does not wish to divulge to anyone now but which, one day after her death and after Harry's, she would like to be known. Of this particular day she wrote:

I paused now and again to watch the early-morning fishermen. I had paid ten thousand francs. At the end of the season the man might go and not return, as he had promised. But I could not be sure.

The morning was beautiful, not yet even faintly hot, the sky a perfect blue. The houses of Beaulieu seemed gracious across the glittering sea, yet the houses of Beaulieu are as ordinary as houses anywhere. A jogger glanced at me as I stood aside to let him pass, perspiration on his nose and chin. He did not speak or smile. I sometimes hate it on Cap Ferrat.

On the coastal path that morning I thought about Harry and myself when we were both eleven; I was in love with him even then. In Holland Falls he'd brought me to his mother's bedroom to show me the rings she crowded on to her plump fingers, her heavily-stoppered scent bottles, her garish silk stockings. But I wasn't interested in his mother's things. Harry told me to take my clothes off, which I shyly did, wanting to because he'd asked me and yet keeping my head averted. Everyone knew that Harry loathed his mother, but no one thought about it or blamed him particularly, she being huge and pink and doting on her only child in a shaming way. 'God!' he remarked, looking at my scrawny nakedness among his mother's frills. 'God, *Jesus!*' I had wires on my teeth, and freckles which I still have: I didn't have breasts of any size. I took off Harry's red windcheater, and after that the rest of his clothes and his shoes. We lay side by side between his mother's scented sheets, while two floors down she talked to Mrs Gilliland. 'Now, that's just a damned lie!' she afterwards shrieked at Rose when Rose said what she'd seen. I'll never forget poor Rose's pretty black face in the bedroom doorway, her eyes as round as tea-cups, bulging from her head. Harry's mother got rid of her because of it, but the story ran all over Holland Falls and someone told my own mother, who sat down and cried. My father bawled at me, his fury a single crimson explosion of lips and tongue, his dotted necktie gulping up and down. It wasn't Harry's fault, I said, I'd tempted Harry because I loved him. Besides, I added, nothing had happened. 'At eleven years of age?' my father yelled. 'It's not the point, for God's sake, that nothing happened!'

On the coastal path that morning I told myself it wasn't

fair to remember my father in the moment of his greatest rage. He'd been a gentle man, at his gentlest when operating his high-speed dentist's drill, white-jacketed and happy. Even so, he never forgave me.

We ran away from Holland Falls when we were twenty-two. Harry had already inherited the paper-mill but it was run by a manager, by whom it has been run ever since. We drove about for a year, from town to town, motel to motel. We occupied different rooms because Harry had begun to compose his cycle and liked to be alone with it at night. I loved him more than I could ever tell him but never again, for Harry, did I take my clothes off. Harry has never kissed me, though I, in passing, cannot even now resist bending down to touch the side of his face with my lips. A mother's kiss, I dare say you would call it, and yet when I think of Harry and me I think as well of Héloïse and Abelard, Beatrice and Dante, and all the others. Absurd, of course.

I left the coastal path and went down to the rocks again, gazing into the depths of the clear blue water. 'You're never cross enough,' Harry said, with childish petulance in the City Hotel, Harrisburg, when we were still twenty-two. I had come into my room to find the girl lying on my bed, as I had lain on his mother's with him. In my presence he paid her forty dollars, but I knew he had not laid a finger on her, any more than he had on me when I was her age.

We went to England because Harry was frightened when a police patrol stopped our car one day and asked us if we'd ever been in Harrisburg. I denied it and they let us go, but that was why Harry thought of England, which he took to greatly as soon as we arrived. It became one of the games in our marriage to use only English phrases and to speak in the English way: Harry enjoyed that enormously, almost as much as working on his cycle. And loving him so, I naturally did my best to please him. Any distraction a harmless little game could provide, any compensation: that was how I saw my duty, if in the circumstances that is not too absurd a word. Anyway, the games and the distractions worked, sometimes for years on end. A great deal of time went by, for instance, between the incident in Harrisburg and the first of the two in England. 'It's all right,' the poor child cried out in London when I entered my room. 'Please don't tell, Mrs Vansittart.' Harry paid her the money he had promised her, and when she had gone I broke down and wept. I didn't even want to look at Harry, I didn't want to hear him speak. In an hour or so he brought me up a cup of tea.

It was, heaven knows, simple enough on the surface of things: I could not leave Harry because I loved him too much. I loved his chubby white hands and tranquil smile, and the weakness in his eyes when he took his spectacles off. If I'd left him, he would have ended up in prison because Harry needs to be loved. And then, besides, there has been so much happiness, at least for me: our travelling together, the pictures and the furniture we've so fondly collected, and of course the Villa Teresa. It's the strangest thing in the world, all that.

A fisherman brought his boat near to the rocks where I was sitting. I had lit a cigarette and put my sunglasses on because the glare of daytime was beginning. I watched the fisherman unloading his modest catch, his brown fingers expertly arranging nets and hooks. How different, I thought, marriage would have been with that stranger. And yet could I, with anyone else, have experienced such feelings of passion as I have known?

'I'm sorry,' Harry began to say, a catch-phrase almost, in the 1950s. He's always sorry when he comes in from the flowerbeds with clay on his shoes, or puts the teapot on a polished surface, or breaks the promises he makes. In a way that's hard to communicate Harry likes being sorry.

'*Bonjour, madame,*' the fisherman said, going by with his baskets of sole or whatever fish it was.

'*Bonjour,*' I replied, smiling at him.

Harry would be still in bed, having worked on his cycle until three or four in the morning. Old Pierre and Carola and Madame Spad would not arrive for another hour, and in any case I did not have to be there when they did. But at the back of my mind there's always the terror that when I return to the Villa Teresa Harry will be dead.

I clambered back to the coastal path and continued on my way. In England, after the first occasion, there was the convent girl in her red gymslip, who wasn't docile like the other ones but shouted at me that she loved Harry more than I did. Sometimes she was there when I returned from shopping in the afternoons, sometimes there was only the rumpling of my bed to remind me of her visit. We had to leave England because of the scenes she made, and after the awful melancholy that had seized him Harry promised that none of it would ever happen again.

My presence at the lighthouse that morning had to do with a German girl in Switzerland eleven years ago. The waiter who is at the Grand-Hotel for the season was at the Bon Accueil in Château d'Oex. The German girl was given wine at dinner-time and suddenly burst into tears, hysterically flinging her accusations about. I simply laughed. I said it was ridiculous.

We were gone by breakfast-time and Harry has kept his promise since, frightened for eleven years. Dear, gentle Harry, who never laid a finger on any of those girls, who never would.

Later that morning Joe-John's friend shopped in St Jean, with Joe-John's terrier on a lead. When he had finished he sat down to rest at the café by the bus stop to have a *jus d'abricot*. He watched the tourists and the young people from the yachts. The terrier, elderly now, crept beneath his chair in search of shade.

'Ah, Mrs Bloch!' Joe-John's friend called out after a little while, for the lean South African lady was shopping also. He persuaded her to join him – rather against her will, since Mrs Bloch does not at all care for Joe-John's friend. He then related what Joe-John had earlier related to him: that Mrs Vansittart now paid money for the intimate services she received from men. He described in detail, with some natural exaggeration, the transaction by the lighthouse. Repelled by the account, Mrs Bloch tightened her lips.

On the way back to the Villa Hadrian she called in at the Villa Japhico with two mouse-traps which she had promised last night she would purchase for Mrs Cecil. The Cecils, with neither gardener nor cleaning woman, do not easily find the time for daily shopping and the chandler's store in St Jean will not deliver mouse-traps. Mrs Bloch waited to be thanked and then began.

'To think that man came last night for money! With Harry there and everyone else!'

Mrs Cecil shook her head in horror. Joe-John was a trouble-maker and so was his rather unpleasant friend, yet neither would surely tell an outright lie. It was appalling to think of Mrs Vansittart conducting such business with a waiter. The satisfying of lust in a woman was most unpleasant.

'I really can't think why he doesn't leave her,' she said.

'Oh, he never would. That simply isn't Harry's style.'

'Yes, Harry's loyal.'

That morning the Cecils had discussed the dropping of the Vansittarts, but had in the end agreed that the result of such a course of action would be that Harry would suffer. So they had decided against it, a decision which Mrs Cecil now passed on to her friend.

Mrs Bloch gloomily agreed.

*

Mrs Vansittart plays an ace and wins the trick. It is autumn, the season is over, the swarthy waiter has gone.

Harry enters the salon with his tray of tea, and the pâtisseries he has made that morning. He is so quiet in the shadows of the room that Mrs Bloch recalls how strangers to the villa have occasionally taken him for a servant. Mrs Cecil throws a smile in his direction.

Mr Bloch and Mr Cecil and Signor Borromeo, all of whom know about the transaction that took place near the lighthouse, prefer not to think about it. Joe-John hopes that Mrs Vansittart will commit some further enormity shortly, so that the gossip it trails may while away the winter. It would be awfully dull, he often remarks to his friend, if Mrs Vansittart was like Mrs Bloch and Mrs Cecil and Signora Borromeo.

'Oh, my dear, don't pour it yet!' she cries across the room, and then with some asperity, 'We really aren't quite ready, old thing.'

Harry apologises, enjoying the wave of sympathy her protest engenders. He waits until the hand is played, knowing that then her voice will again command him. He can feel the stifled irritation in the room, and then the sympathy.

He pours the tea and hands the cups around. She lights a cigarette. Once, at the beginning of their time in the Villa Teresa, she had a way of getting up and helping him with the tea-cups, but then she sensed that that was wrong. She senses things in a clumsy kind of way. She is not clever.

'Oh, look, you've made marzipan ones again! You *know* no one likes marzipan, dear.'

But Mrs Cecil and Mrs Bloch both select the marzipan ones, and Harry is apologetic. He is not aware that people have ever said his wife had three affairs and sundry casual conjunctions when they lived in England; nor does he know it is categorically stated that a peasant woman once spat in her face. It would not upset him to hear all this because it's only gossip and its falsity doesn't matter. It is a long time now since she sensed his modest wish, and in answer to it developed the rhythmic swing of her hips and the look in her eyes. Unconsciously, of course, she developed them; not quite in the way she allows the English intonations to creep into her voice. When he looks at her in the company of these people it's enjoyable to imagine the swarthy waiter undressing her among the rocks, even Signor Borromeo trying something on beneath the bridge table.

Harry smiles. He goes around with the teapot, refilling the cups. He wishes she would say again that an avenue on Cap Ferrat would be called after him. It's enjoyable, the feeling in the room then, the people thinking she shouldn't have said it. It's enjoyable when they think she shouldn't swing her hips so and when they come to conclusions about her made-up English voice. It's enjoyable when she listens to his saga of Soaring Cloud the child-wife, and when her face is worried because yet another song has a theme of self-inflicted death. Harry enjoys that most of all.

Mrs Vansittart loses, for her attention had briefly wandered, as it sometimes does just after he has brought the tea around. She tried not to love him when her father was so upset. She tried to forget him, but he was always there, wordlessly pleading from a distance, so passionately demanding the love she passionately felt. She'd felt it long before the day she took her clothes off for him, and she remembers perfectly how it was.

For a moment at the bridge table the thoughts that have slipped beneath her guard make her so light-headed that she wants to jump up and run after him to the kitchen. She sees herself, gazing at him from the doorway, enticing him with her eyes, as first of all she did in Holland Falls. He puts his arms around her, and she feels on hers the lips she never has felt.

'Diamonds,' someone says, for she has asked what trumps are. Her virginal longing still warms her as the daydream dissipates. From its fragments Harry thanks her for the companion she has been, and her love is calm again at the bridge table.

Downstairs at Fitzgerald's

Cecilia's father would sit there, slowly eating oysters. Cecilia would tell him about school and about her half-brothers, and of course she'd have to mention her mother because it was impossible to have a conversation without doing that. She'd mention Ronan also, but because of her father's attitude to her stepfather this was never an embarrassment.

'Aren't they good today?' Tom, the waiter at Fitzgerald's, would remark, always at the same moment, when placing in front of Cecilia's father his second pint of jet-black stout.

'Great, Tom,' her father would unhesitatingly reply, and then Tom would ask Cecilia how her bit of steak was and if the chips were crisp. He'd mention the name of a racehorse and Cecilia's father would give his opinion of it, drawing a swift breath of disapproval or thoughtfully pursing his lips.

These occasions in Fitzgerald's Oyster Bar – downstairs at the counter – were like a thread of similar beads that ran through Cecilia's childhood, never afterwards to be forgotten. Dublin in the 1940s was a different city from the city it later became; she'd been different herself. Cecilia was five when her father first took her to Fitzgerald's, the year after her parents were divorced.

'And tell me,' he said some time later, when she was growing up a bit, 'have you an idea at all about what you'll do with yourself?'

'When I leave school, d'you mean?'

'Well, there's no hurry, I'm not saying there is. Still and all, you're nearly thirteen these days.'

'In June.'

'Ah, I know it's June, Cecilia.' He laughed, with his glass halfway to his lips. He looked at her over the rim, his light-blue eyes twinkling in a way she was fond of. He was a burly man with a brown bald head and freckles on the back of his hands and all over his forehead and his nose.

'I don't know what I'll do,' she said.

'Some fellow'll snap you up. Don't worry about that.' He swallowed another oyster and wiped his mouth with his napkin. 'How's your mother?'

'She's fine.'

He never spoke disparagingly of her mother, nor she of him. When Cecilia was younger he used to drive up the short avenue of the house in Chapelizod in his old sloping-backed Morris, and Cecilia would always be ready for him. Her mother would say hullo to him and they'd have a little chat, and if Ronan opened the door or happened to be in the garden her father would ask him how he was, as though nothing untoward had ever occurred between them. Cecila couldn't understand any of it, but mistily there was the memory of her father living in the house in Chapelizod, and fragments from that time had lodged in her recollection. By the fire in the dining-room he read her a story she had now forgotten. 'Your jersey's inside out,' he said to her mother and then he laughed because it was April Fools' Day. Her father and Ronan had run a furniture-making business together, two large workshops in Chapelizod, not far from the house.

'Lucky,' he said in Fitzgerald's. 'Any fellow you'd accept.'

She blushed. At school a few of her friends talked of getting married, but in a way that wasn't serious. Maureen Finnegan was in love with James Stewart, Betsy Bloom with a boy called George O'Malley: silly, really, it all was.

'The hard case,' a man in a thick overcoat said to her

father, pausing on his way to the other end of the bar. 'Would I chance money on Persian Gulf?'

Cecilia's father shook his head and the man, accepting this verdict, nodded his. He winked at Cecilia in the way her father's friends sometimes did after such an exchange, an acknowledgement of her father's race-track wisdom. When he had gone her father told her that he was a very decent person who had come down in the world due to heavy drinking. Her father often had such titbits to impart and when he did so his tone was matter-of-fact, neither malicious nor pitying. In return, Cecilia would relate another fact or two about school, about Miss O'Shaughnessy or Mr Horan or the way Maureen Finnegan went on about James Stewart. Her father always listened attentively.

He hadn't married again. He lived on his own in a flat in Waterloo Road, his income accumulating from a variety of sources, several of them to do with horse-racing. He'd explained that to her when she'd asked him once about this, wondering if he went to an office every day. She had never been to his flat, but he had described it to her because she'd wondered about that too.

'We'll take the trifle?' he suggested, the only alternative offered by Fitzgerald's being something called Bonanza Cream, over which Tom the waiter had years ago strenuously shaken his head.

'Yes, please,' she said.

When they'd finished it her father had a glass of whiskey and Cecilia another orange soda, and then he lit the third of his afternoon's cigarettes. They never had lunch upstairs at Fitzgerald's, where the restaurant proper was. 'Now come and I'll show you,' her father had offered a year or so ago, and they had stared through a glass door that had the word *Fitzgerald's* in elaborate letters running diagonally across

it. Men and women sat at tables covered with pink table-
cloths and with scarlet-shaded electric lamps on them, the
lamps alight even though it was the afternoon. 'Ah no, it's
nicer downstairs,' her father had insisted, but Cecilia hadn't
entirely agreed, for downstairs in Fitzgerald's possessed
none of that cosiness. There were green tiles instead of the
pink peacock wallpaper of the upper room, and stark rows of
gin and whiskey bottles, and a workmanlike mahogany
food-lift that banged up and down loaded with plates of
oysters. Tom the waiter was really a barman, and the
customers were all men. Cecilia had never seen a woman
downstairs in Fitzgerald's.

'Bedad, isn't her ladyship growing up,' Tom said when
her father had finished his whiskey and they both stood up.
'Sure, it's hardly a day ago she was a chiseler.'

'Hardly a day,' Cecilia's father agreed, and Cecilia blushed
again, glancing down at her wrists because she didn't know
where else to look. She didn't like her wrists. They were the
thinnest in Class Three, which was a fact she knew because a
week ago one of the boys had measured everyone's wrists
with a piece of string. She didn't like the black hair that
hung down on either side of her face because it wasn't curly
like her mother's. She didn't like her eyes and she didn't
like the shape of her mouth, but the boy who had measured
her wrists said she was the prettiest girl in Class Three.
Other people said that too.

'She's a credit to yourself, sir,' Tom said, scooping up
notes and coins from the bar. 'Thanks very much.'

Her father held her coat for her, taking it from a peg by the
door. It and the hat he handed her were part of her school
uniform, both of them green, the hat with a pale blue band.
He didn't put on his own overcoat, saying that the afternoon
wasn't chilly. He never wore a hat.

They walked past Christ Church Cathedral, towards Grafton Street. Their lunchtime encounters always took place on a Saturday, and sometimes in the middle of one Cecilia's father would reveal that he had tickets for a rugby international at Lansdowne Road, or a taxi-driver would arrive in Fitzgerald's to take them to the races at Phoenix Park. Sometimes they'd walk over to the Museum or the National Gallery. Cecilia's father no longer drove a car.

'Will we go to the pictures?' he said today. '*Reap the Wild Wind* at the Grafton?'

He didn't wait for an answer because he knew she'd want to go. He walked a little ahead of her, tidy in his darkish suit, his overcoat over his arm. On the steps of the cinema he gave her some money to go up to Noblett's to buy chocolate and when she returned he was waiting with the tickets in his hand. She smiled at him, thanking him. She often wondered if he was lonely in his flat, and at the back of her mind she had an idea that what she'd like best when she left school would be to look after him there. It gave her a warm feeling in her stomach when she imagined the flat he had described and thought about cooking meals for him in its tiny kitchen.

After the cinema they had tea in Roberts' and then he walked with her to the bus stop in the centre of the city. On the way he told her about an elderly couple in the café who'd addressed him by name, people who lived out in Greystones and bred Great Danes. 'Till next time then,' he said as the bus drew in, and kissed her shyly, in the manner of someone not used to kissing people.

She waved to him from her seat by the window and watched him turn and become lost in the crowded street. He would call in at a few public houses on his way back to the flat in Waterloo Road, places he often referred to by name, Toner's and O'Donoghue's and the upstairs lounge of

Mooney's, places where he met his friends and talked about racing. She imagined him there, with men like the man who'd asked if he should chance his money on Persian Gulf. But again she wondered if he was lonely.

*

It was already dark and had begun to rain by the time Cecilia reached the white house in Chapelizod where her father had once lived but which was occupied now by her mother and Ronan, and by Cecilia and her two half-brothers. A stove, with baskets of logs on either side of it, burned in the square, lofty hall where she took her coat and hat off. The brass door-plates and handles gleamed in the electric light. From the drawing-room came the sound of the wireless. 'Ah, the wanderer's returned,' Ronan murmured when she entered, smiling, making her welcome.

Her half-brothers were constructing a windmill out of Meccano on the floor. Her mother and Ronan were sitting close together, he in an armchair, she on the hearthrug. They were going out that night, Cecilia could tell because her mother's face was already made up: cerise lipstick and mascara, smudges of shadow beneath her eyes that accentuated their brownness, the same brown as her own. Her mother was petite and dark-haired – like Claudette Colbert, as Maureen Finnegan had once said.

'Hullo,' her mother said. 'Nice time?'

'Yes, thanks.'

She didn't say anything else because they were listening to the wireless. Her father would be drinking more stout, she thought, his overcoat on a chair beside him, a fresh cigarette in his mouth. There wasn't a public house between Stephen's Green and Waterloo Road in which he wouldn't know somebody. Of course he wasn't lonely.

The voices on the wireless told jokes, a girl sang a song about a nightingale. Cecilia glanced at her mother and Ronan, she snuggling against his legs, his hand on her shoulder. Ronan was very thin, with a craggy face and a smile that came languidly on to his lips and died away languidly also. He was never cross: in the family, anger didn't play the part it did in the households of several of Cecilia's school friends, where there was fear of a father or a mother. Every Sunday she went with Ronan to the workshops where the furniture was made and he showed her what had been begun or completed during the week. She loved the smell of wood-shavings and glue and French polish.

When the programme on the wireless came to an end her mother rose to go upstairs, to finish getting ready. Ronan muttered lazily that he supposed he'd have to get himself into a suit. He stacked logs on to the fire and set the fireguard in place. 'Your tweed one's ironed,' Cecilia's mother reminded him sternly before she left the room. He grimaced at the boys, who were showing him their completed windmill. Then he grimaced at Cecilia. It was a joke in the family that Ronan never wanted to put on a suit.

*

Cecilia went to a school across the city from Chapelizod, in Ranelagh. It was an unusual place in the Dublin of that time, catering for both boys and girls, for Catholics and Protestants and Jews, and for Mohammedans when that rare need arose. Overflowing from a large suburban house into the huts and prefabricated buildings that served as extra classrooms, it was run by a headmaster, assisted by a staff of both sexes. There were sixty-eight pupils.

In spite of the superficially exotic nature of this establishment Cecilia was the only child whose parents had been divorced and in the kind of conversations she began to have when she was twelve the details of that were increasingly a subject of curiosity. Divorce had a whiff of Hollywood and wickedness. Betsy Bloom claimed to have observed her parents naked on their bed, engaged in the act of love; Enid Healy's father had run amok with a sofa leg. What had happened within the privacy of Cecilia's family belonged in that same realm, and Cecilia was questioned closely. Even though her parents' divorce had had to be obtained in England owing to the shortcomings of the Irish law, the events leading up to it must clearly have occurred in Chapelizod. Had Cecilia ever walked into a room and found her mother and her stepfather up to something? Was it true that her mother and her stepfather used to meet for cocktails in the Gresham Hotel? What exactly *were* cocktails? Had detectives been involved? Her mother and Ronan were glanced at with interest on the very few occasions when they put in an appearance at a school function, and it was agreed that they lived up to the roles they had been cast in. The clothes her mother wore were not like the all-purpose garments of Mrs O'Reilly-Hamilton or Kitty Benson's mother. 'Sophisticated,' Maureen Finnegan had pronounced. 'Chic.'

But in the end Cecilia was aware of her school-fellows' disappointment. There had been no detectives that she could recall, and she didn't know if there had been meetings in the Gresham Hotel. She had never walked into a room to find something untoward taking place and she could remember no quarrels – nothing that was even faintly in the same category as Enid Healy's father brandishing a sofa leg. In America, so the newspapers said, kidnappings occasionally took place when the estranged couples of divorce could not accept the dictates of the law where their children were concerned. 'Your daddy never try that?' Maureen Finnegan hopefully prompted, and Cecilia had to laugh at the absurdity of it. A satisfactory arrangement had been made, she explained for the umpteenth time, knowing it sounded dreary: everyone was content.

The headmaster of the school once spoke to her of the divorce also, though only in passing. He was a massively proportioned man known as the Bull, who shambled about the huts and prefabricated buildings calling out names in the middle of a lesson, ticking his way down the columns of his enormous roll-book. Often he would pause as if he had forgotten what he was about and for a moment or two would whistle through his breath 'The British Grenadiers', the marching song of the regiment in which he had once served with distinction. The only tasks he had ever been known to perform were the calling out of names and the issuing of an occasional vague announcement at the morning assemblies which were conducted by Mr Horan. Otherwise he remained lodged in his own cloudlands, a faint, blue-suited presence, benignly unaware of the feuds that stormed among his staff or the nature of the sixty-eight children whose immediate destinies had been placed in his care.

To Cecilia's considerable surprise the Bull sent for her one morning, the summons interrupting one of Miss O'Shaughnessy's science periods. Miss O'Shaughnessy was displaying how a piece of litmus paper had impressively changed colour, and when Mickey, the odd-job boy, entered the classroom and said that the headmaster wanted Cecilia an immediate whispering broke out. The substance of this was that a death must have taken place.

'Ah,' the Bull said when Cecilia entered the study where he ate all his meals, read the *Irish Times* and interviewed prospective parents. His breakfast tray was still on his desk, a paper-backed Sexton Blake adventure story beside it. 'Ah,' he said again, and did not continue. His bachelor existence was nicely expressed by the bleak furnishings of the room, the row of pipes above a damply smouldering fire, the insignia of the Grenadier Guards scattered on darkly panelled walls.

'Is anything the matter, sir?' Cecilia eventually enquired, for the suggestion that a death might have occurred still echoed as she stood there.

The headmaster regarded her without severity. The breathy whistling of the marching song began as he reached for a pipe and slowly filled it with tobacco. The whistling ceased. He said:

'The fees are sometimes a little tardy. The circumstances are unusual, since you are not regularly in touch with your father. But I would be obliged, when next you see him, if you would just say that the fees have of late been tardy.'

A match was struck, the tobacco ignited. Cecilia was not formally dismissed, but the headmaster's immense hand seized the Sexton Blake adventure story, indicating that the interview was over. It had never occurred to her before that it was her father, not her mother and Ronan, who paid her school fees. Her father had never in his life visited the school, as her mother and Ronan had. It was strange that he should be responsible for the fees, and Cecilia resolved to thank him when next she saw him. It was also embarrassing that they were sometimes late.

'Ah,' the Bull said when she had reached the door. 'You're – ah – all right, are you? The – ah – family trouble . . .?'

'Oh, that's all over, sir.'

'So it is. So it is. And everything . . .?'

'Everything's fine, sir.'

'Good. Good.'

Interest in the divorce had dwindled and might even have dissipated entirely had not the odd behaviour of a boy called Abrahamson begun. Quite out of the blue, about a month after the Saturday on which Cecilia and her father had gone to see *Reap the Wild Wind*, Abrahamson began to stare at her.

In the big classroom where Mr Horan's morning assemblies were held his eyes repeatedly darted over her features, and whenever they met in a corridor or by the tennis-courts he would glance at her sharply and then glance away again, trying to do so before she noticed. Abrahamson's father was the solicitor to the furniture-making business and because of that Abrahamson occasionally turned up in the house in Chapelizod. No one else from the school did so, Chapelizod being too distant from the neighbourhoods where most of the school's sixty-eight pupils lived. Abrahamson was younger than Cecilia, a small olive-skinned boy whom Cecilia had many times entertained in the nursery while his parents sat downstairs, having a drink. He was an only child, self-effacing and anxious not to be a nuisance: when he came to Chapelizod now he obligingly played with Cecilia's half-brothers, humping them about the garden on his back or acting the unimportant parts in the playlets they composed.

At school he was always called by his surname and was famous for his brains. He was neither popular nor unpopular, content to remain on the perimeter of things. Because of this, Cecilia found it difficult to approach him about his staring, and the cleverness that was reflected in the liquid depths of his eyes induced a certain apprehension. But since his interest in her showed no sign of diminishing she decided she'd have to point out that she found it discomfiting.

One showery afternoon, on the way down the shrubbed avenue of the school, she questioned him.

Being taller than the boy and his voice being softly pitched, Cecilia had to bend over him to catch his replies. He had a way of smiling when he spoke – a smile, so everyone said, that had to do with his thoughts rather than with any conversation he happened to be having at the time.

'I'm sorry,' he said. 'I'm really sorry, Cecilia. I didn't know I was doing it.'

'You've been doing it for weeks, Abrahamson.'

He nodded, obligingly accepting the truth of the accusation. And since an explanation was required, he obligingly offered one.

'It's just that when you reach a certain age the features of your face aren't those of a child any more. I read it in a book: a child's face disguises its real features, but at a certain age the disguise falls off. D'you understand, Cecilia?'

'No, I don't. And I don't know why you've picked on me just because of something you read in a book.'

'It happens to everyone, Cecilia.'

'You don't go round staring at everyone.'

'I'm sorry. I'm terribly sorry, Cecilia.'

Abrahamson stopped and opened the black case in which he carried his school books. Cecilia thought that in some clever way he was going to produce from it an explanation that made more sense. She waited without pressing the matter. On the avenue boys kicked each other, throwing caps about. Miss O'Shaughnessy passed on her motorised bicycle. Mr Horan strode by with his violin.

'Like one?' Abrahamson had taken from his case a carton containing two small, garishly iced cakes. 'Go on, really.'

She took the raspberry-coloured one, after which Abrahamson meticulously closed the carton and returned it to his case. Every day he came to school with two of these cakes, supplied by his mother for consumption during the eleven o'clock break. He sold them to anyone who had a few pence to spare, and if he didn't sell them at school he did so to a girl in a newsagent's shop which he passed on his journey home.

'I don't want to tell you,' he said as they walked on. 'I'm sorry you noticed.'

'I couldn't help noticing.'

'Call it quits now, will we?' There was the slightest of gestures towards the remains of the cake, sticky in Cecilia's hand. Abrahamson's tone was softer than ever, his distant smile an echo from his private world. It was said that he played chess games in his head.

'I'd like to know, Abrahamson.'

His thin shoulders just perceptibly shifted up and down. He appeared to be stating that Cecilia was foolish to insist, and to be stating as well that if she continued to insist he did not intend to waste time and energy in argument. They had passed through the gates of the school and were standing on the street, waiting for a number 11 bus.

'It's odd,' he said, 'if you want to know. Your father and all that.'

'Odd?'

The bus drew up. They mounted to the upper deck. When they sat down Abrahamson stared out of the window. It was as if he had already said everything that was necessary, as if Cecilia should effortlessly be able to deduce the rest. She had to nudge him with her elbow, and then – politely and very swiftly – he glanced at her, silently apologising for her inability to understand the obvious. A pity, his small face declared, a shame to have to carry this burden of stupidity.

'When people get divorced,' he said, carefully spacing the

words, 'there's always a reason. You'll observe that in films. Or if you read in the paper about the divorce of, say, William Powell and Carole Lombard. They don't actually bother with divorce if they only dislike one another.'

The conductor came to take their fares. Again the conversation appeared to have reached its termination.

'But what on earth's that got to do with what we're talking about, Abrahamson?'

'Wouldn't there have been a reason why your parents got divorced? Wouldn't the reason be the man your mother married?'

She nodded vehemently, feeling hot and silly. Abrahamson said:

'They'd have had a love affair while your father was still around. In the end there would have been the divorce.'

'I know all that, Abrahamson.'

'Well, then.'

Impatiently, she began to protest again but broke off in the middle of a sentence and instead sat there frowning. She sensed that the last two words her companion had uttered contained some further declaration, but was unable to grasp it.

'Excuse me,' Abrahamson said, politely, before he went.

*

'Aren't you hungry?' her mother asked, looking across the lace-trimmed white cloth on the dining-room table. 'You haven't been gorging yourself, have you?'

Cecilia shook her head, and the hair she didn't like swung about. Her half-brothers giggled, a habit they had recently developed. They were years younger than Cecilia, yet the briskness in her mother's voice placed her in a category with them, and she suddenly wondered if her mother could somehow guess what had come into her mind and was telling her not to be silly. Her mother was wearing a red dress and her fingernails had been freshly tinted. Her black bobbed hair gleamed healthily in watery afternoon sunshine, her dimples came and went.

'How was the Latin?'

'All right.'

'Did you get the passive right?'

'More or less.'

'Why're you so grumpy, Cecilia?'

'I'm not.'

'Well, I think I'd disagree with that.'

Cecilia's cheeks had begun to burn, which caused her half-brothers to giggle again. She knew they were kicking one another beneath the table and to avoid their scrutiny she stared through the French windows, out into the garden. She'd slept in a pram beneath the apple-tree and once had crawled about among the flowerbeds: she could just remember that, she could remember her father laughing as he picked her up.

Cecilia finished her cup of tea and rose, leaving half a piece of coffee cake on her plate. Her mother called after her when she reached the door.

'I'm going to do my homework,' Cecilia said.

'But you haven't eaten your cake.'

'I don't want it.'

'That's rude, you know.'

She didn't say anything. She opened the door and closed it softly behind her. Locked in the bathroom, she examined in the looking-glass the features Abrahamson had spoken of. She made herself smile. She squinted, trying to see her profile. She didn't want to think about any of it, yet she couldn't help herself. She hated being here, with the door locked at five o'clock in the evening, yet she couldn't help that either. She stared at herself for minutes on end, performing further contortions, glancing and grimacing, catching herself unawares. But she couldn't see anywhere a look of her stepfather.

*

'Well, you wouldn't,' Abrahamson explained. 'It's difficult to analyse your own face.'

They walked together slowly, on the cinder-track that ran around the tennis-courts and the school's single hockey pitch. She was wearing her summer uniform, a green and blue dress, short white socks. Abrahamson wore flannel shorts and the elaborate school blazer.

'Other people would have noticed, Abrahamson.'

He shook his head. Other people weren't so interested in things like that, he said. And other people weren't so familiar with her family.

'It isn't a likeness or anything, Cecilia. Not a strong resemblance, nothing startling. It's only a hint, Cecilia, an inkling you could call it.'

'I wish you hadn't told me.'

'You wanted me to.'

'Yes, I know.'

They had reached the end of the cinder-track. They turned and walked back towards the school buildings in silence. Girls were playing tennis. 'Love, forty,' called the elderly English master, No-teeth Carroll as he was known as.

'I've looked and looked,' Cecilia said. 'I spend hours in the bathroom.'

'Even if I hadn't read about the development of the

features I think I'd have stumbled on it for myself. "Now, what on earth is it about that girl?" I kept saying to myself. "Why's her face so interesting all of a sudden?" '

'I think you're imagining it.'

'Well, maybe I am.'

They watched the tennis-players. He wasn't someone who made mistakes, or made things up; he wasn't like that at all. She wished she had her father's freckles, just a couple, anywhere, on her forehead or her nose. 'Deuce,' No-teeth Carroll called. 'No it's definitely deuce,' he insisted, but an argument continued. The poor old fellow was on a term's notice, Abrahamson said.

They walked on. She'd heard it too, she agreed, about the term's notice. Pity, because he wasn't bad, the way he let you do anything you liked provided you were quiet.

'Would you buy one of my cakes today?' Abrahamson asked.

'Please don't tell anyone, Abrahamson.'

'You could buy them *every* day, you know. I never eat them myself.'

★

A little time went by. On the fifteenth of June Cecilia became thirteen. A great fuss was made of the occasion, as was usual in the family whenever there was a birthday. Ronan gave her *A Tale of Two Cities*, her mother a dress which she had made herself, with rosebuds on it, and her half-brothers gave her a red bangle. There was chicken for her birthday lunch, with roast potatoes and peas, and then lemon meringue pie. All of them were favourites of hers.

'Happy birthday, darling,' Ronan whispered, finding a special moment to say it when everyone else was occupied.

She knew he was fond of her, she knew that he enjoyed their Sunday mornings in the workshops. She liked him too. She'd never thought of not liking him.

'*Really* happy birthday,' he said and it was then, as he smiled and turned away, that something occurred to her which she hadn't thought of before, and which Abrahamson clearly hadn't thought of either: when you'd lived for most of your life in a house with the man whom your mother had married you could easily pick up some of his ways. You could pick them up without knowing it, like catching a cold, his smile or some other hint of himself. You might laugh the way he did, or say things with his voice. You'd never guess you were doing it.

'Oh, of course,' Abrahamson obligingly agreed when she put it to him. 'Of course, Cecilia.'

'But wouldn't that be it then? I mean, mightn't that account –'

'Indeed it might.'

His busy, unassuming eyes looked up into hers and then at the distant figure of No-teeth Carroll, who was standing dismally by the long-jump pit.

'Indeed,' Abrahamson said again.

'I'm *certain* that's it. I mean, I still can't see anything myself in my looks –'

'Oh, there's definitely something.' He interrupted sharply, his tone suggesting that it was illogical and ridiculous to question what had already been agreed upon. 'It's very interesting, what you're saying about growing like someone you live with and quite like. It's perfectly possible, just as the other is perfectly possible. If you asked your mother, Cecilia, she probably wouldn't know what's what any more than anyone else does. On account of the circumstances.'

He was bored by the subject. He had acceded to her

request about not telling anyone. It was best to let the subject go.

'Chocolate and strawberry today,' he said, smiling again as he passed over the two small cakes.

*

There was another rendezvous in Fitzgerald's Oyster Bar. Cecilia wore her new rosebud dress and her red bangle. On her birthday a ten-shilling note had arrived from her father, which she now thanked him for.

'When I was thirteen myself,' he said, pulling the cellophane from a packet of Sweet Afton, 'I didn't know whether I was coming or going.'

Cecilia kept her head averted. At least the light wasn't strong. There was a certain amount of stained glass in the windows and only weak bulbs burned in the globe-topped brass lamps that were set at intervals along the mahogany bar. She tried not to smile in case the inkling in her face had something to do with that.

'Well, I see your man's going up in front of the stewards,' Tom the waiter remarked. 'Sure, isn't it time they laid down the law on that fellow?'

'Oh, a terrible chancer that fellow, Tom.'

Their order was taken, and shouted down the lift-shaft.

'We might indulge in a drop of wine, Tom. On account of her ladyship's birthday.'

'I have a great little French one, sir. Mâcon, sir.'

'That'll suit us fine, Tom.'

It was early, the bar was almost empty. Two men in camel-coloured coats were talking in low voices by the door. Cecilia had seen them before. They were bookies, her father had told her.

'Are you all right?' he enquired. 'You haven't got the toothache or anything?'

'No, I'm all right, thanks.'

The bar filled up. Men stopped to speak to her father and then sat at the small tables behind them or on stools by the bar itself. Her father lit another cigarette.

'I didn't realise you paid the fees,' she said.

'What fees do you mean?'

She told him in order to thank him, because she thought they could laugh over the business of the fees being late every term. But her father received the reprimand solemnly. He was at fault, he confessed: the headmaster was quite right, and must be apologised to on his behalf.

'He's not someone you talk to,' Cecilia explained, realising that although she'd so often spoken about school to her father she'd never properly described the place, the huts and prefabricated buildings that were its classrooms, the Bull going round every morning with his huge roll-book.

She watched Tom drawing the cork from the bottle of red wine. She said that only yesterday Miss O'Shaughnessy's motorised bicycle had given up the ghost and she repeated the rumour that poor old No-teeth Carroll was on a term's notice. She couldn't say that she'd struck a silent bargain with a boy called Abrahamson, who brought to the school each day two dainty little cakes in a carton. She'd have liked just to tell about the cakes because her father would have appreciated the oddity of it. It was strange that she hadn't done so before.

'Now,' said Tom, placing the oysters in front of her father and her steak in front of her. He filled up their wine-glasses and drew a surplus of foam from the surface of someone else's stout.

'Is your mother well, Cecilia?'

'Oh, yes.'

'And everyone in Chapelizod?'

'They're all well.'

He looked at her. He had an oyster on the way to his mouth and he glanced at her and then he ate the oyster. He took a mouthful of wine to wash it down.

'Well, that's great,' he said.

Slowly he continued to consume his oysters. 'If we felt like it,' he said, 'we could catch the races at the Park.'

He had been through all of it, just as she had. Ever since the divorce he must have wondered, looking at her as he had looked at her just now, for tell-tale signs. 'They'd have had a love affair while your father was still around,' came the echo of Abrahamson's confident voice, out of place in the oyster bar. Her father had seen Abrahamson's inkling and had felt as miserable as she had. He had probably even comforted himself with the theory about two people in the same house, she picking up her stepfather's characteristics. He had probably said all that to himself over and over again but the doubt had lingered, as it had lingered with her. Married to one man, her mother had performed with another the same act of passion which Betty Bloom had witnessed in her parents' bedroom. As Abrahamson had fairly pointed out, in confused circumstances such as these no one would ever know what was what.

'We'll take the trifle, will we?' her father said.

'Two trifle,' Tom shouted down the lift-shaft.

'You're getting prettier all the time, girl.'

'I don't like my looks at all.'

'Nonsense, girl. You're lovely.'

His eyes, pinched a bit because he was laughing, twinkled. He was much older than her mother, Cecilia suddenly realised, something which had never struck her before.

Were the fees not paid on time because he didn't always have the money? Was that why he had sold his car?

'Will we settle for the races, or something else? You're the birthday lady today.'

'The races would be lovely.'

'Could you ever put that on for me, sir?' Tom requested in a whisper, passing a pound note across the bar. 'Amazon Girl, the last race.'

'I will of course, Tom.'

His voice betrayed nothing of the pain which Cecilia now knew must mark these Saturday occasions for him. The car that was due to collect them was late, he said, and as he spoke the taximan entered.

'Step on it,' her father said, 'like a good man.'

*

He gave her money and advised her which horses to gamble on. He led her by the hand when they went to find a good place to watch from. It was a clear, sunny day, the sky without a cloud in it, and in the noise and bustle no one seemed unhappy.

'There's a boy at school,' she said, 'who brings two little cakes for the eleven o'clock lunch. He sells them to me every day.'

He wagged his head and smiled. But in a serious voice he said he hoped she didn't pay too much for the cakes, and she explained that she didn't.

It was odd the way Maureen Finnegan and all the others, even the Bull, had suspected the tidy settlement there'd been. It would be ridiculous, now, ever to look after him in his flat.

'I hate to lose poor Tom's money for him.'

49

'Won't Amazon Girl win?'

'Never a hope.'

Women in brightly coloured dresses passed by as Cecilia's father paused for a moment by a bookmaker's stand to examine the offered odds. He ran a hand over his jaw, considering. A woman with red hair and sunglasses came up. She said it was good to see him and then passed on.

'We'll take a small little flutter on Gillian's Choice,' he finally said. 'D'you like the sound of that, Cecilia?'

She said she did. She put some of the money he had given her on the horse and waited for him while he transacted with another bookmaker. He approached a third one with Tom's pound for Amazon Girl. It was a habit of his to bet with different bookmakers.

'That red-haired woman's from Carlow,' he said as they set off to their vantage point. 'The widow of the county surveyor.'

'Yes,' she said, not caring much about the red-haired woman.

'Gillian's Choice is the one with the golden hoops,' he said. 'Poor Tom's old nag is the grey one.'

The horses went under starter's orders and then, abruptly, were off. In the usual surprisingly short space of time the race was over.

'What did I tell you?' He laughed down at her as they went to collect the winnings from their two different bookmakers. He had won more than three hundred pounds, she fourteen and sixpence. They always counted at the end; they never lost when they went together. He said she brought him luck, but she knew it was the other way round.

'You'll find your way to the bus, Cecilia?'

'Yes, I will. Thanks very much.'

He nodded. He kissed her in his awkward way and then

disappeared into the crowd, as he always seemed to do when they parted. It was standing about in the sun, she thought, that caused him to have so many freckles. She imagined him at other race-courses, idling between races without her, sunning himself while considering a race-card. She imagined him in his flat in Waterloo Road and wondered if he ever cried.

She walked slowly away, the money clenched in her hand because the rosebud dress had no pockets. He did cry, she thought: on the Saturdays when they met, when he was on his own again. It was easy to imagine him because she wanted to cry herself, because on all their occasions in the future there would be the doubt. Neither of them would ever really know what being together meant, downstairs at Fitzgerald's or anywhere else.

Mulvihill's Memorial

The man, naked himself, slowly removed the woman's clothes: a striped red and black dress, a petticoat, stockings, further underclothes. In an armchair he took the woman on to his knees, nuzzling her neck with his mouth.

A second man entered the room and divested himself of his clothes. A second woman, in a grey skirt and jersey, was divested of hers. The four sprawled together on the armchair and the floor. Complex sexual union took place.

The film ended; a square of bright light replaced the sexual antics on the sheet of cartridge paper which Mulvihill had attached to the back of his drawing-office door. He switched on a green-shaded desk-light, removed the cartridge paper and the drawing-pins that had held it in place. Packing away his projector in the bottom drawer of his filing-cabinet, he hummed beneath his breath an old tune from his childhood, *I'll Be Around*. The projector and Mulvihill's films were naturally kept under lock and key. Some of his films he could project at home and often did so; others he did not feel he could. 'Whatever are you doing, dear?' his sister sometimes called through the door of the garden shed where now and again he did a bit of carpentry, and of course it would be terrible if ever she discovered the stuff. So every Friday evening, when everyone else had left the Ygnis and Ygnis building – and before the West Indian cleaners arrived in the corridor where his office was – Mulvihill locked the door and turned the lights out. He'd been doing it for years.

He was a man with glasses, middle-aged, of medium height, neither fat nor thin. Given to wearing Harris tweed jackets and looking not unlike an advertisement for the Four Square tobacco he smoked, he travelled every day to the centre of London from the suburb of Purley, where his relationship with his slightly older sister was cemented by the presence in their lives of a sealyham called Pasco. By trade Mulvihill was a designer of labels – labels for soup-tins and coffee in plastic packets, for seed-packets and sachets of shampoo. The drawing-office he shared with a Hungarian display artist called Wilkinski reflected the work of both of them. The walls were covered with enlarged versions of designs that had in the past been used to assist in the selling of a variety of products; cardboard point-of-sale material stood on all the office's surfaces except the two sloping drawing-boards, each with its green-shaded light. Paint-brushes and pencils filled jam-jars, different-coloured papers were stored in a corner. In different colours also, sheaves of cellophane hung from bulldog-clips. Tins of Cow paper-adhesive were everywhere.

Being at the ordinary end of things, neither Mulvihill nor Wilkinski created the Ygnis and Ygnis glamour that appeared on the television screen and in the colour supplements: their labels and display material were merely echoes of people made marvellous with a red aperitif on the way to their lips, of women enriched by the lather of a scented soap, and men invigorated by the smooth operation of a razor-blade. From Ygnis and Ygnis came images lined always with a promise, of happiness or ecstasy. Girls stood aloof by castle walls, beautiful in silk. Children laughed as they played, full of the beans that did them good. Ygnis and Ygnis was of the present, but the past was never forgotten: the hot days of summer before the worst of the wars, brown bread and jam, and faded flowered dresses. The future was simple with plain white furniture and stainless steel and Japanese titbits. In the world of wonders that was Ygnis and Ygnis's, empresses ate Turkish Delight and men raced speedboats. For ever and for ever there was falling in love.

Mulvihill took his mackintosh from a peg on the wall, and picked up the two short pieces of timber he'd purchased during the lunch hour and with which, that weekend, he hoped to repair a bookcase. He didn't light his pipe, although while watching *Confessions of a Housewife* he had filled it with Four Square, ready to ignite it in the lift. 'Evening, Violet,' he said to the big West Indian lady who was just beginning to clean the offices of the corridor. He listened for a moment while she continued what she had been telling him last Friday, about a weakness her son had developed in his stomach. He nodded repeatedly and several times spoke sympathetically before moving on. He would call in at the Trumpet Major for a glass of red wine, as he did every Friday evening, and chat for a quarter of an hour to the usual people. It was all part of the weekend, but this time it wasn't to be. In the lift which Mulvihill always took – the one at the back of the building, which carried him to the garage and the mews – he died as he was lighting his pipe.

*

In the Trumpet Major nobody missed Mulvihill. His regular presence on Friday evenings was too brief to cause a vacuum when it did not occur. Insisting that a single glass of wine was all he required, he never became involved in rounds of drinks, and it was accepted that that was his way. R. B. Strathers was in the lounge bar, as always on Friday, with Tip Dainty and Capstick and Lilia. Other employees of

Ygnis and Ygnis were there also, two of the post-boys in the public bar, Fred Stein the art buyer. At a quarter past eight Ox-Banham joined Strathers and his companions, who had made a place for themselves in a corner. Like Mulvihill, Ox-Banham was known to work late on Fridays, presumed to be finishing anything that had become outstanding during the week. In fact, like Mulvihill, he indulged a private hobby: the seduction, on the floor of his office, of his secretary, Rowena.

'Well, how are we all?' Ox-Banham demanded. 'And, more to the point, what are we having?'

Everyone was having the same as usual. Lilia, the firm's most important woman copywriter, was drunk, as she had been since lunchtime. R. B. Strathers, who had once almost played rugby for South Africa and was now the managing director of Ygnis and Ygnis, was hoping to be drunk shortly. Tip Dainty occasionally swayed.

Ox-Banham took a long gulp of his whisky and water and gave a little gasp of satisfaction. Rowena would be leaving the building about now, since the arrangement was that she stayed behind for ten minutes or so after he'd left her so that they wouldn't be seen together. In normal circumstances it didn't matter being seen together, an executive and his secretary, but just after sexual congress had taken place it might well be foolish: some telltale detail in their manner with one another might easily be still floating about on the surface. 'Point taken of course,' Rowena had said, being given to speaking in that masculine way. Hard as glass she was, in Ox-Banham's view.

'The confectionery boys first thing Monday,' he said now. 'Neat little campaign we've got for them, I think.'

Lilia, who was middle-aged and untidy, talked about shoes. She was clutching a bundle of papers in her left hand, pressing it tightly against her breast as if she feared someone might snatch it from her. Her grey hair had loosened, her eyes were glazed. 'How about Cliff Hangers?' she said to Tip Dainty, offering the term as a name for a new range of sandals.

Lilia's bundle of papers was full of such attempts to find a title for the new range. The sandals were well designed, so Ygnis and Ygnis had been told, with a definite no-nonsense look. Tip Dainty said Cliff Hangers sounded as if something dreadful might happen to you if you wore the things, and Lilia grinned extravagantly, her lean face opening until it seemed entirely composed of teeth. 'Hangers?' she suggested. 'Just Hangers?' But Tip Dainty said Hangers would make people think of death.

Ox-Banham talked to Capstick and R. B. Strathers about the confectionery people and the preparations that had been made by Ygnis and Ygnis to gain the advertising of a new chocolate bar. Again there had been the que~tion of a name and Ygnis and Ygnis in the end had settleᴅ for Go. It was Mulvihill who had designed the wrapper and the various cartons in which the bar would be delivered to the shops, as well as window-stickers and other point-of-sale material.

'I like that Go idea,' Ox-Banham said, 'and I like the moody feel of that scene in the cornfield.' His back was a little painful because Rowena had a way of digging her fingernails into whatever flesh she could find, but of course it was worth it. Rowena had been foisted on him by her father, Bloody Smithson, the awful advertising manager of McCulloch Paints, and when Ox-Banham had first seduced her he'd imagined he was getting his own back for years of Smithson's awkwardness. But in no time at all he'd realised Rowena was using him as much as he was using her: she wanted him to get her into the copywriting department.

'How about Strollers?' Lilia was asking, and Tip Dainty pointed out that Clarke's were using it already. 'Cliff Hangers, Strath?' Lilia repeated, but in his blunt, rugby-playing way R. B. Strathers said Cliff Hangers was useless.

★

Mulvihill's sister, who was the manageress of an Express Dairy, was surprised when Mulvihill didn't put in an appearance at a quarter to nine, his usual time on Fridays. Every other evening he was back by ten past seven, in time for most of the Archers, but on Fridays he liked to finish off his week's work so as to have a clean plate on Monday. He smelt a little of the wine he drank in the Trumpet Major, but since he always told her the gossip he'd picked up she never minded in the least having to keep their supper back. She knew it wasn't really for the gossip he went to the public house but in order to pass a few moments with Ox-Banham and R. B. Strathers, to whom he owed his position at Ygnis and Ygnis. Not that either Ox-Banham or R. B. Strathers had employed him in the first place – neither had actually been at Ygnis and Ygnis in those days – but Ox-Banham had since become the executive to whom Mulvihill was mainly responsible and R. B. Strathers was naturally important, being the managing director. Miss Mulvihill had never met these men, but imagined them easily enough from the descriptions that had been passed on to her: Ox-Banham tight-faced in a striped dark suit, R. B. Strathers big, given to talking about rugby matches he had played in. Lilia was peculiar by the sound of her, and Capstick, who designed the best advertisements in Ygnis and Ygnis, was a bearded little creature with a tendency to become insulting when he reached a certain stage in drunkenness. Tip Dainty became genial.

Miss Mulvihill missed these people, her Friday people as she thought of them: she felt deprived as she impatiently waited, she even felt a little cross. Her brother had said he was going to pick up the timber pieces for the bookcase, but he'd have done that in his lunchtime. Never in a million years would he just stay on drinking, he didn't even like the taste. Shortly after ten o'clock the sealyham, Pasco, became agitated, and at eleven Miss Mulvihill noticed that her crossness had turned to fear. But it wasn't until the early hours of the morning that she telephoned the police.

*

On the following Monday morning the employees of Ygnis and Ygnis arrived at the office building variously refreshed after their weekend. The body had been removed from the back lift, no trace of the death remained. The Hungarian, Wilkinski, was surprised that Mulvihill was not already in the office they shared, for normally he was the first of the two to arrive. He was still pondering the cause of this when the tea-woman, Edith, told him she'd heard Mulvihill had died. She handed Wilkinski his tea, with two lumps of sugar in the saucer, and even while she released the news she poured from her huge, brown enamel teapot a cup for the deceased. 'Oh, stupid thing!' she chided herself.

'But however dead, Edith? However he die, my God?'

Edith shook her head. It was terrible, she said, placing the edge of the teapot on Mulvihill's drawing-board because it was heavy to hold. She still couldn't believe it, she said, laughing and joking he'd been Friday, right as rain. 'Well, it just goes to show,' she said. 'Poor man!'

'Are you sure of this, Edith?' The fat on Wilkinski's face was puckered in mystification, his thick spectacles magnifying the confusion in his eyes. 'Dead?' he said again.

'Definitely,' Edith added, and moved on to spread the news.

My God, dead! Wilkinski continued to reflect, for several minutes unable to drink his tea and finding it cold when he did so. Mulvihill had been the easiest man in the world to share an office with, neither broody nor a bore, a pleasant unassuming fellow, perhaps a little over-worried about the safety of his job, but then who doesn't have faults in this world? He'd been happy, as far as Wilkinski had ever made out, with his sister and their dog in Purley, a few friends in on a Saturday night to cheese and wine, old films on the television. Anything to do with films had interested him, photography being as much of a hobby as his do-it-yourself stuff. In 1971, when Wilkinski's elder daughter married, Mulvihill had recorded the occasion with the camera he'd just bought. He'd made an excellent job of it, with titles he'd lettered himself, and a really impressive shot of the happy couple coming down the steps of the reception place. Unfortunately the marriage had broken up a year ago, and the film was no longer of interest. As dead as poor old Mulvihill, Wilkinski thought sadly: my God, it just goes to show. Ernie Taplow, the art buyer's assistant, came in at that point, shaking his head over the shock of it. And then Len Billings came in, and Harry Plant, and Agnes Trotter the typographer.

Elsewhere in the building life continued normally that morning. The confectionery manufacturers arrived to see the proposals Ygnis and Ygnis had to put to them concerning the promotion of their new chocolate bar. Ox-Banham displayed posters and advertisements, and the labels and window-stickers Mulvihill had designed. 'Go,' one of the confectionery men said. 'Yes, I like that.' Ox-Banham took them down to the television theatre and showed them a series of commercials in which children were dressed up as cowboys and Indians. Afterwards his secretary, Rowena, poured them all drinks in his office, smiling at them and murmuring because it was part of her duty to be charming. Just occasionally as she did so she recalled the conjunction that had taken place in the office on Friday evening, Ox-Banham's wiry body as brown as a nut in places, the smell of his underarm-odour preventive. She liked it to take place in the dark, but he preferred the lights on and had more than once mentioned mirrors, although there were no mirrors in the office. They took it in turns, his way one week, hers the next. The only trouble was that personally she didn't much care for him. 'I want you to fix it immediately,' she'd said in her no-nonsense voice on Friday, and this morning he'd arranged for her to be moved into the copy department at the end of the month. 'I'll need a new girl,' he'd said, meaning a secretary. 'I'll leave that to you.'

Ox-Banham introduced the confectionery men to R. B. Strathers, in whose office they had another drink. He then took them to lunch, referring in the taxi to the four times Strathers had been a reserve for the South African rugby team: often a would-be client was impressed by this fact. He didn't mention Mulvihill's death, even though there might have been a talking point in the fact that the chap who'd designed the wrapper for the Go bar had had a heart attack in a lift. But it might also have cast a gloom, you never could tell, so he concentrated instead on making sure that each of the confectionery men had precisely what he wished to have in the way of meat and vegetables, solicitously filling up the wine-glass of the one who drank more than the others. He saw that cigars and brandy were at hand when the moment came, and in the end the most important man said, 'I think we buy it.' All the others agreed: the image that had been devised for the chocolate bar was an apt one, its future safe in the skilful hands of Ygnis and Ygnis.

'Wednesday,' said Miss Mulvihill on the telephone to people who rang with messages of sympathy. 'Eleven-thirty, Putney Vale Crematorium.'

*

As the next few weeks went by so life continued smoothly in the Ygnis and Ygnis building. Happy in the copywriting department, Rowena practised the composition of slogans and thought up trade names for shoes, underwear and garden seeds. She wrote a television commercial for furniture polish, and explained to Ox-Banham that there would now be no more Friday evenings. She began to spend her lunchtimes with a new young man in market research. Unlike Ox-Banham, he was a bachelor.

Bloody Smithson telephoned Strathers to say he was dissatisfied with Ygnis and Ygnis's latest efforts for McCulloch Paints. Typical, Ox-Banham said when Strathers sent for him: as soon as little Rowena's home and dry the old bugger starts doing his nut again. 'Let us just look into all that,' he murmured delicately to Bloody Smithson on the telephone.

'There are private possessions,' Wilkinski said to Mulvihill's sister, on the telephone also. 'Maybe we send a messenger to your house with them?'

'That's very kind, Mr Wilkinski.'

'No, no. But the filing cabinet he had is locked. Maybe the key was on his person?'

'Yes, I have his bunch of keys. If I may, I'll post it to you, Mr Wilkinski.'

Everything else Wilkinski had tidied up: Mulvihill's paintbrushes and his pencils, his paints and his felt pens. Strictly speaking, they were the property of Ygnis and Ygnis, but Wilkinski thought Miss Mulvihill should have them. The filing-cabinet itself, the drawing-board and the green-shaded light, would pass on to Mulvihill's successor.

When the keys arrived, Wilkinski found that Mulvihill had retained samples of every label and sticker and wrapper, every packet and point-of-sale item he had ever designed. The samples were stuck on to sheets of white card, one to a sheet, and the sheets neatly documented and filed. Wilkinski decided that Mulvihill's sister would wish to have this collection, as well as the old Four Square tobacco tins containing drawing-pins and rubber bands, a pair of small brass hinges, several broken pipes, some dental fixative, and two pairs of spectacles. Mulvihill's camera was there, side by side with his projector. And in the bottom drawer, beneath ideas for the lettering on a toothpaste tube, were his films.

Pleased to have an excuse to walk about the building, Wilkinski made his way to the basement and asked Mr Betts, the office maintenance man, for a large, strong cardboard carton, explaining why he wanted it. Mr Betts did his best to supply what was necessary and Wilkinski returned to his office with it. He packed the projector and the camera with great care and when he came to the vast assortment of neatly titled films, all in metal containers, he looked out for one that Agnes Trotter wanted, to do with her father's retirement party. 'A Day in the Life of a Sealyham', he read, and then 'A Sealyham Has His Say' and 'A Sealyham at Three'. A note was attached to the label, 'Mr Trotter's Retirement

Occasion', a reminder that the film still needed some editing. Wilkinski put it aside for Agnes Trotter and then, to his surprise, noticed that the label on the next tin said, 'Confessions of a Housewife'. He examined some of the others and was even more surprised to read, 'Virgins' Delight', 'Naughty Nell' and 'Bedtime with Bunny'.

Closer examination of the metal film-containers convinced Wilkinski that while most of the more exotic titles were not Mulvihill's own work, two or three of them were. 'Easy Lady', for instance, had a reminder stuck to it indicating that editing was necessary; 'Let's Go, Lover' and two untitled containers had a note about splicing. 'My God!' Wilkinski said.

He didn't know what to think. He imagined Mulvihill wandering about Soho in his lunch-hour, examining the pictures that advertised the strip joints, entering the pornographic shops where blue films were discreetly for sale. None of that fitted Mulvihill, none of it was like him. Quite often Wilkinski had accompanied him and his camera to Green Park, to catch the autumn, or the ducks in springtime.

Wilkinski sat down. He ran the tip of his tongue over his rather thick lips. They had shared an office since 1960, yet he had never known a thing about this man. Clearly Mulvihill had bought 'Virgins' Delight' and 'Bedtime with Bunny' to see how it was done, and then he had begun to make blue films himself. Being in terror of losing his job, he had every day passed humbly through the huge reception area of Ygnis and Ygnis, its walls enriched by pictures of shoes and seed-packets and ironworks, and biscuits and whisky bottles. Humbly he had walked the corridors that rattled with the busyness of typewriters and voices in trivial conversation; humbly he had done his duty by the words and images that

63

were daily created. Wilkinski recalled his saying that he'd always wanted to be a photographer: had he decided in the end to attempt to escape from his treadmill by becoming a pornographer instead? It was a sad thing to have happened to a man. It was an ugly thing as well.

Still, Wilkinski had a job to do and he knew that in the carton destined for Purley he must not include such items as 'Let's Go, Lover' and 'Confessions of a Housewife' because of the embarrassment they would cause. His first thought was that he should simply throw the pornographic films away, but even though he had emigrated from Hungary in 1955 Wilkinski was still aware that he had to be careful in a foreign country. Assiduously he avoided all trouble and was notably polite in tube trains and on the street: it seemed a doubtful procedure, to destroy the possessions of a dead man.

'Films?' Ox-Banham said on the telephone. 'You mean they're dirty?'

'Some you might call domestic. Others I think they could offend a lady.'

'I'll come and have a look.'

'Some are of a dog.'

Later that day Ox-Banham arrived in Wilkinski's small office and took charge of the films, including the ones of the dog. He locked them away in his own office, for he was personally not in the least interested in pornography and certainly not curious to investigate this private world of a label-designer who had remotely been in his charge. He didn't destroy the films because you never could tell: an occasion might quite easily arise when some client or would-be client would reveal, even without meaning to, an interest in such material. Topless waitresses, gambling clubs, or just getting drunk: where his clients were concerned, Ox-Banham was endlessly solicitous, a guide and a listener. It was unbecoming that Mulvihill should have titillated himself in this way, he reflected as he stood that evening in the Trumpet Major, getting more than a little drunk himself. Nasty he must have been, in spite of his pipe and his Harris tweed jackets.

*

In time the carton containing Mulvihill's effects was delivered to Purley. Miss Mulvihill returned from the Express Dairy one evening to find it on the doorstep. In the hall, where she opened it, she discovered that her brother's keys had been returned to her, Sellotaped on to one of the carton's flaps; only the key of the filing-cabinet had been removed, but Miss Mulvihill didn't even notice that. She looked through the white cards on which her brother had mounted the items he had designed at Ygnis and Ygnis; she wondered what to do with his old pipes. In the end she put everything back into the carton and hauled it into the cubbyhole beneath the stairs. Pasco bustled about at her feet, delighted to be able to make a foray into a cupboard that was normally kept locked.

An hour or so later, scrambling an egg for herself in the kitchen, Miss Mulvihill reflected that this was truly the end of her brother. The carton in the cubbyhole reminded her of the coffin that had slid away towards the fawn-coloured curtains in the chapel of the crematorium. She'd been through her brother's clothes, setting most of them aside for Help the Aged. She'd told the man next door that he could have the contents of the workshed in the garden, asking him to leave her only a screwdriver and a hammer and a pair of pliers.

She had always been fond of her brother; being the older one, she had looked after him as a child, taking him by the hand when they crossed a street together, answering his questions. Their mother had died when he was eight, and when their father died thirty years later it had seemed natural that they should continue to live together in the house in Purley. 'Let's have a dog,' her brother had said one Saturday morning nine years ago, and soon after that Pasco had entered their lives. The only animal the house had known before was Miss Muffin, their father's cat, but they'd agreed immediately about Pasco. Never once in their lives had they quarrelled, her brother being too nervous and she too even-tempered. Neither had ever wished to marry.

She'd put a rose in, she thought as she ate her scrambled egg, the way you could in the grounds of the crematorium, a living thing to remember him by.

*

A year went by in Ygnis and Ygnis. The new man who shared Wilkinski's office was young and given to whistling. On the telephone he addressed his wife as 'chick', which began to grate on Wilkinski's nerves. He possessed a 1951 Fiat, which he talked about; and a caravan, which he talked about also.

Established now in the copy department, Rowena Smithson was responsible for a slogan which won a prize. She had been put in charge of a frozen foods account and had devised a television campaign which displayed an ordinary family's preference for a packet of fish to a banquet. In Ygnis and Ygnis it was said more than once that Rowena Smithson was going places. Foolish in her dishevelled middle age, Lilia was said to be slipping.

During the course of that year Ox-Banham interested himself in one of Ygnis and Ygnis's three receptionists, a girl who wanted to get into the art department. The Trumpet Major continued to profit from the drinking requirements of Capstick, Lilia, Tip Dainty and R. B. Strathers. Several office parties took place during the year and at the end of it the Ygnis and Ygnis chairman was awarded an OBE.

'Well, I quite appreciate that of course,' Ox-Banham said on the telephone one morning after that year had passed. He was speaking to Bloody Smithson, who had not ceased to give him a bad time, forgetful of all that had been arranged in the matter of placing his daughter in her chosen career. Rowena was shortly to marry the man she'd begun to go out with, from the market research department. The man was welcome to her as far as Ox-Banham was concerned, but when her father was disagreeable it gave him no satisfaction whatsoever to recall how he'd repeatedly pleasured himself with her on the floor of his office. 'Let's iron it out over lunch,' he urged Bloody Smithson.

The lunch that took place was a sticky one, bitter with Bloody Smithson's acrimony. Only when coffee and glasses of Hine arrived on the table did the man from McCulloch Paints desist and Ox-Banham cease inwardly to swear. Then, quite unexpectedly, Bloody Smithson mentioned blue films. His mood was good by now, for he'd enjoyed being a bully for two hours; he described at length some material he'd been shown on a trip to Sweden. 'Awfully ripe,' he said, his large blood-red face inches from his companion's.

Until that moment Ox-Banham had forgotten about the metal containers he had locked away after Mulvihill's death. He didn't mention them, but that evening he read through their neatly labelled titles, and a week later he borrowed a projector. He found what he saw distasteful, as he'd known he would, but was aware that his own opinion didn't matter in the least. 'I've got hold of a few ripe ones that might interest you,' he said on the telephone to Bloody Smithson when he next had occasion to speak to him.

In the comfort of the television theatre they watched 'Confessions of a Housewife', 'Virgins' Delight' and 'Naughty Nell'. Bloody Smithson liked 'Virgins' Delight' best. Ox-Banham explained how the cache had fallen into his hands and how some of the films were apparently the late Mulvihill's own work. 'Let's try this "Day in the Life of a Sealyham",' he suggested. 'Goodness knows what all *that's* about.' But Bloody Smithson said he'd rather have another showing of 'Virgins' Delight'.

Ox-Banham told the story in the Trumpet Major. 'Not a word to my daughter, mind,' Bloody Smithson had insisted, chortling in a way that was quite unlike him. The next day all of it went around the Ygnis and Ygnis building, but it naturally never reached the ears of Rowena because no one liked to tell her that her father had a penchant for obscene films. Mulvihill's name was used again, his face and clothing recalled, a description supplied to newcomers at Ygnis and Ygnis. Wilkinski heard the story and it hurt him that Mulvihill should be remembered in this way. It was improper, Wilkinski considered, and it made him feel guilty himself: he should have thrown the films away, as his first instinct had been. 'Mulvihill's Memorial' the pornography came to be called, and the employees of Ygnis and Ygnis laughed when they thought of an overweight advertising manager being shown 'Virgins' Delight' in the television theatre. It seemed to Wilkinski that the dead face of Mulvihill was being rubbed in the dirt he had left behind him. It

worried Wilkinski, and eventually he plucked up his courage and went to speak to Ox-Banham.

'We shared the office since 1960,' he said, and Ox-Banham
looked at him in astonishment. 'It isn't very nice to call it
"Mulvihill's Memorial".'

'Mulvihill's dead and gone. What d'you expect us to do
with his goodies?'

'Maybe put them down Mr Betts' incinerator.'

Ox-Banham laughed and suggested that Wilkinski was
being a bit Hungarian about the matter. The smile that
appeared on his face was designed to be reassuring, but
Wilkinski found this reference to his origins offensive. It
seemed that if Mulvihill's wretched pornography brought
solace to a recalcitrant advertising manager, then Mulvihill
had not died in vain. The employees had to be paid, profits
had to be made. 'It isn't very nice,' Wilkinski said again,
quietly in the middle of one night. No one heard him, for
though he addressed his wife she was dreaming at the time
of something else.

*

Then two things happened at once. Wilkinski had a telephone call from Miss Mulvihill, and Ox-Banham made a
mistake.

'It's just that I was wondering,' Miss Mulvihill said. 'I
mean, he definitely made these little films and there's absolutely no trace of them.'

'About a dog maybe?'

'And a little one about the scouts. Then again one concerning Purley.'

'Leave the matter with me, Miss Mulvihill.'

The telephone call came late in the day, and when

Wilkinski tried to see Ox-Banham it was suggested that he should try again in the morning. It pleased him that Miss Mulvihill had phoned, that she had sought to have returned to her what was rightfully hers. He'd considered it high-handed at the time that Ox-Banham hadn't bothered to di-vide the films into two groups, as he had done himself. 'Oh, let's not bother with all that,' Ox-Banham had said with a note of impatience in his voice.

Wilkinski hurried to catch his train on the evening of Miss Mulvihill's call; Ox-Banham entertained Bloody Smithson in the television theatre. 'No, no, no,' Bloody Smithson protested. 'We'll stick with our Virgins, Ox.'

But Ox-Banham was heartily sick of 'Virgins' Delight', which he had seen by now probably sixty times. He thought he'd die if he had to watch, yet again, the three schoolgirls putting down their hockey sticks and beginning to take off their gymslips. 'I thought we were maybe wearing it out,' he said. 'I thought I'd better have a copy made.'

'You mean it's not here?'

'Back in a week or so, Smithy.'

They began to go through the others. 'Let's try this "Day in the Life of a Sealyham",' Ox-Banham suggested, and shortly afterwards a dog appeared on the screen, ambling about a kitchen. Then the dog was put on a lead and taken for a walk around a suburb by a middle-aged woman. Back in the kitchen again, the dog begged with its head on one side and was given a titbit. There was another walk, a bus shelter, the dog smelling at bits of paper on the ground. 'Well, for God's sake!' Bloody Smithson protested when the animal was fin-ally given a meal to eat and put to bed.

'Sorry, Smithy.'

'I thought she and the dog –'

'I know. So did I.'

'Some bloody nut made that one.'

Ox-Banham then showed 'Naughty Nell', followed by 'Country Fun', 'Oh Boy!' and 'Girlie'. But Bloody Smithson wasn't in the least impressed. He didn't care for 'Confessions of a Housewife' any more than he had the first time he'd seen it. He didn't care for 'Nothing on Tonight' and wasn't much impressed by anything else. Ox-Banham regretted that he'd said 'Virgins' Delight' was being copied. This tedious search for excitement could go on all night, for even though Smithson continued to say that everything was less good than 'Virgins' Delight' Ox-Banham had a feeling that some enjoyment at least was being derived from the continuous picture show.

'You're sure there isn't another reel or something to that dog stuff?' the advertising manager even enquired. 'I wouldn't mind seeing that dame with her undies off.' He gave a loud laugh, draining his glass of whisky and poking it out at Ox-Banham for a refill.

'I think that's the bloke's sister actually. I don't think she takes anything off.' Ox-Banham laughed himself, busy with glasses and ice. 'Call it a day after this one, shall we?'

'Might as well run through the lot, Ox.'

They saw 'Come and Get It', 'Girls on the Rampage', 'A Sealyham Has His Say', 'Street of Desire', a film of boy scouts camping, scenes on a golf course, 'Saturday Morning, Purley', and 'Flesh for Sale'. It was then, after a few moments of a film without a title, that Ox-Banham realised something was wrong. Unfortunately he realised it too late.

'Great God almighty,' said Bloody Smithson.

*

'You opened the filing-cabinet, Wilkinski, you took the

films out. What did you do next?' Ox-Banham ground his teeth together, struggling with his impatience.

'I say myself it's not nice for the sister. The sister phoned up yesterday, I came down to see you –'

'You didn't project any of the films?'

'No, no. I think of Mulvihill lying dead and I think of the sister. What the sister wants is the ones about the dog, and anything else, maybe boy scouts, is there?'

'You are absolutely certain that you did not project any of the films? Not one called "Easy Lady" or another, "Let's Go, Lover"? Neither of the two untitled ones?'

'No, no. I have no interest in this. I get the box from Mr Betts –'

'Is it possible that someone else might have examined the films? Did you leave the filing-cabinet unlocked, for instance?'

'No, no. I get the box from Mr Betts, maybe ten minutes. The cabinet is closed and locked then. The property of a dead man, I say myself –'

'So no one could possibly have projected one of these films?'

'No, no. The sister rings me yesterday. She is anxious for the dog ones, also boy scouts, and others.'

'Oh, for God's sake, Wilkinski!'

'I promise I find –'

'They've all been destroyed. Everything's been destroyed.'

'Destroyed? But I thought –'

'I destroyed them myself last night.'

Returning to his office, Wilkinski paused for a moment in a corridor, removed his spectacles and polished them with his handkerchief. People hurried by him with proofs of new advertisements and typewritten pages of copy, but it was easier to think in the corridor than it would be in the office because of the whistling of Mulvihill's successor. Ox-Banham had looked almost ill, his voice had been shaky. Wilkinski shook his head and slowly padded back to his drawing-board, baffled by the turn of events. He didn't know what he was going to say to Mulvihill's sister.

What happened next was that Bloody Smithson removed the McCulloch Paints account from Ygnis and Ygnis. Then Rowena Smithson walked out. She didn't hand in her notice, she simply didn't return after lunch one day. The man in market research to whom she was engaged let it be known that the engagement had been broken off, and made it clear that it was he who had done the breaking. A rumour went round that the big shoe account – a Quaker concern and one of Ygnis and Ygnis's mainstays – was about to go, and a week later it did. Questions were asked by the men of the chocolate account which Ox-Banham had gained a year ago, and by the toiletries people, and by the men of Macclesfield Metals. Hasty lunches were arranged, explanations pressed home over afternoon brandy. *Ygnis and Ygnis in Trouble* a headline in a trade magazine was ready to state, but the headline – and the report that went with it – was abandoned at the eleventh hour because it appeared that Ygnis and Ygnis had weathered their storm.

Wilkinski tried to piece things together, and so did the other employees. In the Trumpet Major it was said that for reasons of his own Bloody Smithson had sworn to bring Ygnis and Ygnis to its knees, but neither Wilkinski nor anyone else knew why he had become so enraged. Then, making a rare appearance in the Trumpet Major, the market research man to whom Rowena Smithson had been engaged drank an extra couple of Carlsbergs while waiting for the rain to cease. Idling at the bar, he told Tip Dainty in the strictest confidence of a scene which had taken place at the time of the crisis in the Smithsons' house in Wimbledon: how he'd been about to leave, having driven Rowena home, when Bloody Smithson had thundered his way into the sitting-room, 'literally like a bull'. Mrs Smithson had been drinking a glass of Ovaltine at the time, Rowena had not yet taken off her coat. 'You filthy young prostitute!' Bloody Smithson had roared at her. 'You cheap whore!' It apparently hadn't concerned him that his daughter's fiancé was present, he hadn't even noticed when the cup of Ovaltine fell from his wife's grasp. He had just stood there shouting, oaths and obscenities bursting out of him, his face the colour of ripe strawberries.

By half past ten the following morning the story was known to every Ygnis and Ygnis employee: Mulvihill had made a film of Ox-Banham and Rowena Smithson banging away on the floor of Ox-Banham's office. Mulvihill had apparently hidden himself behind the long blue Dralon curtains, which in the circumstances had naturally been drawn. The lights in the room had been on and neither protagonist in the proceedings had been wearing a stitch.

At lunchtime that day, passing through the large, chic reception area, the people of Ygnis and Ygnis hardly noticed the images displayed on its walls. The messages that murmured at them were rich in sexual innuendo, but the hard facts of a dead pornographer briefly interested them more. 'Mulvihill!' some exclaimed in uneasy admiration, for to a few at least it seemed that Mulvihill had dealt in an honesty that just for a moment made the glamour of the images and the messages appear to be a little soiled. Wilkinski thought so, and longed to telephone Mulvihill's sister to tell her of what had occurred, but of course it was impossible to do that. He wrote a letter instead, apologising for taking so

74

long in replying to her query and informing her that the films she'd mentioned had been destroyed in error. It was not exactly a lie, and seemed less of one as the day wore on, as the glamour glittered again, undefeated when it came to the point.

Beyond the Pale

We always went to Ireland in June.

Ever since the four of us began to go on holidays together, in 1965 it must have been, we had spent the first fortnight of the month at Glencorn Lodge in Co. Antrim. Perfection, as Dekko put it once, and none of us disagreed. It's a Georgian house by the sea, not far from the village of Ardbeag. It's quite majestic in its rather elegant way, a garden running to the very edge of a cliff, its long rhododendron drive – or avenue, as they say in Ireland. The English couple who bought the house in the early sixties, the Malseeds, have had to build on quite a bit but it's all been discreetly done, the Georgian style preserved throughout. Figs grow in the sheltered gardens, and apricots, and peaches in the greenhouses which old Mr Saxton presides over. He's Mrs Malseed's father actually. They brought him with them from Surrey, and their Dalmatians, Charger and Snooze.

It was Strafe who found Glencorn for us. He'd come across an advertisement in the *Lady* in the days when the Malseeds still felt the need to advertise. 'How about this?' he said one evening at the end of the second rubber, and then read out the details. We had gone away together the summer before, to a hotel that had been recommended on the Costa del Sol, but it hadn't been a success because the food was so appalling. 'We could try this Irish one,' Dekko suggested cautiously, which is what eventually we did.

The four of us have been playing bridge together for ages, Dekko, Strafe, Cynthia and myself. They call me Milly, though strictly speaking my name is Dorothy Milson. Dekko picked up his nickname at school, Dekko Deakin sounding rather good, I dare say. He and Strafe were in fact at school together, which must be why we all call Strafe by his surname: Major R. B. Strafe he is, the initials standing for Robert Buchanan. We're of an age, the four of us, all in the early fifties: the prime of life, so Dekko insists. We live quite close to Leatherhead, where the Malseeds were before they decided to make the change from Surrey to Co. Antrim. Quite a coincidence, we always think.

'How *very* nice,' Mrs Malseed said, smiling her welcome again this year. Some instinct seems to tell her when guests are about to arrive, for she's rarely not waiting in the large low-ceilinged hall that always smells of flowers. She dresses beautifully, differently every day, and changing of course in the evening. Her blouse on this occasion was scarlet and silver, in stripes, her skirt black. This choice gave her a brisk look, which was fitting because being so busy she often has to be a little on the brisk side. She has smooth grey hair which she once told me she entirely looks after herself, and she almost always wears a black velvet band in it. Her face is well made up, and for one who arranges so many vases of flowers and otherwise has to use her hands she manages to keep them marvellously in condition. Her fingernails are varnished a soft pink, and a small gold bangle always adorns her right wrist, a wedding present from her husband.

'Arthur, take the party's luggage,' she commanded the old porter, who doubles as odd-job man. 'Rose, Geranium, Hydrangea, Fuchsia.' She referred to the titles of the rooms reserved for us: in winter, when no one much comes to Glencorn Lodge, pleasant little details like that are seen to. Mrs Malseed herself painted the flower-plaques that are attached to the doors of the hotel instead of numbers; her

77

husband sees to redecoration and repairs.

'Well, well, well,' Mr Malseed said now, entering the hall through the door that leads to the kitchen regions. 'A hundred thousand welcomes,' he greeted us in the Irish manner. He's rather shorter than Mrs Malseed, who's handsomely tall. He wears Donegal tweed suits and is brown as a berry, including his head, which is bald. His dark brown eyes twinkle at you, making you feel rather more than just another hotel guest. They run the place like a country house, really.

'Good trip?' Mr Malseed enquired.

'Super,' Dekko said. 'Not a worry all the way.'

'Splendid.'

'The wretched boat sailed an hour early one day last week,' Mrs Malseed said. 'Quite a little band were left stranded at Stranraer.'

Strafe laughed. Typical of that steamship company, he said. 'Catching the tide, I dare say?'

'They caught a rocket from me,' Mrs Malseed replied good-humouredly. 'A couple of old dears were due with us on Tuesday and had to spend the night in some awful Scottish lodging-house. It nearly finished them.'

Everyone laughed, and I could feel the others thinking that our holiday had truly begun. Nothing had changed at Glencorn Lodge, all was well with its Irish world. Kitty from the dining-room came out to greet us, spotless in her uniform. 'Ach, you're looking younger,' she said, paying the compliment to all four of us, causing everyone in the hall to laugh again. Kitty's a bit of a card.

Arthur led the way to the rooms called Rose, Geranium, Hydrangea and Fuchsia, carrying as much of our luggage as he could manage and returning for the remainder. Arthur has a beaten, fisherman's face and short grey hair. He wears a green baize apron, and a white shirt with an imitation-silk scarf tucked into it at the neck. The scarf, in different swirling greens which blend nicely with the green of his apron, is an idea of Mrs Malseed's and one appreciates the effort, if not at a uniform, at least at tidiness.

'Thank you very much,' I said to Arthur in my room, smiling and finding him a coin.

★

We played a couple of rubbers after dinner as usual, but not of course going on for as long as we might have because we were still quite tired after the journey. In the lounge there was a French family, two girls and their parents, and a honeymoon couple – or so we had speculated during dinner – and a man on his own. There had been other people at dinner of course, because in June Glencorn Lodge is always full: from where we sat in the window we could see some of them strolling about the lawns, a few taking the cliff path down to the seashore. In the morning we'd do the same: we'd walk along the sands to Ardbeag and have coffee in the hotel there, back in time for lunch. In the afternoon we'd drive somewhere.

I knew all that because over the years this kind of pattern had developed. We had our walks and our drives, tweed to buy in Cushendall, Strafe's and Dekko's fishing day when Cynthia and I just sat on the beach, our visit to the Giant's Causeway and one to Donegal perhaps, though that meant an early start and taking pot-luck for dinner somewhere. We'd come to adore Co. Antrim, its glens and coastline, Rathlin Island and Tievebulliagh. Since first we got to know it, in 1965, we'd all four fallen hopelessly in love with every variation of this remarkable landscape. People in England thought us mad of course: they see so much of the troubles on television that it's naturally difficult for them to realise that most places are just as they've always been. Yet coming as we did, taking the road along the coast, dawdling through Ballygally, it was impossible to believe that somewhere else the unpleasantness was going on. We'd never seen a thing, nor even heard people talking about incidents that might have taken place. It's true that after a particularly nasty carry-on a few winters ago we did consider finding somewhere else, in Scotland perhaps, or Wales. But as Strafe put it at the time, we felt we owed a certain loyalty to the Malseeds and indeed to everyone we'd come to know round about, people who'd always been glad to welcome us back. It seemed silly to lose our heads, and when we returned the following summer we knew immediately we'd been right. Dekko said that nothing could be further away from all the violence than Glencorn Lodge, and though his remark could hardly be taken literally I think we all knew what he meant.

'Cynthia's tired,' I said because she'd been stifling yawns. 'I think we should call it a day.'

'Oh, not at all,' Cynthia protested. 'No, please.'

But Dekko agreed with me that she was tired, and Strafe said he didn't mind stopping now. He suggested a nightcap, as he always does, and as we always do also, Cynthia and I declined. Dekko said he'd like a Cointreau.

The conversation drifted about. Dekko told us an Irish joke about a drunk who couldn't find his way out of a telephone box, and then Strafe remembered an incident at school concerning his and Dekko's housemaster, A. D. Cowley-Stubbs, and the house wag, Thrive Major. A. D. Cowley-Stubbs had been known as Cows and often featured in our after-bridge reminiscing. So did Thrive Major.

'Perhaps I *am* sleepy,' Cynthia said. 'I don't think I closed my eyes once last night.'

She never does on a sea crossing. Personally I'm out like a light the moment my head touches the pillow; I often think it must be the salt in the air because normally I'm an uneasy sleeper at the best of times.

'You run along, old girl,' Strafe advised.

'Brekky at nine,' Dekko said.

Cynthia said good-night and went, and we didn't remark on her tiredness because as a kind of unwritten rule we never comment on one another. We're four people who play bridge. The companionship it offers, and the holidays we have together, are all part of that. We share everything: the cost of petrol, the cups of coffee or drinks we have; we even each make a contribution towards the use of Strafe's car because it's always his we go on holiday in, a Rover it was on this occasion.

'Funny, being here on your own,' Strafe said, glancing across what the Malseeds call the After-Dinner Lounge at the man who didn't have a companion. He was a red-haired man of about thirty, not wearing a tie, his collar open at the neck and folded back over the jacket of his blue serge suit. He was uncouth-looking, though it's a hard thing to say, not at all the kind of person one usually sees at Glencorn Lodge. He sat in the After-Dinner Lounge as he had in the dining-room, lost in some concentration of his own, as if calculating sums in his mind. There had been a folded newspaper on his table in the dining-room. It now reposed tidily on the arm of his chair, still unopened.

'Commercial gent,' Dekko said. 'Fertilisers.'

'Good heavens, never. You wouldn't get a rep in here.'

I took no part in the argument. The lone man didn't much interest me, but I felt that Strafe was probably right: if there was anything dubious about the man's credentials he might have found it difficult to secure a room. In the hall of Glencorn Lodge there's a notice which reads: *We prefer not to feature in hotel guides, and we would be grateful to our guests if they did not seek to include Glencorn Lodge in the Good Food Guide, the Good Hotel Guide, the Michelin, Egon Ronay or any others. We have not advertised Glencorn since our early days, and prefer our recommendations to be by word of mouth.*

'Ah, thank you,' Strafe said when Kitty brought his whisky and Dekko's Cointreau. 'Sure you won't have something?' he said to me, although he knew I never did.

Strafe is on the stout side, I suppose you could say, with a gingery moustache and gingery hair, hardly touched at all by grey. He left the Army years ago, I suppose because of me in a sense, because he didn't want to be posted abroad again. He's in the Ministry of Defence now.

I'm still quite pretty in my way, though nothing like as striking as Mrs Malseed, for I've never been that kind of woman. I've put on weight, and wouldn't have allowed myself to do so if Strafe hadn't kept saying he can't stand a bag of bones. I'm careful about my hair and, unlike Mrs Malseed, I have it very regularly seen to because if I don't it gets a salt and pepper look, which I hate. My husband, Ralph, who died of food-poisoning when we were still quite young, used to say I wouldn't lose a single look in middle age, and to some extent that's true. We were still putting off having children when he died, which is why I haven't any. Then I met Strafe, which meant I didn't marry again.

Strafe is married himself, to Cynthia. She's small and ineffectual, I suppose you'd say without being untruthful or unkind. Not that Cynthia and I don't get on or anything like that, in fact we get on extremely well. It's Strafe and Cynthia who don't seem quite to hit it off, and I often think how much happier all round it would have been if Cynthia had married someone completely different, someone like Dekko in a way, except that that mightn't quite have worked out either. The Strafes have two sons, both very like their father, both of them in the Army. And the very sad thing is they think nothing of poor Cynthia.

'Who's that chap?' Dekko asked Mr Malseed, who'd come over to wish us good-night.

'Awfully sorry about that, Mr Deakin. My fault entirely, a booking that came over the phone.'

'Good heavens, not at all,' Strafe protested, and Dekko looked horrified in case it should be thought he was objecting to the locals. 'Splendid-looking fellow,' he said, overdoing it.

Mr Malseed murmured that the man had only booked in for a single night, and I smiled the whole thing away, reassuring him with a nod. It's one of the pleasantest of the traditions at Glencorn Lodge that every evening Mr Malseed makes the rounds of his guests just to say good-night. It's because of little touches like that that I, too, wished Dekko hadn't questioned Mr Malseed about the man because it's the kind of thing one doesn't do at Glencorn Lodge. But Dekko is a law unto himself, very tall and gangling, always immaculately suited, a beaky face beneath mousy hair in which flecks of grey add a certain distinction. Dekko has money of his own and though he takes out girls who are half his age he has never managed to get around to marriage. The uncharitable might say he has a rather gormless laugh; certainly it's sometimes on the loud side.

We watched while Mr Malseed bade the lone man good-night. The man didn't respond, but just sat gazing. It was ill-mannered, but this lack of courtesy didn't appear to be intentional: the man was clearly in a mood of some kind, miles away.

'Well, I'll go up,' I said. 'Good-night, you two.'

'Cheery-bye, Milly,' Dekko said. 'Brekky at nine, remember.'

'Good-night, Milly,' Strafe said.

The Strafes always occupy different rooms on holidays, and at home also. This time he was in Geranium and she in Fuchsia. I was in Rose, and in a little while Strafe would come to see me. He stays with her out of kindness, because he fears for her on her own. He's a sentimental, good-hearted man, easily moved to tears: he simply cannot bear the thought of Cynthia with no one to talk to in the evenings, with no one to make her life around. 'And besides,' he often says when he's being jocular, 'it would break up our bridge four.' Naturally we never discuss her shortcomings or in any way analyse the marriage. The unwritten rule that exists among the four of us seems to extend as far as that.

He slipped into my room after he'd had another drink or two, and I was waiting for him as he likes me to wait, in bed but not quite undressed. He has never said so, but I know that that is something Cynthia would not understand in him, or ever attempt to comply with. Ralph, of course, would not have understood either; poor old Ralph would have been shocked. Actually it's all rather sweet, Strafe and his little ways.

'I love you, dear,' I whispered to him in the darkness, but just then he didn't wish to speak of love and referred instead to my body.

★

If Cynthia hadn't decided to remain in the hotel the next morning instead of accompanying us on our walk to Ardbeag everything might have been different. As it happened, when she said at breakfast she thought she'd just potter about the garden and sit with her book out of the wind somewhere, I can't say I was displeased. For a moment I hoped Dekko might say he'd stay with her, allowing Strafe and myself to go off on our own, but Dekko – who doesn't go in for saying what you want him to say – didn't. 'Poor old sausage,' he said instead, examining Cynthia with a solicitude that suggested she was close to the grave, rather than just a little lowered by the change of life or whatever it was.

'I'll be perfectly all right,' Cynthia assured him. 'Honestly.'

'Cynthia likes to mooch, you know,' Strafe pointed out, which of course is only the truth. She reads too much, I always think. You often see her putting down a book with the most melancholy look in her eyes, which can't be good for her. She's an imaginative woman, I suppose you would say, and of course her habit of reading so much is often useful on our holidays: over the years she has read her way through dozens of Irish guide-books. 'That's where the garrison pushed the natives over the cliffs,' she once remarked on a drive. 'Those rocks are known as the Maidens,' she remarked on another occasion. She has led us to places of interest which we had no idea existed: Garron Tower on Garron Point, the mausoleum at Bonamargy, the Devil's Backbone. As well as which, Cynthia is extremely knowledgeable about all matters relating to Irish history. Again she has read endlessly: biographies and autobiographies, long accounts of the centuries of battling and politics there've been. There's hardly a town or village we ever pass through that hasn't some significance for Cynthia, although

I'm afraid her impressive fund of information doesn't always receive the attention it deserves. Not that Cynthia ever minds; it doesn't seem to worry her when no one listens. My own opinion is that she'd have made a much better job of her relationship with Strafe and her sons if she could have somehow developed a bit more character.

We left her in the garden and proceeded down the cliff path to the shingle beneath. I was wearing slacks and a blouse, with the arms of a cardigan looped round my neck in case it turned chilly: the outfit was new, specially bought for the holiday, in shades of tangerine. Strafe never cares how he dresses and of course she doesn't keep him up to the mark: that morning, as far as I remember, he wore rather shapeless corduroy trousers, the kind men sometimes garden in, and a navy-blue fisherman's jersey. Dekko as usual was a fashion plate: a pale green linen suit with pleated jacket pockets, a maroon shirt open at the neck, revealing a medallion on a fine gold chain. We didn't converse as we crossed the rather difficult shingle, but when we reached the sand Dekko began to talk about some girl or other, someone called Juliet who had apparently proposed marriage to him just before we'd left Surrey. He'd told her, so he said, that he'd think about it while on holiday and he wondered now about dispatching a telegram from Ardbeag saying, *Still thinking*. Strafe, who has a simple sense of humour, considered this hugely funny and spent most of the walk persuading Dekko that the telegram must certainly be sent, and other telegrams later on, all with the same message. Dekko kept laughing, throwing his head back in a way that always reminds me of an Australian bird I once saw in a nature film on television. I could see this was going to become one of those jokes that would accompany us all through the holiday, a man's thing really, but of course I didn't mind. The girl called Juliet was nearly thirty years younger than Dekko. I supposed she knew what she was doing.

Since the subject of telegrams had come up, Strafe recalled the occasion when Thrive Major had sent one to A. D. Cowley-Stubbs: *Darling regret three months gone love Rowena.* Carefully timed, it had arrived during one of Cows' Thursday evening coffee sessions. Rowena was a maid, known as the Bicycle, who had been sacked the previous term, and old Cows had something of a reputation as a misogynist. When he read the message he apparently went white and collapsed into an armchair. Warrington P. J. managed to read it too, and after that the fat was in the fire. The consequences went on rather, but I never minded listening when Strafe and Dekko drifted back to their schooldays. I just wish I'd known Strafe then, before either of us had gone and got married.

We had our coffee at Ardbeag, the telegram was sent off, and then Strafe and Dekko wanted to see a man called Henry O'Reilly whom we'd met on previous holidays, who organises mackerel-fishing trips. I waited on my own, picking out postcards in the village shop that sells almost everything, and then I wandered down towards the shore. I knew that they would be having a drink with the boatman because a year had passed since they'd seen him last. They joined me after about twenty minutes, Dekko apologising but Strafe not seeming to be aware that I'd had to wait because Strafe is not a man who notices little things. It was almost one o'clock when we reached Glencorn Lodge and were told by Mr Malseed that Cynthia needed looking after.

*

The hotel, in fact, was in a turmoil. I have never seen anyone as ashen-faced as Mr Malseed; his wife, in a forget-me-not dress, was limp. It wasn't explained to us immediately what had happened, because in the middle of telling us that Cynthia needed looking after Mr Malseed was summoned to the telephone. I could see through the half-open door of their little office a glass of whisky or brandy on the desk and Mrs Malseed's bangled arm reaching out for it. Not for ages did we realise that it all had to do with the lone man whom we'd speculated about the night before.

'He just wanted to talk to me,' Cynthia kept repeating hysterically in the hall. 'He sat with me by the magnolias.'

I made her lie down. Strafe and I stood on either side of her bed as she lay there with her shoes off, her rather unattractively cut plain pink dress crumpled and actually damp from her tears. I wanted to make her take it off and to slip under the bed-clothes in her petticoat but somehow it seemed all wrong, in the circumstances, for Strafe's wife to do anything so intimate in my presence.

'I couldn't stop him,' Cynthia said, the rims of her eyes crimson by now, her nose beginning to run again. 'From half past ten till well after twelve. He had to talk to someone, he said.'

I could sense that Strafe was thinking precisely the same as I was: that the red-haired man had insinuated himself into Cynthia's company by talking about himself and had then put a hand on her knee. Instead of simply standing up and going away Cynthia would have stayed where she was, embarrassed or tongue-tied, at any rate unable to cope. And when the moment came she would have turned hysterical. I could picture her screaming in the garden, running across the lawn to the hotel, and then the pandemonium in the hall. I could sense Strafe picturing that also.

'My God, it's terrible,' Cynthia said.

'I think she should sleep,' I said quietly to Strafe. 'Try to sleep, dear,' I said to her, but she shook her head, tossing her jumble of hair about on the pillow.

'Milly's right,' Strafe urged. 'You'll feel much better after a little rest. We'll bring you a cup of tea later on.'

'My God!' she cried again. 'My God, how could I sleep?'

I went away to borrow a couple of mild sleeping pills from Dekko, who is never without them, relying on the things too much in my opinion. He was tidying himself in his room, but found the pills immediately. Strangely enough, Dekko's always sound in a crisis.

I gave them to her with water and she took them without asking what they were. She was in a kind of daze, one moment making a fuss and weeping, the next just peering ahead of her, as if frightened. In a way she was like someone who'd just had a bad nightmare and hadn't yet completely returned to reality. I remarked as much to Strafe while we made our way down to lunch, and he said he quite agreed.

'Poor old Cynth!' Dekko said when we'd all ordered lobster bisque and entrecôte béarnaise. 'Poor old sausage.'

You could see that the little waitress, a new girl this year, was bubbling over with excitement; but Kitty, serving the other half of the dining-room, was grim, which was most unusual. Everyone was talking in hushed tones and when Dekko said, 'Poor old Cynth!' a couple of heads were turned in our direction because he can never keep his voice down. The little vases of roses with which Mrs Malseed must have decorated each table before the fracas had occurred seemed strangely out of place in the atmosphere which had developed.

The waitress had just taken away our soup-plates when Mr Malseed hurried into the dining-room and came straight to our table. The lobster bisque surprisingly hadn't been quite up to scratch, and in passing I couldn't help wondering if the fuss had caused the kitchen to go to pieces also.

'I wonder if I might have a word, Major Strafe,' Mr Malseed said, and Strafe rose at once and accompanied him from the dining-room. A total silence had fallen, everyone in the dining-room pretending to be intent on eating. I had an odd feeling that we had perhaps got it all wrong, that because we'd been out for our walk when it had happened all the other guests knew more of the details than Strafe and Dekko and I did. I began to wonder if poor Cynthia had been raped.

Afterwards Strafe told us what occurred in the Malseeds' office, how Mrs Malseed had been sitting there, slumped, as he put it, and how two policemen had questioned him. 'Look, what on earth's all this about?' he had demanded rather sharply.

'It concerns this incident that's taken place, sir,' one of the policemen explained in an unhurried voice. 'On account of your wife –'

'My wife's lying down. She must not be questioned or in any way disturbed.'

'Ach, we'd never do that, sir.'

Strafe does a good Co. Antrim brogue and in relating all this to us he couldn't resist making full use of it. The two policemen were in uniform and their natural slowness of intellect was rendered more noticeable by the lugubrious air the tragedy had inspired in the hotel. For tragedy was what it was: after talking to Cynthia for nearly two hours the lone man had walked down to the rocks and been drowned.

*

When Strafe finished speaking I placed my knife and fork together on my plate, unable to eat another mouthful. The facts appeared to be that the man, having left Cynthia by the magnolias, had clambered down the cliff to a place no one ever went to, on the other side of the hotel from the sands we had walked along to Ardbeag. No one had seen him except Cynthia, who from the cliff-top had apparently witnessed his battering by the treacherous waves. The tide had been coming in, but by the time old Arthur and Mr Malseed reached the rocks it had begun to turn, leaving behind it the fully dressed corpse. Mr Malseed's impression was that the man had lost his footing on the seaweed and accidentally stumbled into the depths, for the rocks were so slippery it was difficult to carry the corpse more than a matter of yards. But at least it had been placed out of view, while Mr Malseed hurried back to the hotel to telephone for assistance. He told Strafe that Cynthia had been most confused, insisting that the man had walked out among the rocks and then into the sea, knowing what he was doing.

Listening to it all, I no longer felt sorry for Cynthia. It was typical of her that she should so sillily have involved us in all this. Why on earth had she sat in the garden with a man of that kind instead of standing up and making a fuss the moment he'd begun to paw her? If she'd acted intelligently the whole unfortunate episode could clearly have been avoided. Since it hadn't, there was no point whatsoever in insisting that the man had committed suicide when at that distance no one could possibly be sure.

'It really does astonish me,' I said at the lunch table, unable to prevent myself from breaking our unwritten rule. 'Whatever came over her?'

'It can't be good for the hotel,' Dekko commented, and I was glad to see Strafe giving him a little glance of irritation.

'It's hardly the point,' I said coolly.

'What I meant was, hotels occasionally hush things like this up.'

'Well, they haven't this time.' It seemed an age since I had waited for them in Ardbeag, since we had been so happily laughing over the effect of Dekko's telegram. He'd included his address in it so that the girl could send a message back, and as we'd returned to the hotel along the seashore there'd been much speculation between the two men about the form this would take.

'I suppose what Cynthia's thinking,' Strafe said, 'is that after he'd tried something on with her he became depressed.'

'Oh, but he could just as easily have lost his footing. He'd have been on edge anyway, worried in case she reported him.'

'Dreadful kind of death,' Dekko said. His tone suggested that that was that, that the subject should now be closed, and so it was.

After lunch we went to our rooms, as we always do at Glencorn Lodge, to rest for an hour. I took my slacks and blouse off, hoping that Strafe would knock on my door, but he didn't and of course that was understandable. Oddly enough I found myself thinking of Dekko, picturing his long form stretched out in the room called Hydrangea, his beaky face in profile on his pillow. The precise nature of Dekko's relationship with these girls he picks up has always privately intrigued me: was it really possible that somewhere in London there was a girl called Juliet who was prepared to marry him for his not inconsiderable money?

I slept and briefly dreamed. Thrive Major and Warrington P. J. were running the post office in Ardbeag, sending telegrams to everyone they could think of, including Dekko's friend Juliet. Cynthia had been found dead beside the magnolias and people were waiting for Hercule Poirot to arrive. 'Promise me you didn't do it,' I whispered to Strafe, but when Strafe replied it was to say that Cynthia's body reminded him of a bag of old chicken bones.

*

Strafe and Dekko and I met for tea in the tea-lounge. Strafe had looked in to see if Cynthia had woken, but apparently she hadn't. The police officers had left the hotel, Dekko said, because he'd noticed their car wasn't parked at the front any more. None of the three of us said, but I think we presumed, that the man's body had been removed from the rocks during the quietness of the afternoon. From where we sat I caught a glimpse of Mrs Malseed passing quite briskly through the hall, seeming almost herself again. Certainly our holiday would be affected, but it might not be totally ruined. All that remained to hope for was Cynthia's recovery, and then everyone could set about forgetting the unpleasantness. The nicest thing would be if a jolly young couple turned up and occupied the man's room, exorcising the incident, as newcomers would.

The family from France – the two little girls and their parents – were chattering away in the tea-lounge, and an elderly trio who'd arrived that morning were speaking in American accents. The honeymoon couple appeared, looking rather shy, and began to whisper and giggle in a corner. People who occupied the table next to ours in the dining-room, a Wing-Commander Orfell and his wife, from Guildford, nodded and smiled as they passed. Everyone was making an effort, and I knew it would help matters further if Cynthia felt up to a rubber or two before dinner. That life should continue as normally as possible was essential for Glencorn Lodge, the example already set by Mrs Malseed.

Because of our interrupted lunch I felt quite hungry, and the Malseeds pride themselves on their teas. The chef, Mr McBride, whom of course we've met, has the lightest touch I know with sponge cakes and little curranty scones. I was, in fact, buttering a scone when Strafe said:

'Here she is.'

And there indeed she was. By the look of her she had simply pushed herself off her bed and come straight down. Her pink dress was even more crumpled than it had been. She hadn't so much as run a comb through her hair, her face was puffy and unpowdered. For a moment I really thought she was walking in her sleep.

Strafe and Dekko stood up. 'Feeling better, dear?' Strafe said, but she didn't answer.

'Sit down, Cynth,' Dekko urged, pushing back a chair to make room for her.

'He told me a story I can never forget. I've dreamed about it all over again.' Cynthia swayed in front of us, not even attempting to sit down. To tell the truth, she sounded inane.

'Story, dear?' Strafe enquired, humouring her.

She said it was the story of two children who had apparently ridden bicycles through the streets of Belfast, out into Co. Antrim. The bicycles were dilapidated, she said; she didn't know if they were stolen or not. She didn't know about the children's homes because the man hadn't spoken of them, but she claimed to know instinctively that they had ridden away from poverty and unhappiness. 'From the clatter and the quarrelling,' Cynthia said. 'Two children who later fell in love.'

'Horrid old dream,' Strafe said. 'Horrid for you, dear.'

She shook her head, and then sat down. I poured another cup of tea. 'I had the oddest dream myself,' I said. 'Thrive Major was running the post office in Ardbeag.'

Strafe smiled and Dekko gave his laugh, but Cynthia didn't in any way acknowledge what I'd said.

'A fragile thing the girl was, with depths of mystery in her wide brown eyes. Red-haired of course he was himself, thin as a rake in those days. Glencorn Lodge was derelict then.'

'You've had a bit of a shock, old thing,' Dekko said.

Strafe agreed, kindly adding, 'Look, dear, if the chap actually interfered with you –'

'Why on earth should he do that?' Her voice was shrill in the tea-lounge, edged with a note of hysteria. I glanced at Strafe, who was frowning into his tea-cup. Dekko began to say something, but broke off before his meaning emerged. Rather more calmly Cynthia said:

'It was summer when they came here. Honeysuckle he described. And mother of thyme. He didn't know the name of either.'

No one attempted any kind of reply, not that it was necessary, for Cynthia just continued.

'At school there were the facts of geography and arithmetic. And the legends of scholars and of heroes, of Queen Maeve and Finn MacCool. There was the coming of St Patrick to a heathen people. History was full of kings and high-kings, and Silken Thomas and Wolfe Tone, the Flight of the Earls, the Siege of Limerick.'

When Cynthia said that, it was impossible not to believe that the unfortunate events of the morning had touched her with some kind of madness. It seemed astonishing that she had walked into the tea-lounge without having combed her hair, and that she'd stood there swaying before sitting down, that out of the blue she had started on about two children. None of it made an iota of sense, and surely she could see that the nasty experience she'd suffered should not be dwelt upon? I offered her the plate of scones, hoping that if she began to eat she would stop talking, but she took no notice of my gesture.

'Look, dear,' Strafe said, 'there's not one of us who knows what you're talking about.'

'I'm talking about a children's story, I'm talking about a girl and a boy who visited this place we visit also. He hadn't been here for years, but he returned last night, making one final effort to understand. And then he walked out into the sea.'

She had taken a piece of her dress and was agitatedly crumpling it between the finger and thumb of her left hand. It was dreadful really, having her so grubby-looking. For some odd reason I suddenly thought of her cooking, how she wasn't in the least interested in it or in anything about the house. She certainly hadn't succeeded in making a home for Strafe.

'They rode those worn-out bicycles through a hot afternoon. Can you feel all that? A newly surfaced road, the snap of chippings beneath their tyres, the smell of tar? Dust from a passing car, the city they left behind?'

'Cynthia dear,' I said, 'drink your tea, and why not have a scone?'

'They swam and sunbathed on the beach you walked along today. They went to a spring for water. There were no magnolias then. There was no garden, no neat little cliff paths to the beach. Surely you can see it clearly?'

'No,' Strafe said. 'No, we really cannot, dear.'

'This place that is an idyll for us was an idyll for them too:

96

the trees, the ferns, the wild roses near the water spring, the very sea and sun they shared. There was a cottage lost in the middle of the woods: they sometimes looked for that. They played a game, a kind of hide and seek. People in a white farmhouse gave them milk.'

For the second time I offered Cynthia the plate of scones and for the second time she pointedly ignored me. Her cup of tea hadn't been touched. Dekko took a scone and cheerfully said:

'All's well that's over.'

But Cynthia appeared to have drifted back into a daze, and I wondered again if it could really be possible that the experience had unhinged her. Unable to help myself, I saw her being led away from the hotel, helped into the back of a blue van, something like an ambulance. She was talking about the children again, how they had planned to marry and keep a sweetshop.

'Take it easy, dear,' Strafe said, which I followed up by suggesting for the second time that she should make an effort to drink her tea.

'Has it to do with the streets they came from? Or the history they learnt, he from his Christian Brothers, she from her nuns? History is unfinished in this island; long since it has come to a stop in Surrey.'

Dekko said, and I really had to hand it to him:

'Cynth, we have to put it behind us.'

It didn't do any good. Cynthia just went rambling on, speaking again of the girl being taught by nuns, and the boy by Christian Brothers. She began to recite the history they might have learnt, the way she sometimes did when we were driving through an area that had historical connections. 'Can you imagine,' she embarrassingly asked, 'our very favourite places bitter with disaffection, with plotting and revenge? Can you imagine the treacherous murder of Shane O'Neill the Proud?'

Dekko made a little sideways gesture of his head, politely marvelling. Strafe seemed about to say something, but changed his mind. Confusion ran through Irish history, Cynthia said, like convolvulus in a hedgerow. On May 24th, 1487, a boy of ten called Lambert Simnel, brought to Dublin by a priest from Oxford, was declared Edward VI of all England and Ireland, crowned with a golden circlet taken from a statue of the Virgin Mary. On May 24th, 1798, here in Antrim, Presbyterian farmers fought for a common cause with their Catholic labourers. She paused and looked at Strafe. Chaos and contradiction, she informed him, were hidden everywhere beneath nice-sounding names. 'The Battle of the Yellow Ford,' she suddenly chanted in a sing-song way that sounded thoroughly peculiar, 'the Statutes of Kilkenny. The Battle of Glenmama, the Convention of Drumceat. The Act of Settlement, the Renunciation Act. The Act of Union, the Toleration Act. Just so much history it sounds like now, yet people starved or died while other people watched. A language was lost, a faith forbidden. Famine followed revolt, plantation followed that. But it was people who were struck into the soil of other people's land, not forests of new trees; and it was greed and treachery that spread as a disease among them all. No wonder unease clings to these shreds of history and shots ring out in answer to the mockery of drums. No wonder the air is nervy with suspicion.'

There was an extremely awkward silence when she ceased to speak. Dekko nodded, doing his best to be companionable. Strafe nodded also. I simply examined the pattern of roses on our tea-time china, not knowing what else to do. Eventually Dekko said:

'What an awful lot you know, Cynth!'

'Cynthia's always been interested,' Strafe said. 'Always had a first-rate memory.'

'Those children of the streets are part of the battles and the Acts,' she went on, seeming quite unaware that her talk was literally almost crazy. 'They're part of the blood that flowed around those nice-sounding names.' She paused, and for a moment seemed disinclined to continue. Then she said:

'The second time they came here the house was being rebuilt. There were concrete-mixers, and lorries drawn up on the grass, noise and scaffolding everywhere. They watched all through another afternoon and then they went their different ways: their childhood was over, lost with their idyll. He became a dockyard clerk. She went to London, to work in a betting shop.'

'My dear,' Strafe said very gently, 'it's interesting, everything you say, but it really hardly concerns us.'

'No, of course not.' Quite emphatically Cynthia shook her head, appearing wholly to agree. 'They were degenerate, awful creatures. They must have been.'

'No one's saying that, my dear.'

'Their story should have ended there, he in the docklands of Belfast, she recording bets. Their complicated childhood love should just have dissipated, as such love often does. But somehow nothing was as neat as that.'

Dekko, in an effort to lighten the conversation, mentioned a boy called Gollsol who'd been at school with Strafe and himself, who'd formed a romantic attachment for the daughter of one of the groundsmen and had later actually married her. There was a silence for a moment, then Cynthia, without emotion, said:

'You none of you care. You sit there not caring that two people are dead.'

'Two people, Cynthia?' I said.

'For God's sake, I'm telling you!' she cried. 'That girl was murdered in a room in Maida Vale.'

Although there is something between Strafe and myself, I do try my best to be at peace about it. I go to church and take communion, and I know Strafe occasionally does too, though not as often as perhaps he might. Cynthia has no interest in that side of life, and it rankled with me now to hear her blaspheming so casually, and so casually speaking about death in Maida Vale on top of all this stuff about history and children. Strafe was shaking his head, clearly believing that Cynthia didn't know what she was talking about.

'Cynthia dear,' I began, 'are you sure you're not muddling something up here? You've been upset, you've had a nightmare: don't you think your imagination, or something you've been reading –'

'Bombs don't go off on their own. Death doesn't just happen to occur in Derry and Belfast, in London and Amsterdam and Dublin, in Berlin and Jerusalem. There are people who are murderers: that is what this children's story is about.'

A silence fell, no one knowing what to say. It didn't matter of course because without any prompting Cynthia continued.

'We drink our gin with Angostura bitters, there's lamb or chicken Kiev. Old Kitty's kind to us in the dining-room and old Arthur in the hall. Flowers are everywhere, we have our special table.'

'Please let us take you to your room now,' Strafe begged, and as he spoke I reached out a hand in friendship and placed it on her arm. 'Come on, old thing,' Dekko said.

'The limbless are left on the streets, blood spatters the

car-parks. *Brits Out* it says on a rockface, but we know it doesn't mean us.'

I spoke quietly then, measuring my words, measuring the pause between each so that its effect might be registered. I felt the statement had to be made, whether it was my place to make it or not. I said:

'You are very confused, Cynthia.'

The French family left the tea-lounge. The two Dalmatians, Charger and Snooze, ambled in and sniffed and went away again. Kitty came to clear the French family's tea things. I could hear her speaking to the honeymoon couple, saying the weather forecast was good.

'Cynthia,' Strafe said, standing up, 'we've been very patient with you but this is now becoming silly.'

I nodded just a little. 'I really think,' I softly said, but Cynthia didn't permit me to go on.

'Someone told him about her. Someone mentioned her name, and he couldn't believe it. She sat alone in Maida Vale, putting together the mechanisms of her bombs: this girl who had laughed on the seashore, whom he had loved.'

'Cynthia,' Strafe began, but he wasn't permitted to continue either. Hopelessly, he just sat down again.

'Whenever he heard of bombs exploding he thought of her, and couldn't understand. He wept when he said that; her violence haunted him, he said. He couldn't work, he couldn't sleep at night. His mind filled up with images of her, their awkward childhood kisses, her fingers working neatly now. He saw her with a carrier-bag, hurrying it through a crowd, leaving it where it could cause most death. In front of the mouldering old house that had once been Glencorn Lodge they'd made a fire and cooked their food. They'd lain for ages on the grass. They'd cycled home to their city streets.'

It suddenly dawned on me that Cynthia was knitting this whole fantasy out of nothing. It all worked backwards from the moment when she'd had the misfortune to witness the man's death in the sea. A few minutes before he'd been chatting quite normally to her, he'd probably even mentioned a holiday in his childhood and some girl there'd been: all of it would have been natural in the circumstances, possibly even the holiday had taken place at Glencorn. He'd said good-bye and then unfortunately he'd had his accident. Watching from the cliff edge, something had cracked in poor Cynthia's brain, she having always been a prey to melancholy. I suppose it must be hard having two sons who don't think much of you, and a marriage not offering you a great deal, bridge and holidays probably the best part of it. For some odd reason of her own she'd created her fantasy about a child turning into a terrorist. The violence of the man's death had clearly filled her imagination with Irish violence, so regularly seen on television. If we'd been on holiday in Suffolk I wondered how it would have seemed to the poor creature.

I could feel Strafe and Dekko beginning to put all that together also, beginning to realise that the whole story of the red-haired man and the girl was clearly Cynthia's invention. 'Poor creature,' I wanted to say, but did not do so.

'For months he searched for her, pushing his way among the people of London, the people who were her victims. When he found her she just looked at him, as if the past hadn't even existed. She didn't smile, as if incapable of smiling. He wanted to take her away, back to where they came from, but she didn't reply when he suggested that. Bitterness was like a disease in her, and when he left her he felt the bitterness in himself.'

Again Strafe and Dekko nodded, and I could feel Strafe

thinking that there really was no point in protesting further. All we could hope for was that the end of the saga was in sight.

'He remained in London, working on the railways. But in the same way as before he was haunted by the person she'd become, and the haunting was more awful now. He bought a gun from a man he'd been told about and kept it hidden in a shoe-box in his rented room. Now and again he took it out and looked at it, then put it back. He hated the violence that possessed her, yet he was full of it himself: he knew he couldn't betray her with anything but death. Humanity had left both of them when he visited her again in Maida Vale.'

To my enormous relief and, I could feel, to Strafe's and Dekko's too, Mr and Mrs Malseed appeared beside us. Like his wife, Mr Malseed had considerably recovered. He spoke in an even voice, clearly wishing to dispose of the matter. It was just the diversion we needed.

'I must apologise, Mrs Strafe,' he said. 'I cannot say how sorry we are that you were bothered by that man.'

'My wife is still a little dicky,' Strafe explained, 'but after a decent night's rest I think we can say she'll be as right as rain again.'

'I only wish, Mrs Strafe, you had made contact with my wife or myself when he first approached you.' There was a spark of irritation in Mr Malseed's eyes, but his voice was still controlled. 'I mean, the unpleasantness you suffered might just have been averted.'

'Nothing would have been averted, Mr Malseed, and certainly not the horror we are left with. Can you see her as the girl she became, seated at a chipped white table, her wires and fuses spread around her? What were her thoughts in that room, Mr Malseed? What happens in the mind of anyone who wishes to destroy? In a back street he bought his gun for too much money. When did it first occur to him to kill her?'

'We really are a bit at sea,' Mr Malseed replied without the slightest hesitation. He humoured Cynthia by displaying no surprise, by speaking very quietly.

'All I am saying, Mr Malseed, is that we should root our heads out of the sand and wonder about two people who are beyond the pale.'

'My dear,' Strafe said, 'Mr Malseed is a busy man.'

Still quietly, still perfectly in control of every intonation, without a single glance around the tea-lounge to ascertain where his guests' attention was, Mr Malseed said:

'There is unrest here, Mrs Strafe, but we do our best to live with it.'

'All I am saying is that perhaps there can be regret when two children end like this.'

Mr Malseed did not reply. His wife did her best to smile away the awkwardness. Strafe murmured privately to Cynthia, no doubt beseeching her to come to her senses. Again I imagined a blue van drawn up in front of Glencorn Lodge, for it was quite understandable now that an imaginative woman should go mad, affected by the ugliness of death. The garbled speculation about the man and the girl, the jumble in the poor thing's mind – a children's story as she called it – all somehow hung together when you realised they didn't have to make any sense whatsoever.

'Murderers are beyond the pale, Mr Malseed, and England has always had its pales. The one in Ireland began in 1395.'

'Dear,' I said, 'what has happened has nothing whatsoever to do with calling people murderers and placing them beyond some pale or other. You witnessed a most unpleasant accident, dear, and it's only to be expected that you've become just a little lost. The man had a chat with you when you were sitting by the magnolias and then the shock of seeing him slip on the seaweed –'

'He didn't slip on the seaweed,' she suddenly screamed. 'My God, he didn't slip on the seaweed.'

Strafe closed his eyes. The other guests in the tea-lounge had fallen silent ages ago, openly listening. Arthur was standing near the door and was listening also. Kitty was waiting to clear away our tea things, but didn't like to because of what was happening.

'I must request you to take Mrs Strafe to her room, Major,' Mr Malseed said. 'And I must make it clear that we cannot tolerate further upset in Glencorn Lodge.'

Strafe reached for her arm, but Cynthia took no notice.

'An Irish joke,' she said, and then she stared at Mr and Mrs Malseed, her eyes passing over each feature of their faces. She stared at Dekko and Strafe, and last of all at me. She said eventually:

'An Irish joke, an unbecoming tale: of course it can't be true. Ridiculous, that a man returned here. Ridiculous, that he walked again by the seashore and through the woods, hoping to understand where a woman's cruelty had come from.'

'This talk is most offensive,' Mr Malseed protested, his calmness slipping just a little. The ashen look that had earlier been in his face returned. I could see he was beside himself with rage. 'You are trying to bring something to our doorstep which most certainly does not belong there.'

'On your doorstep they talked about a sweetshop: Cadbury's bars and different-flavoured creams, nut-milk toffee, Aero and Crunchie.'

'For God's sake pull yourself together,' I clearly heard Strafe whispering, and Mrs Malseed attempted to smile. 'Come along now, Mrs Strafe,' she said, making a gesture.

'Just to please us, dear. Kitty wants to clear away the dishes. Kitty!' she called out, endeavouring to bring matters down to earth.

Kitty crossed the lounge with her tray and gathered up the cups and saucers. The Malseeds, naturally still anxious, hovered. No one was surprised when Cynthia began all over again, by crazily asking Kitty what she thought of us.

'I think, dear,' Mrs Malseed began, 'Kitty's quite busy really.'

'Stop this at once,' Strafe quietly ordered.

'For fourteen years, Kitty, you've served us with food and cleared away the tea-cups we've drunk from. For fourteen years we've played our bridge and walked about the garden. We've gone for drives, we've bought our tweed, we've bathed as those children did.'

'Stop it,' Strafe said again, a little louder. Bewildered and getting red in the face, Kitty hastily bundled china on to her tray. I made a sign at Strafe because for some reason I felt that the end was really in sight. I wanted him to retain his patience, but what Cynthia said next was almost unbelievable.

'In Surrey we while away the time, we clip our hedges. On a bridge night there's coffee at nine o'clock, with macaroons or *petits fours*. Last thing of all we watch the late-night News, packing away our cards and scoring-pads, our sharpened pencils. There's been an incident in Armagh, one soldier's had his head shot off, another's run amok. Our lovely Glens of Antrim, we all four think, our coastal drives: we hope that nothing disturbs the peace. We think of Mr Malseed, still busy in Glencorn Lodge, and Mrs Malseed finishing her flower-plaques for the rooms of the completed annexe.'

'Will you for God's sake shut up?' Strafe suddenly

shouted. I could see him struggling with himself, but it didn't do any good. He called Cynthia a bloody spectacle, sitting there talking rubbish. I don't believe she even heard him.

'Through honey-tinted glasses we love you and we love your island, Kitty. We love the lilt of your racy history, we love your earls and heroes. Yet we made a sensible pale here once, as civilised people create a garden, pretty as a picture.'

Strafe's outburst had been quite noisy and I could sense him being ashamed of it. He muttered that he was sorry, but Cynthia simply took advantage of his generosity, continuing about a pale.

'Beyond it lie the bleak untouchables, best kept as dots on the horizon, too terrible to contemplate. How can we be blamed if we make neither head nor tail of anything, Kitty, your past and your present, those battles and Acts of Parliament? We people of Surrey: how can we know? Yet I stupidly thought, you see, that the tragedy of two children could at least be understood. He didn't discover where her cruelty had come from because perhaps you never can: evil breeds evil in a mysterious way. That's the story the red-haired stranger passed on to me, the story you huddle away from.'

Poor Strafe was pulling at Cynthia, pleading with her, still saying he was sorry.

'Mrs Strafe,' Mr Malseed tried to say, but got no further. To my horror Cynthia abruptly pointed at me.

'That woman,' she said, 'is my husband's mistress, a fact I am supposed to be unaware of, Kitty.'

'My God!' Strafe said.

'My husband is perverted in his sexual desires. His friend, who shared his schooldays, has never quite recovered from that time. I myself am a pathetic creature who has closed her eyes to a husband's infidelity and his mistress's viciousness. I am dragged into the days of Thrive Major and A. D. Cowley-Stubbs: mechanically I smile. I hardly exist, Kitty.'

There was a most unpleasant silence, and then Strafe said: 'None of that's true. For God's sake, Cynthia,' he suddenly shouted, 'go and rest yourself.'

Cynthia shook her head and continued to address the waitress. She'd had a rest, she told her. 'But it didn't do any good, Kitty, because hell has invaded the paradise of Glencorn, as so often it has invaded your island. And we, who have so often brought it, pretend it isn't there. Who cares about children made into murderers?'

Strafe shouted again. 'You fleshless ugly bitch!' he cried. 'You bloody old fool!' He was on his feet, trying to get her on to hers. The blood was thumping in his bronzed face, his eyes had a fury in them I'd never seen before. 'Fleshless!' he shouted at her, not caring that so many people were listening. He closed his eyes in misery and in shame again, and I wanted to reach out and take his hand but of course I could not. You could see the Malseeds didn't blame him, you could see them thinking that everything was ruined for us. I wanted to shout at Cynthia too, to batter the silliness out of her, but of course I could not do that. I could feel the tears behind my eyes, and I couldn't help noticing that Dekko's hands were shaking. He's quite sensitive behind his joky manner, and had quite obviously taken to heart her statement that he had never recovered from his schooldays. Nor had it been pleasant, hearing myself described as vicious.

'No one cares,' Cynthia said in the same unbalanced way, as if she hadn't just been called ugly and a bitch. 'No one cares, and on our journey home we shall all four be silent. Yet is the truth about ourselves at least a beginning? Will we wonder in the end about the hell that frightens us?'

Strafe still looked wretched, his face deliberately turned away from us. Mrs Malseed gave a little sigh and raised the fingers of her left hand to her cheek, as if something tickled it. Her husband breathed heavily. Dekko seemed on the point of tears.

Cynthia stumbled off, leaving a silence behind her. Before it was broken I knew she was right when she said we would just go home, away from this country we had come to love. And I knew as well that neither here nor at home would she be led to a blue van that was not quite an ambulance. Strafe would stay with her because Strafe is made like that, honourable in his own particular way. I felt a pain where perhaps my heart is, and again I wanted to cry. Why couldn't it have been she who had gone down to the rocks and slipped on the seaweed or just walked into the sea, it didn't matter which? Her awful rigmarole hung about us as the last of the tea things were gathered up – the earls who'd fled, the famine and the people planted. The children were there too, grown up into murdering riff-raff.

The Blue Dress

My cinder-grey room has a window, but I have never in all
my time here looked out of it. It's easier to remember, to
conjure up this scene or that, to eavesdrop. Americans give
arms away, Russians promise tanks. In Brussels an English
politician breakfasts with his mistress; a pornographer pre-
tends he's selling Christmas cards. Carefully I listen, as in
childhood I listened to the hushed conversation of my
parents.

I stand in the cathedral at Vézelay, whose bishops once
claimed it possessed the mortal remains of Mary Magdalene,
a falseness which was exposed by Pope Boniface VIII. I
wonder about that Pope, and then the scene is different.

I sit in the Piazza San Marco on the day when I discovered a
sea of corruption among the local Communists. The music
plays, visitors remark upon the pigeons.

Scenes coalesce: Miss MacNamara passes along the promenade, Major Trubstall lies, the blue dress flutters and is
still. In Rotterdam I have a nameless woman. *'Feest wezen
vieren?'* she says. *'Gedronken?'* In Corniglia the wine is
purple, the path by the coast is marked as a lover's lane
I am silly, Dorothea says, the dress is just a dress. She
laughs, like water running over pebbles.

I must try, they tell me; it will help to write it down. I do
not argue, I do precisely as they say. Carefully, I remember.
Carefully, I write it down.

★

It was Bath, not Corniglia, not Rotterdam or Venice, not Vézelay: it was in Bath where Dorothea and I first met, by chance in the Pump Room. 'I'm sorry,' I said, actually bumping into her.

She shook her head, saying that of course I hadn't hurt her. She blamed the crowds, tourists pushing like mad things, always in a hurry. But nothing could keep her out of the Pump Room because of its Jane Austen associations.

'I've never been here before.'

'Goodness! You poor thing!'

'I was on the way to have some coffee. Would you like some?'

'I always have coffee when I come.'

She was small and very young – twenty-one or -two, I guessed – in a plain white dress without sleeves. She carried a basket, and had very fair hair, quite straight and cut quite short. Her oval face was perfect, her eyes intense, the blue of a washed-out sky. She smiled when she told me about herself, as though she found the subject a little absurd. She was studying the history of art but when she finished that she didn't know what on earth she was going to do next. I said I was in Bath because my ex-wife's mother, who'd only come to live there six months ago, had died. The funeral had taken place that morning and my ex-wife, Charlotte, had been furious that I'd attended it. But I'd always been fond of her mother, fonder in fact than Charlotte had ever been. I'd known of course that I would have to meet her at the funeral. She'd married again, a man who ran a wine business: he had been there too.

'Is it horrible, a divorce?' the girl asked me while we drank our weak, cool coffee. 'I can never think of my parents divorcing.'

'It's nice you can't. Yes, it's horrible.'

'Did you have children?'

'No.'

'There's that at least. But isn't it odd, to make such a very rudimentary mistake?'

'Extraordinary.'

I don't know what it was about her manner that first morning, but something seemed to tell me that this beautiful creature would not be outraged if I said – which I did – that we might go somewhere else in search of a better cup of coffee. And when I said, 'Let's have a drink,' I said it confidently. She telephoned her parents' house. We had lunch together in the Francis Hotel.

'I went to a boarding-school I didn't like,' she told me. 'Called after St Catherine but without her charity. I was bad at maths and French and geography. I didn't like a girl called Angela Tate and I didn't like the breakfasts. I missed my brothers. What about you? What was your wife like?'

'Fond of clothes. Very fine tweed, a certain shade of scarlet, scarves of every possible variation. She hated being abroad, trailing after me.' I didn't add that Charlotte had been unfaithful with anyone she had a fancy for; I didn't even want to think about that.

The waiter brought Dorothea veal *escalope* and steak *au poivre* for me. It was very like being in a dream. The funeral of my ex-mother-in-law had taken place at ten o'clock, there had been Charlotte's furious glances and her husband's disdain, my walking away when the ceremony was over without a word to anyone. I'd felt wound up, like a watch-spring, seeing vividly in my mind's eye an old, grey woman who'd always entertained me with her gossip, who'd written to me when Charlotte went to say how sorry she was, adding in a postscript that Charlotte had always been a handful. She and I had shared the truth about her daughter, and it was that that I'd honoured by making the journey to her funeral.

'They say I am compulsively naughty,' Dorothea said, as if guessing that I wondered what she had said to her parents on the telephone. I suspected she had not confessed the truth. There'd been some excuse to account for her delay, and already that fitted in with what I knew of her. Certainly she would not have said that she'd been picked up by a middle-aged journalist who had come to Bath to attend a funeral. She spoke again of Jane Austen, of Elizabeth Bennet, and Emma and Elinor. She spoke as though these fictional characters were real. She almost loved them, she said, but that of course could not have been quite true.

'Who were encumbered with low connections and gave themselves airs? Who bestowed their consent with a most joyful alacrity?'

I laughed, and waited for her to tell me. I walked with her to a parked car, a white Mini that had collected a traffic warden's ticket. Formally we shook hands and all the way to London on the train I thought of her. I sat in the bar drinking one after another of those miniature bottles of whisky that trains go in for, while her face jumped about in my imagination, unnerving me. Again and again her white, even teeth smiled at me.

*

Within a day or two I was in Belfast, sending reports to a Washington newspaper and to a syndicate in Australia. As always, I posted photo-copies of everything I wrote to Stoyckov, who operates a news bureau in Prague. Stoyckov used to pay me when he saw me, quite handsomely in a sense, but it was never the money that mattered: it was simply that I saw no reason why the truth about Northern Ireland should not be told behind the Iron Curtain as well as in Washington and Adelaide.

I had agreed to do a two-months stint – no longer, because from experience I knew that Belfast becomes depressing. Immediately afterwards I was to spend three days in Madrid, trying to discover if there was truth in the persistent rumour that the Pope was to visit Spain next year. 'Great Christ alive,' Charlotte used to scream at me, 'call this a marriage?'

In Belfast the army was doing its best to hush up a rape case. I interviewed a man called Ruairi O Baoill, whom I'd last seen drilling a gang of terrorists in the Syrian desert. 'My dear fellow, you can hardly call this rape,' a Major Trubstall insisted. 'The girl was yelling her head off for it.' But the girl had been doing no such thing; the girl was whey-faced, unable to stop crying; the girl was still in pain, she'd been rushed to hospital to have stitches. 'Listen,' Major Trubstall said, pushing a great crimson face into mine. 'If a girl goes out drinking with four soldiers, d'you think she isn't after something?' The Red Hand of Ulster meant what it said, O Baoill told me: the hand was waiting to grasp the hammer and the sickle. He didn't say it to his followers, and later he denied that he had said it at all.

Ruairi O Baoill is a sham, I wrote. *And so, it would appear, is a man called Major Trubstall. Fantasy rules*, I wrote, knowing it was the truth.

All the time in Northern Ireland and for three days in Spain Dorothea's voice continued about Emma and Elinor and Elizabeth Bennet, and Mrs Elton and Mr Woodhouse. I kept imagining us together in a clean, empty house that appeared to be our home. Like smoke evaporating, my failed marriage wasn't there any more. And my unhappy child-hood slipped away also, as though by magic.

*

'Dorothea?'

'No, this is her mother. Please hold on. I'll fetch her.'

I waited for so long I began to fear that this was Mrs Lysarth's way of dealing with unwelcome telephone callers. I felt that perhaps the single word I'd spoken had been enough to convey an image of my unsuitableness, and my presumption.

'Yes?' Dorothea's voice said.

'It's Terris. Do you remember?'

'Of course I remember. Are you in Bath again?'

'No. But at least I've returned from Northern Ireland. I'm in London. How are you, Dorothea?'

'I'm very well. Are you well?'

'Yes.' I paused, not knowing how to put it.

'It's kind of you to ring, Terris.'

'D'you think we might meet?'

'Meet?'

'It would be nice to see you.'

She didn't answer. I felt I had proposed marriage already, that it was that she was considering. 'It doesn't matter,' I began to say.

'Of course we must meet. Would Thursday do? I have to be in London then.'

'We could have lunch again.'

'That would be lovely.'

And so it was. We sat in the bow window of an Italian restaurant in Romilly Street, and when anyone glanced in I felt inordinately proud. It was early September, a warm, clear day without a hint of autumn. Afterwards we strolled through Leicester Square and along Piccadilly. We were still in Green Park at six o'clock. 'I love you, Terris,' Dorothea said.

*

Her mother smiled a slanting smile at me, head a little on one side. She laid down an embroidery on a round, cane frame. She held a hand out.

'We've heard so much,' she said, still smiling, and then she introduced her sons. While we were drinking sherry Dorothea's father appeared, a thin, tall man, with spectacles on a length of leather, dancing on a tweed waistcoat.

'My dear fellow.' Vaguely he smiled and held a hand out: an amateur archaeologist, though by profession a medical doctor. That I was the divorced middle-aged man whom his young daughter wished to marry was not a fact that registered in his face. Dorothea had shown me a photograph of him, dusty in a crumpled linen suit, holding between finger and thumb a piece of glazed terracotta. 'A pleasure,' he continued as vaguely as before. 'A real pleasure.'

'A pleasure to meet *you*, Dr Lysarth.'

'Oh, not at all.'

'More sherry?' Dorothea suggested, pouring me whisky because she knew I probably needed it.

'That's whisky in that decanter, Dorothea,' her brother Adam pointed out and while I was saying it didn't matter, that whisky actually was what I preferred, her other brother, Jonathan, laughed.

'I'm sure Mr Terris knows what he wants,' Mrs Lysarth remarked, and Dorothea said:

'Terris is his Christian name.'

'Oh, I'm so sorry.'

'You must call him Terris, Mother. You cannot address a prospective son-in-law as Mister.'

'Please do,' I urged, feeling a word from me was necessary.

'Terris?' Adam said.

'Yes, it is an odd name.'

The brothers stood on either side of Dorothea's chair in that flowery drawing-room. There were pale blue delphiniums in two vases on the mantelpiece, and roses and sweet-peas in little vases everywhere. The mingled scent was delicious, and the room and the flowers seemed part of the family the Lysarths were, as did the way in which Adam and Jonathan stood, protectively, by their sister.

They were twins, both still at Cambridge. They had their mother's oval face, the pale blue eyes their parents shared, their father's languid tallness. I was aware that however protective they might seem they were not protecting Dorothea from me: I was not an interloper, they did not resent me. But their youth made me feel even older than I was, more knocked about and less suitable than ever for the role I wished to play.

'You've travelled a great deal,' Mrs Lysarth said. 'So Dorothea says.'

'Yes, I have.'

I didn't say I'd been an only child. I didn't mention the seaside town where I'd spent my childhood, or reveal that we'd lived in a kind of disgrace really, that my father worked ignominiously in the offices of the trawling business which the family had once owned. Our name remained on the warehouses and the fish-boxes, a daily reminder that we'd slipped down in the world. I'd told Dorothea, but I didn't really think all that would interest the other Lysarths.

'Fascinating, to travel so,' Mrs Lysarth remarked, politely smiling.

After dinner Dr Lysarth and I were left alone in the dining-room. We drank port in a manner which suggested that had I not been present Dr Lysarth would have sat there drinking it alone. He talked about a Roman pavement, twenty feet below the surface somewhere. Quite suddenly he said:

'Dorothea wants to marry you.'

'We both actually –'

'Yes, so she's told us.'

I hesitated. I said:

'I'm – I'm closer to your age, in a way, than to hers.'

'Yes, you probably are. I'm glad you like her.'

'I love her.'

'Of course.'

'I hope,' I began.

'My dear fellow, we're delighted.'

'I'm a correspondent, Dr Lysarth, as Dorothea, I think, has told you. I move about a bit, but for the next two years I'll be in Scandinavia.'

'Ah, yes.' He pushed the decanter towards me. 'She's a special girl, you know.'

'Yes, I do know, Dr Lysarth.'

'We're awfully fond of her. We're a tightly bound family – well, you may have noticed. We're very *much* a family.'

'Yes, indeed.'

'But of course we've always known that Dorothea would one day wish to marry.'

'I know I'm not what you must have imagined, Dr Lysarth, when you thought of Dorothea's husband. I assure you I'm aware of that.'

'It's just that she's more vulnerable than she seems to be:

I just want to say that. She's really a very vulnerable girl.'

The decanter was again moved in my direction. The tone of voice closed the subject of Dr Lysarth's daughter. We returned to archaeological matters.

I spent that night at Wistaria Lodge and noticed at breakfast-time how right Dr Lysarth had been when he'd said that the family was a tightly bound one. Conversation drifted from one Lysarth to the next in a way that was almost artificial, as though the domestic scenes I witnessed belonged in the theatre. I formed the impression that the Lysarths invariably knew what was coming next, as though their lines had been learnt. My presence was accommodated through a telepathy that was certainly as impressive, another piece of practised theatre.

'Yes, we're like that,' Dorothea said in the garden after breakfast. 'We never seem to quarrel.'

She taught me how to play croquet and when we'd finished one game we were joined by her brothers. Adam was the best of the three and he, partnering Dorothea, easily beat Jonathan and myself. Mrs Lysarth brought a tray of drinks to a white table beside the lawn and we sat and sipped in the sunshine, while I was told of other games of croquet there had been, famous occasions when the tempers of visitors had become a little ragged.

'It's a perfect training for life,' Mrs Lysarth said, 'the game of croquet.'

'Cunning pays,' Adam continued. 'Generosity must know its place.'

'Not that we are against generosity, Terris,' Adam said. 'Not that we're on the side of cunning.'

'What a family poor Terris is marrying into!' Dorothea cried, and on cue her mother smiled and added:

'Terris is a natural croquet-player. He will one day put you all to shame.'

'I doubt that very much.' And as I spoke I felt I said precisely what was expected of me.

'You must teach the Scandinavians, Dorothea,' Adam said. 'Whatever else, you must flatten out a lawn in your little Scandinavian garden.'

'Oh yes, of course we shall. So there.'

After lunch Dorothea and I went for a walk. We had to say good-bye because that evening I was to go away; when I returned it would almost be the day we'd set for our wedding. We walked slowly through the village and out into the country. We left the road and passed along a track by the side of a cornfield. We rested by a stream which Dorothea had often told me about, a place she'd come to with her brothers as a child. We sat there, our backs against the same ivy-covered tree-stump. We talked about being married, of beginning our life together in Copenhagen. I made love to Dorothea by her stream, and it was afterwards that she told me the story of Agnes Kemp. She began it as we lay there, and continued while we washed and tidied ourselves and began the journey back to Wistaria Lodge.

'She was twelve at the time, staying with us while her parents were abroad. She fell from the beech-tree. Her neck was broken.'

I only nodded because there isn't much anyone can say when a fact like that is related.

'I had always wanted to climb that tree, I had been told I never must. "I dare you," she said. "I dare you, Dorothea." I was frightened, but when no one was looking we climbed it together, racing one another to the top.'

She spoke of the funeral of Agnes Kemp, how the dead child's parents had not been present because it had been impossible to contact them in time. 'We don't much hear of them now,' Dorothea said. 'A card at Christmas. Agnes was an only child.'

We walked a little in silence. Then I said:

'What was she like?'

'Oh, she was really awfully spoilt. The kind of person who made you furious.'

I suppose it was that last remark that started everything off, that and the feeling that Wistaria Lodge was a kind of theatre. The remark passed unnoticed at the time, for even as she made it Dorothea turned round, and smiled and kissed me. 'It's all forgotten now,' she said when that was over, 'but of course I had to tell you.'

It was certainly forgotten, for when we arrived in the garden the white table had been moved beneath the beech-tree out of the glare of the sun, and tea with scones and sandwiches and cake was spread all over it. I felt a dryness in my mouth that was not dispelled when I drank. I found it hard to eat, or even to smile in unison with the smiling faces around me. I kept seeing the spoilt child on the grass and Dr Lysarth bending over her, saying she was dead, as no doubt he must have. I kept thinking that the beech-tree should have been cut down years ago, no matter how beautiful it was.

*

'You're mad,' Charlotte shouted at me more than once. 'You're actually mad.' Her voice in its endless repetition is always a reminder of my parents' faces, that worry in their eyes. All I had wanted to know was the truth about our-selves: why did the offices and the warehouses still bear our name, what had my grandfather done? 'Best just left,' my mother said. 'Best not bothered with.' But in the end they told me because naturally I persisted – at eight and twelve and eighteen: naturally I persisted. My grandfather had been a criminal and that was that: a drunkard and an embezzler, a gambler who had run through a fortune in a handful of years: I'd guessed, of course, by the time they told me. I didn't know why they'd been so reluctant, or why they'd displayed concern when I persisted about Miss MacNamara: why did she weep when she walked along the promenade? I had to guess again, because all my childhood Miss MacNamara's tears possessed me so: she wept for the music teacher, who was married and had a family, and I did not forgive my parents for wishing to keep that covered up. Passionately I did not forgive them, although my mother begged me, saying I made myself unhappy. 'You sound so noble,' Charlotte snapped at me. 'Yet what's so marvellous about exposing a brothel-keeper for peddling drugs? Or a grimy pederast and a government minister?' Charlotte's mother called her 'a tricky kind of customer'. And tricky was just the word. Tricky, no doubt, with bank tellers and men met idly in bars. Tricky in beds all over the place, when I was so often away, having to be away.

I crossed the bedroom to the window. The beech-tree was lit by moonlight now. Gazing at it, I heard the voices that had haunted me ever since Dorothea told me the story.

'Then I dare you to,' Dorothea angrily shouts, stopping suddenly and confronting the other girl.

'You're frightened of it, Dorothea. You're frightened of a tree.'

'Of course I'm not.'

'Then I dare you to.'

In the garden the boys, delighted, listen. Their sister's cheeks have reddened. Agnes Kemp is standing on one foot and then the other, balancing in a way she has, a way that infuriates Dorothea.

'You're a horrid person,' Dorothea says. 'You aren't even pretty. You're stupid and spoilt and greedy. You always have two helpings. There's something the matter with your eyes.'

'There isn't, Dorothea Lysarth. You're jealous, that's all.'

'They're pig's eyes.'

'You're just afraid of a tree, Dorothea.'

They climb it, both at the same time, from different sides. There's a forked branch near the top, a sprawling knobbly crutch, easily distinguishable from the ground: they race to that.

The boys watch, expecting any moment that an adult voice will cry out in horror from the house, but no voice does. The blue dress of Agnes Kemp and the white one of Dorothea disappear into a mass of leaves, the boys stand further back, the dresses reappear. Agnes Kemp is in front, but their sister has chosen a different route to the top, a shorter one it seems. The boys long for their sister to win because if she does Agnes Kemp will at least be quiet for a day or two. They don't call out, although they want to: they want to advise Dorothea that in a moment she will have overtaken her challenger; they don't because their voices might attract attention from the house. From where they stand they can hear the grandfather clock in the hall striking ten. Most of the windows are open.

Dorothea slips and almost falls. Her shoes aren't right for climbing and when she glances to her left she can see that Agnes's are: Agnes has put on tennis shoes, knowing she will succeed that morning in goading Dorothea. This is typical of her, and when it is all over Dorothea will be blamed because of course Agnes will blurt it out, in triumph if she wins, in revenge if she doesn't.

The blue dress reaches the fork and then advances along one of its prongs, further than is necessary. Dorothea is a yard behind. She waits, crouched at the knobbly juncture, for Agnes Kemp's return. The boys don't understand that. They stare, wondering why their sister doesn't climb down again so that they can all three run away from Agnes Kemp, since it is running away from her that has been in their minds since breakfast-time. They watch while Agnes Kemp reaches a point at which to pose triumphantly. They watch while slowly she creeps backwards along the branch. Their sister's hand reaches out, pulling at the blue dress, at the child who has been such a nuisance all summer, who'll be worse than ever after her victory. There is a clattering among the leaves and branches. Like a stone, the body strikes the ground.

*

'Now what did anyone dream?' Mrs Lysarth enquired at breakfast. Knives rattled on plates, toast crackled, Dr Lysarth read *The Times*. It was a family thing to talk about dreams. I had been told that there were dreaming seasons, a period when dreams could be remembered easily and a time when they could not be. It was all another Lysarth game.

'I'd been skipping French classes again,' Adam said. 'For a year or even longer I'd been keeping so low a profile that Monsieur Bertain didn't even know I existed. And then some examination or other loomed.'

'Adam often has that dream,' Dorothea confided to me.

'I was in Istanbul,' Jonathan said, 'or at least it seemed like Istanbul. A man was selling me a stolen picture. A kind of goat, by Marc Chagall.'

'I had only a wisp of a thing,' Mrs Lysarth contributed. 'A bit out of Dorothea's birth.'

'I dreamed that Terris's wife was picking scallions in the garden,' Dorothea said. ' "You're wrong to think there's been a divorce," she said.'

'Did you dream, Terris?' Mrs Lysarth asked, buttering toast, but I was so confused about the night that had passed that I thought it better to say I hadn't.

'What's the criterion for *As You Like It*, ten letters, beginning with "T"?' Dr Lysarth asked.

'Touchstone,' Dorothea said, and another Lysarth game began. 'Lord of Eden End' was 'North', 'poet's black tie ruined by vulcanised rubber' was 'ebonite'. Within ten minutes the crossword puzzle was complete.

The faces laughed and smiled around the breakfast table, the conversation ran about. Especially for my benefit a description of Monsieur Bertain, Adam's French master, was engaged upon. His accent was imitated, his war wound designated as the cause of his short temper. Dr Lysarth looked forward to a dig in Derbyshire in the autumn; his wife was to accompany him and would, as always on archaeological occasions, spend her time walking and reading. Jonathan said he intended to visit us in Scandinavia. Dorothea pressed him and I found myself doing the same.

In the sunny room, while marmalade was passed and the flowered china had all the prettiness of a cottage garden, the horror was nonsensical. Mrs Lysarth's elegance, her perfect features and her burnished hair, would surely not be as they were. No wrinkles creased her face; the Doctor's eyes were honestly untroubled, forget-me-not blue, a darker shade than Dorothea's. And Dorothea's hands would surely be less beautiful? The fingers clawing at the blue dress would have acquired some sign, a joint arthritic, a single bitten

125

nail. The faces of the boys could not have shed all traces of the awful ugliness. 'Dear, it isn't our affair, why Miss MacNamara is troubled,' my mother agitatedly protested. 'Senseless,' Charlotte shouted. 'You frighten me with your senseless talk.'

On Tuesday afternoon, three days away, we would marry and the car would take us to the station at Bath after the champagne on the lawn. Our flight to Paris was at five past seven, we would have dinner in the Chez les Anges. We would visit Versailles and Rouen, and the Jeu de Paume because Dorothea had never been there. I may for a moment have closed my eyes at the breakfast table, so lost was I in speculation and imaginings.

'Well, I have a surgery,' Dr Lysarth announced, folding the newspaper as he rose from the table.

'And I have Castlereagh to wonder about,' Adam said. 'That fascinating figure.'

For a moment in the sunny room the brothers again stood by Dorothea, an accidental conjunction or perhaps telepathy came into play: perhaps they guessed the contents of my mind. There was defiance in their stance, or so I thought, a reason for it now.

*

'When I was little I used to ride here on my ponies. On Jess first. Later on Adonis.'

We walked as we had on the day we'd made love, through a spinney, along the track by the cornfield. Poppies, not in bloom before, were everywhere now, cow-parsley whitened the hedges.

'The first thing I remember,' Dorothea said, 'is that bits of grass had got into my pram.'

I told myself that I should mention Agnes Kemp, but I did not do so. And when we reached the stream I did not embrace the girl who was to be my bride in a few days' time. We sat with our backs against the tree-trunk, watching the ripple of the water.

'I was lifted up,' Dorothea said, 'and there was a great tutting while the grass cuttings were removed. Years went by before I can remember anything else.'

Murder was not like stealing a pencil-sharpener at school, or spilling something. Agnes Kemp had been detested, a secret had afterwards become a way of life. Few words had perhaps been spoken within the family, Dr Lysarth's giving the cause of death as a broken neck being perhaps the only announcement as to how the future was to be. The faces of the boys on the lawn returned to me, and Dorothea's face as she looked down at the still body. Had she afterwards ridden her pony, Jess or Adonis, whichever it happened to be, by the cornfield and the poppies? 'I dreamed of Agnes,' was what she didn't say at breakfast any more, because the family had exorcised the ghost.

*

Alone, Miss MacNamara walks; the winter waves tumble about. 'Sea-spray,' my mother lies. 'Sea-spray on her cheeks, dear.' How can my father, morning after morning, leave our gaunt house in order to perform his ignominious work, pretending it is work like any other? How can he hope that I will not scratch away the falsehoods they tell? My father is caught like a creature in a trap, for ever paying back the debts his own father has incurred. It isn't nice, Miss MacNamara and a music teacher; it isn't nice, the truth in Northern Ireland. None of it is nice. 'No, no,' they tell me, 'you must be quiet, Terris.' But I am always quiet. I make no noise in the small grey room where I have to be alone because, so they say, it is better so. The room is full of falseness: then I must write it down, they tell me, quite triumphantly; it will be easier if I write it down.

Americans give arms away, Russians promise tanks. I stand again in the cathedral at Vézelay, pleased that Pope Boniface exposed the pretence about Mary Magdalene. Charlotte passes me a drink, smiling with *ersatz* affection. Our fingers touch, I know how she has spent that afternoon. 'Poor Dorothea,' Mrs Lysarth comforts, and the boys are angry because Dorothea has always needed looking after, ever since the day of the accident, the wretched death of a nuisance. I know I am right, as that Pope knew also. They hold me and buckle the thing on to me, but still I know I am right. Flowers are arranged in vases, croquet played beneath the beech-tree. Ruairi O Baoill adopts a hero's voice to proclaim his pretence of a cause, Major Trubstall's smile is loaded with hypocrisy. The blue dress flutters and is still, telling me again that I am right.

The Time of Year

All that autumn, when they were both fourteen, they had talked about their Christmas swim. She'd had the idea: that on Christmas morning when everyone was still asleep they would meet by the boats on the strand at Ballyquin and afterwards quite casually say that they had been for a swim on Christmas Day. Whenever they met during that stormy October and November they wondered how fine the day might be, how cold or wet, and if the sea could possibly be frozen. They walked together on the cliffs, looking down at the breaking waves of the Atlantic, shivering in anticipation. They walked through the misty dusk of the town, lingering over the first signs of Christmas in the shops: coloured lights strung up, holly and Christmas trees and tinsel. They wondered if people guessed about them. They didn't want them to, they wanted it to be a secret. People would laugh because they were children. They were in love that autumn.

Six years later Valerie still remembered, poignantly, in November. Dublin, so different from Ballyquin, stirred up the past as autumn drifted into winter and winds bustled around the grey buildings of Trinity College, where she was now a student. The city's trees were bleakly bare, it seemed to Valerie; there was sadness, even, on the lawns of her hall of residence, scattered with finished leaves. In her small room, preparing herself one Friday evening for the Skullys' end-of-term party, she sensed quite easily the Christmas chill of the sea, the chilliness creeping slowly over her calves and knees. She paused with the memory, gazing at herself in the looking-glass attached to the inside of her cupboard door. She was a tall girl, standing now in a white silk petticoat, with a thin face and thin long fingers and an almost classical nose. Her black hair was as straight as a die, falling to her shoulders. She was pretty when she smiled and she did so at her reflection, endeavouring to overcome the melancholy that visited her at this time of year. She turned away and picked up a green corduroy dress which she had laid out on her bed. She was going to be late if she dawdled like this.

*

The parties given by Professor and Mrs Skully were renowned neither for the entertainment they provided nor for their elegance. They were, unfortunately, difficult to avoid, the Professor being persistent in the face of repeated excuses – a persistence it was deemed unwise to strain.

Bidden for half past seven, his History students came on bicycles, a few in Kilroy's Mini, Ruth Cusper on her motorcycle, Bewley Joal on foot. Woodward, Whipp and Woolmer-Mills came cheerfully, being kindred spirits of the Professor's and in no way dismayed by the immediate prospect. Others were apprehensive or cross, trying not to let it show as smilingly they entered the Skullys' house in Rathgar.

'How very nice!' Mrs Skully murmured in a familiar manner in the hall. 'How jolly good of you to come.'

The hall was not yet decorated for Christmas, but the Professor had found the remains of last year's crackers and had stuck half a dozen behind the heavily framed scenes of

Hanover that had been established in the hall since the early days of the Skullys' marriage. The gaudy crêpe paper protruded above the pictures in splurges of green, red and yellow, and cheered up the hall to a small extent. The coloured scarves and overcoats of the History students, already accumulating on the hall-stand, did so more effectively.

In the Skullys' sitting-room the Professor's record-player, old and in some way special, was in its usual place: on a mahogany table in front of the French windows, which were now obscured by brown curtains. Four identical rugs, their colour approximately matching that of the curtains, were precisely arranged on darker brown linoleum. Rexine-seated dining-chairs lined brownish walls.

The Professor's History students lent temporary character to this room, as their coats and scarves did to the hall. Kilroy was plump in a royal-blue suit. The O'Neill sisters' cluster of followers, jostling even now for promises of favours, wore carefully pressed denim or tweed. The O'Neill sisters themselves exuded a raffish, cocktail-time air. They were twins, from Lurgan, both of them blonde and both favouring an excess of eye-shadow, with lipstick that wetly gleamed, the same shade of pink as the trouser suits that nudgingly hugged the protuberances of their bodies. Not far from where they now held court, the rimless spectacles of Bewley Joal had a busy look in the room's harsh light; the complexion of Yvonne Smith was displayed to disadvantage. So was the troublesome fair hair of Honor Hitchcock, who was engaged to a student known as the Reverend because of his declared intention one day to claim the title. Cosily in a corner she linked her arm with his, both of them seeming middle-aged before their time, inmates already of a draughty rectory in Co. Cork or Clare. 'I'll be the first,' Ruth Cusper vowed, 'to visit you in your parish. Wherever it is.' Ruth Cusper was a statuesque English girl, not yet divested of her motor-cycling gear.

The colours worn by the girls, and the denim and tweed, and the royal blue of Kilroy, contrasted sharply with the uncared-for garb of Woodward, Whipp and Woolmer-Mills, all of whom were expected to take Firsts. Stained and frayed, these three hung together without speaking, Woodward very tall, giving the impression of an etiolated newt, Whipp small, his glasses repaired with Sellotape, Woolmer-Mills for ever launching himself back and forth on the balls of his feet.

In a pocket of Kilroy's suit there was a miniature bottle of vodka, for only tea and what the Professor described as 'cup' were served in the course of the evening. Kilroy fingered it, smiling across the room at the Professor, endeavouring to give the impression that he was delighted to be present. He was a student who was fearful of academic failure, his terror being that he would not get a Third: he had set his sights on a Third, well aware that to have set them higher would not be wise. He brought his little bottles of vodka to the Professor's parties as an act of bravado, a gesture designed to display jauntiness, to show that he could take a chance. But the chances he took with his vodka were not great.

Bewley Joal, who would end up with a respectable Second, was laying down the law to Yvonne Smith, who would be grateful to end up with anything at all. Her natural urge to chatter was stifled, for no one could get a word in when the clanking voice of Bewley Joal was in full flow. 'Oh, it's far more than just a solution, dear girl,' he breezily pronounced, speaking of Moral Rearmament. Yvonne Smith nodded and agreed, trying to say that an aunt of hers thought most highly of Moral Rearmament, that she herself had always been meaning to look into it. But the voice of Bewley Joal cut all her sentences in half.

'I thought we'd start,' the Professor announced, having coughed and cleared his throat, 'with the *Pathétique*.' He fiddled with the record-player while everyone sat down, Ruth Cusper on the floor. He was a biggish man in a grey suit that faintly recalled the clothes of Woodward, Whipp and Woolmer-Mills. On a large head hair was still in plentiful supply even though the Professor was fifty-eight. The hair was grey also, bushing out around his head in a manner that suggested professorial vagueness rather than a gesture in the direction of current fashion. His wife, who stood by his side while he placed a record on the turntable, wore a magenta skirt and twin-set, and a string of jade beads. In almost every way – including this lively choice of dress – she seemed naturally to complement her husband, to fill the gaps his personality couldn't be bothered with. Her nervous manner was the opposite of his confident one. He gave his parties out of duty, and having done so found it hard to take an interest in any students except those who had already proved themselves academically sound. Mrs Skully preferred to strike a lighter note. Now and again she made efforts to entice a few of the girls to join her on Saturday evenings, offering the suggestion that they might listen together to Saturday Night Theatre and afterwards sit around and discuss it. Because the Professor saw no point in television there was none in the Skullys' house.

Tchaikovsky filled the sitting-room. The Professor sat down and then Mrs Skully did. The doorbell rang.

*

'Ah, of course,' Mrs Skully said.

'Valerie Upcott,' Valerie said. 'Good evening, Mrs Skully.'

'Come in, come in, dear. The *Pathétique*'s just started.' She remarked in the hall on the green corduroy dress that was revealed when Valerie took off her coat. The green was of so dark a shade that it might almost have been black. It had large green buttons all down the front. 'Oh, how really nice!' Mrs Skully said.

The crackers that decorated the scenes of Hanover looked sinister, Valerie thought: Christmas was on the way, soon there'd be the coloured lights and imitation snow. She smiled at Mrs Skully. She wondered about saying that her magenta outfit was nice also, but decided against it. 'We'll slip in quietly,' Mrs Skully said.

Valerie tried to forget the crackers as she entered the sitting-room and took her place on a chair, but in her mind the brash images remained. They did so while she acknowledged Kilroy's winking smile and while she glanced towards the Professor in case he chose to greet her. But the Professor, his head bent over clasped hands, did not look up.

Among the History students Valerie was an unknown quantity. During the two years they'd all known one another she'd established herself as a person who was particularly quiet. She had a private look even when she smiled, when the thin features of her face were startled out of tranquillity, as if an electric light had suddenly been turned on. Kilroy still tried to take her out, Ruth Cusper was pally. But Valerie's privacy, softened by her sudden smile, unfussily repelled these attentions.

For her part she was aware of the students' curiosity, and yet she could not have said to any one of them that a tragedy which had occurred was not properly in the past yet. She could not mention the tragedy to people who didn't know

about it already. She couldn't tell it as a story because to her
it didn't seem in the least like that. It was a fact you had to
live with, half wanting to forget it, half feeling you could
not. This time of year and the first faint signs of Christmas
were enough to tease it brightly into life.

The second movement of the *Pathétique* came to an end,
the Professor rose to turn the record over, the students
murmured. Mrs Skully slipped away, as she always did at
this point, to attend to matters in the kitchen. While the
Professor was bent over the record-player Kilroy waved his
bottle of vodka about and then raised it to his lips. 'Hullo,
Valerie,' Yvonne Smith whispered across the distance that
separated them. She endeavoured to continue her com-
munication by shaping words with her lips. Valerie smiled
at her and at Ruth Cusper, who had turned her head when
she'd heard Yvonne Smith's greeting. 'Hi,' Ruth Cusper
said.

The music began again. The mouthing of Yvonne Smith
continued for a moment and then ceased. Valerie didn't
notice that, because in the room the students and the Professor were shadows of a kind, the music a distant piping. The
swish of wind was in the room, and the shingle, cold on her
bare feet; so were the two flat stones they'd placed on their
clothes to keep them from blowing away. White flecks in the
air were snow, she said: Christmas snow, what everyone
wanted. But he said the flecks were flecks of foam.

He took her hand, dragging her a bit because the shingle
hurt the soles of her feet and slowed her down. He hurried
on the sand, calling back to her, reminding her that it was
her idea, laughing at her hesitation. He called out something else as he ran into the breakers, but she couldn't hear
because of the roar of the sea. She stood in the icy shallows
and when she heard him shouting again she imagined he

was still mocking her. She didn't even know he was struggling, she wasn't in the least aware of his death. It was his not being there she noticed, the feeling of being alone on the strand at Ballyquin.

'Cup, Miss Upcott?' the Professor offered in the dining-room. Poised above a glass, a jug contained a yellowish liquid. She said she'd rather have tea.

There were egg sandwiches and cakes, plates of crisps, biscuits and Twiglets. Mrs Skully poured tea, Ruth Cusper handed round the cups and saucers. The O'Neill sisters and their followers shared an obscene joke, which was a game that had grown up at the Skullys' parties: one student doing his best to make the others giggle too noisily. A point was gained if the Professor demanded to share the fun.

'Oh, but of course there isn't any argument,' Bewley Joal was insisting, still talking to Yvonne Smith about Moral Rearmament. Words had ceased to dribble from her lips. Instead she kept nodding her head. 'We live in times of decadence,' Bewley Joal pronounced.

Woodward, Whipp and Woolmer-Mills were still to-gether, Woolmer-Mills launching himself endlessly on to the balls of his feet, Whipp sucking at his cheeks. No conversation was taking place among them: when the Professor finished going round with his jug of cup, talk of some kind would begin, probably about a mediaeval document Woodward had earlier mentioned. Or about a reference to *panni streit sine grano* which had puzzled Woolmer-Mills.

'Soon be Christmas,' Honor Hitchcock remarked to Valerie.

'Yes, it will.'

'I love it. I love the way you can imagine everyone doing just the same things on Christmas Eve, tying up presents, running around with holly, listening to the carols. And

Christmas Day: that same meal in millions of houses, and the same prayers. All over the world.

'Yes, there's that.'

'Oh, I think it's marvellous.'

'Christmas?' Kilroy said, suddenly beside them. He laughed, the fat on his face shaking a bit. 'Much overrated in my small view.' He glanced as he spoke at the Professor's profile, preparing himself in case the Professor should look in his direction. His expression changed, becoming solemn.

There were specks of dandruff, Valerie noticed, on the shoulders of the Professor's grey suit. She thought it odd that Mrs Skully hadn't drawn his attention to them. She thought it odd that Kilroy was so determined about his Third. And that Yvonne Smith didn't just walk away from the clanking voice of Bewley Joal.

'Orange or coffee?' Ruth Cusper proffered two cakes that had been cut into slices. The fillings in Mrs Skully's cakes were famous, made with Trex and castor sugar. The cakes themselves had a flat appearance, like large biscuits.

'I wouldn't touch any of that stuff,' Kilroy advised, jocular again. 'I was up all night after it last year.'

'Oh, nonsense!' Ruth Cusper placed a slice of orange cake on Valerie's plate, making a noise that indicated she found Kilroy's attempt at wit a failure. She passed on, and Kilroy without reason began to laugh.

Valerie looked at them, her eyes pausing on each face in the room. She was different from these people of her own age because of her autumn melancholy and the bitterness of Christmas. A solitude had been made for her, while they belonged to each other, separate yet part of a whole.

She thought about them, envying them their ordinary normality, the good fortune they accepted as their due. They trailed no horror, no ghosts or images that wouldn't go away: you could tell that by looking at them. Had she herself already been made peculiar by all of it, eccentric and strange and edgy? And would it never slip away, into the past where it belonged? Each year it was the same, no different from the year before, intent on hanging on to her. Each year she smiled and made an effort. She was brisk with it, she did her best. She told herself she had to live with it, agreeing with herself that of course she had to, as if wishing to be over-heard. And yet to die so young, so pointlessly and so casually, seemed to be something you had to feel unhappy about. It dragged out tears from you; it made you hesitate again, standing in the icy water. Your idea it had been.

'Tea, you people?' Mrs Skully offered.

'Awfully kind of you, Mrs Skully,' Kilroy said. 'Splendid tea this is.'

'I should have thought you'd be keener on the Professor's cup, Mr Kilroy.'

'No, I'm not a cup man, Mrs Skully.'

Valerie wondered what it would be like to be Kilroy. She wondered about his private thoughts, even what he was thinking now as he said he wasn't a cup man. She imagined him in his bedroom, removing his royal-blue suit and meti-culously placing it on a hanger, talking to himself about the party, wondering if he had done himself any damage in the Professor's eyes. She imagined him as a child, plump in bathing-trunks, building a sandcastle. She saw him in a kitchen, standing on a chair by an open cupboard, nibbling the corner of a Chivers' jelly.

She saw Ruth Cusper too, bossy at a children's party, friendlily bossy, towering over other children. She made them play a game and wasn't disappointed when they didn't like it. You couldn't hurt Ruth Cusper; she'd grown an extra skin beneath her motor-cycling gear. At night, she often said, she fell asleep as soon as her head touched the pillow.

You couldn't hurt Bewley Joal, either: a grasping child Valerie saw him as, watchful and charmless. Once he'd been hurt, she speculated: another child had told him that no one enjoyed playing with him, and he'd resolved from that moment not to care about stuff like that, to push his way through other people's opinion of him, not wishing to know it.

As children, the O'Neill sisters teased; their faithful tormentors pulled their hair. Woodward, Whipp and Woolmer-Mills read the *Children's Encyclopaedia*. Honor Hitchcock and the Reverend played mummies and daddies. 'Oh, listen to that chatterbox!' Yvonne Smith's father dotingly cried, affection that Yvonne Smith had missed ever since.

In the room the clanking of Bewley Joal punctuated the giggling in the corner where the O'Neill sisters were. More tea was poured and more of the Professor's cup, more cake was handed round. 'Ah, yes,' the Professor began. *'Panni streit sine grano.'* Woodward, Whipp and Woolmer-Mills bent their heads to listen.

*

The Professor, while waiting on his upstairs landing for Woolmer-Mills to use the lavatory, spoke of the tomatoes he grew. Similarly delayed downstairs, Mrs Skully suggested to the O'Neill sisters that they might like, one Saturday night next term, to listen to Saturday Night Theatre with her. It was something she enjoyed, she said, especially the discussion afterwards. 'Or you, Miss Upcott,' she said. 'You've never been to one of my evenings either.'

Valerie smiled politely, moving with Mrs Skully towards the sitting-room, where Tchaikovsky once more resounded powerfully. Again she examined the arrayed faces. Some eyes were closed in sleep, others were weary beneath a weight of tedium. Woodward's newt-like countenance had not altered, nor had Kilroy's fear dissipated. Frustration still tugged at Yvonne Smith. Nothing much was happening in the face of Mrs Skully.

Valerie continued to regard Mrs Skully's face and suddenly she found herself shivering. How could that mouth open and close, issuing invitations without knowing they were the subject of derision? How could this woman, in her late middle age, officiate at student parties in magenta and jade, or bake inedible cakes without knowing it? How could she daily permit herself to be taken for granted by a man who cared only for students with academic success behind them? How could she have married his pomposity in the first place? There was something wrong with Mrs Skully, there was something missing, as if some part of her had never come to life. The more Valerie examined her the more extraordinary Mrs Skully seemed, and then it seemed extraordinary that the Professor should be unaware that no one liked his parties. It was as if some part of him hadn't come to life either, as if they lived together in the dead wood of a relationship, together in this house because it was convenient.

She wondered if the other students had ever thought that, or if they'd be bothered to survey in any way whatsoever the Professor and his wife. She wondered if they saw a reflection of the Skullys' marriage in the brownness of the room they all sat in, or in the crunchy fillings of Mrs Skully's cakes, or in the Rexine-seated dining-chairs that were not comfortable. You couldn't blame them for not wanting to think about the Skullys' marriage: what good could come of it?

The other students were busy and more organised than she. They had aims in life. They had futures she could sense, as she had sensed their pasts. Honor Hitchcock and the Reverend would settle down as right as rain in a provincial rectory, the followers of the O'Neill sisters would enter various business worlds. Woodward, Whipp and Woolmer-Mills would be the same as the Professor, dandruff on the shoulders of three grey suits. Bewley Joal would rise to heights, Kilroy would not. Ruth Cusper would run a hall of residence, the O'Neill sisters would give two husbands hell in Lurgan. Yvonne Smith would live in hopes.

The music of Tchaikovsky gushed over these reflections, as if to soften some harshness in them. But to Valerie there was no harshness in her contemplation of these people's lives, only fact and a lacing of speculation. The Skullys would go on ageing and he might never turn to his wife and say he was sorry. The O'Neill sisters would lose their beauty and Bewley Joal his vigour. One day Woolmer-Mills would find that he could no longer launch himself on to the balls of his feet. Kilroy would enter a home for the senile. Death would shatter the cotton-wool cosiness of Honor Hitchcock and the Reverend.

She wondered what would happen if she revealed what she had thought, if she told them that in order to keep her melancholy in control she had played about with their lives, seeing them in childhood, visiting them with old age and death. Which of them would seek to stop her while she cited the arrogance of the Professor and the pusillanimity of his wife? She heard her own voice echoing in a silence, telling them finally, in explanation, of the tragedy in her own life.

*

'Please all have a jolly Christmas,' Mrs Skully urged in the hall as scarves and coats were lifted from the hall-stand. 'Please now.'

'We shall endeavour,' Kilroy promised, and the others made similar remarks, wishing Mrs Skully a happy Christmas herself, thanking her and the Professor for the party, Kilroy adding that it had been most enjoyable. There'd be another, the Professor promised, in May.

There was the roar of Ruth Cusper's motor-cycle, and the overloading of Kilroy's Mini, and the striding into the night of Bewley Joal, and others making off on bicycles. Valerie walked with Yvonne Smith through the suburban roads. 'I quite like Joal,' Yvonne Smith confided, releasing the first burst of her pent-up chatter. 'He's all right, isn't he? Quite nice, really, quite clever. I mean, if you care for a clever kind of person. I mean, I wouldn't mind going out with him if he asked me.'

Valerie agreed that Bewley Joal was all right if you cared for that kind of person. It was pleasant in the cold night air. It was good that the party was over.

Yvonne Smith said good-night, still chattering about Bewley Joal as she turned into the house where her lodgings were. Valerie walked on alone, a thin shadow in the gloom. Compulsively now, she thought about the party, seeing again the face of Mrs Skully and the Professor's face and the faces of the others. They formed, like a backdrop in her mind, an assembly as vivid as the tragedy that more grimly visited it. They seemed like the other side of the tragedy, as if she had for the first time managed to peer round a corner. The feeling puzzled her. It was odd to be left with it after the Skullys' end-of-term party.

In the garden of the hall of residence the fallen leaves were sodden beneath her feet as she crossed a lawn to shorten her journey. The bewilderment she felt lifted a little. She had been wrong to imagine she envied other people their normality and good fortune. She was as she wished to be. She paused in faint moonlight, repeating that to herself and then repeating it again. She did not quite add that the tragedy had made her what she was, that without it she would not possess her reflective introspection, or be sensitive to more than just the time of year. But the thought hovered with her as she moved towards the lights of the house, offering what appeared to be a hint of comfort.

The Teddy-bears' Picnic

'I simply don't believe it,' Edwin said. 'Grown-up people?'

'Well, grown-up now, darling. We weren't always grown-up.'

'But *teddy-bears*, Deborah?'

'I'm sure I've told you dozens of times before.'

Edwin shook his head, frowning and staring at his wife. They'd been married six months: he was twenty-nine, swiftly making his way in a stockbroker's office, Deborah was twenty-six and intended to continue being Mr Harridance's secretary until a family began to come along. They lived in Wimbledon, in a block of flats called The Zodiac. 23 The Zodiac their address was and friends thought the title amusing and lively, making jokes about Gemini and Taurus and Capricorn when they came to drinks. A Dane had designed The Zodiac in 1968.

'I'll absolutely tell you this,' Edwin said, 'I'm not attending this thing.'

'But darling –'

'Oh, don't be bloody silly, Deborah.'

Edwin's mother had called Deborah 'a pretty little thing', implying for those who cared to be perceptive a certain reservation. She'd been more direct with Edwin himself, in a private conversation they'd had after Edwin had said he and Deborah wanted to get married. 'Remember, dear,' was how Mrs Chalm had put it then, 'she's not always going to be a pretty little thing. This really isn't a very sensible marriage, Edwin.' Mrs Chalm was known to be a woman who didn't go in for cant when dealing with the lives of the children she had borne and brought up; she made no bones about it and often said so. Her husband, on the other hand, kept out of things.

Yet in the end Edwin and Deborah had married, one Tuesday afternoon in December, and Mrs Chalm resolved to make the best of it. She advised Deborah about this and that, she gave her potted plants for 23 The Zodiac, and in fact was kind. If Deborah had known about her mother-in-law's doubts she'd have been surprised.

'But we've always done it, Edwin. All of us.'

'All of who, for heaven's sake?'

'Well, Angela for one. And Holly and Jeremy of course.'

'*Jeremy*? My God!'

'And Peter. And Enid and Charlotte and Harriet.'

'You've never told me a word about this, Deborah.'

'I'm really sure I have.'

The sitting-room where this argument took place had a single huge window with a distant view of Wimbledon Common. The walls were covered with rust-coloured hessian, the floor with a rust-coloured carpet. The Chalms were still acquiring furniture: what there was, reflecting the style of The Zodiac's architecture, was in bent steel and glass. There was a single picture, of a field of thistles, revealed to be a photograph on closer examination. Bottles of alcohol stood on a glass-topped table, their colourful labels cheering that corner up. Had the Chalms lived in a Victorian flat, or a cottage in a mews, their sitting-room would have been different, fussier and more ornate, dictated by the architectural environment. Their choice of decor and furniture was the choice of newly-weds who hadn't yet discovered a confidence of their own.

'You mean you all sit round with your teddies,' Edwin said, 'having a picnic? And you'll still be doing that at eighty?'

'What d'you mean, eighty?'

'When you're eighty years of age, for God's sake. You're trying to tell me you'll still be going to this garden when you're stumbling about and hard of hearing, a gang of O.A.P.s squatting out on the grass with teddy-bears?'

'I didn't say anything about when we're old.'

'You said it's a tradition, for God's sake.'

He poured some whisky into a glass and added a squirt of soda from a Sparklets syphon. Normally he would have poured a gin and dry vermouth for his wife, but this evening he felt too cross to bother. He hadn't had the easiest of days. There'd been an error in the office about the B.A.T. shares a client had wished to buy, and he hadn't managed to have any lunch because as soon as the B.A.T. thing was sorted out a crisis had blown up over sugar speculation. It was almost eight o'clock when he'd got back to The Zodiac and instead of preparing a meal Deborah had been on the telephone to her friend Angela, talking about teddy-bears.

Edwin was an agile young man with shortish black hair and a face that had a very slight look of a greyhound about it. He was vigorous and athletic, sound on the tennis court, fond of squash and recently of golf. His mother had once stated that Edwin could not bear to lose and would go to ruthless lengths to ensure that he never did. She had even remarked to her husband that she hoped this quality would not one day cause trouble, but her husband replied it was probably just what a stockbroker needed. Mrs Chalm had been thinking more of personal relationships, where losing couldn't be avoided. It was that she'd had on her mind when she'd had doubts about the marriage, for the doubts were not there simply because Deborah was a pretty little thing: it was the conjunction Mrs Chalm was alarmed about.

'I didn't happen to get any lunch,' Edwin snappishly said now. 'I've had a long unpleasant day and when I get back here –'

'I'm sorry, dear.'

Deborah immediately rose from among the rust-coloured cushions of the sofa and went to the kitchen, where she took two pork chops from a Marks and Spencer's carrier-bag and placed them under the grill of the electric cooker. She took a packet of frozen broccoli spears from the carrier-bag as well, and two Marks and Spencer's trifles. While typing letters that afternoon she'd planned to have fried noodles with the chops and broccoli spears, just for a change. A week ago they'd had fried noodles in the new Mexican place they'd found and Edwin said they were lovely. Deborah had kicked off her shoes as soon as she'd come into the flat and hadn't put them on since. She was wearing a dress with scarlet petunias on it. Dark-haired, with a heart-shaped face and blue eyes that occasionally acquired a bewildered look, she seemed several years younger than twenty-six, more like eighteen.

She put on water to boil for the broccoli spears even though the chops would not be ready for some time. She prepared a saucepan of oil for the noodles, hoping that this was the way to go about frying them. She couldn't understand why Edwin was making such a fuss just because Angela had telephoned, and put it down to his not having managed to get any lunch.

In the sitting-room Edwin stood by the huge window, surveying the tops of trees and, in the distance, Wimbledon Common. She must have been on the phone to Angela for an hour and a half, probably longer. He'd tried to ring himself to say he'd be late but each time the line had been engaged. He searched his mind carefully, going back through the three years he'd known Deborah, but no reference to a teddy-bears' picnic came to him. He'd said very positively that she had never mentioned it, but he'd said that in anger, just to make his point: reviewing their many conversations now, he saw he had been right and felt triumphant. Of course he'd have remembered such a thing, any man would.

Far down below, a car turned into the wide courtyard of The Zodiac, a Rover it looked like, a discreet shade of green. It wouldn't be all that long before they had a Rover themselves, even allowing for the fact that the children they hoped for would be arriving any time now. Edwin had not objected to Deborah continuing her work after their marriage, but family life would naturally be much tidier when she no longer could, when the children were born. Eventually they'd have to move into a house with a garden because it was natural that Deborah would want that, and he had no intention of disagreeing with her.

'Another thing is,' he said, moving from the window to the open doorway of the kitchen, 'how come you haven't had a reunion all the years I've known you? If it's an annual thing —'

'It isn't an annual thing, Edwin. We haven't had a picnic since 1975 and before that 1971. It's just when someone feels like it, I suppose. It's just a bit of fun, darling.'

'You call sitting down with teddy-bears a bit of fun? Grown-up people?'

'I wish you wouldn't keep on about grown-ups. I know we're grown-ups. That's the whole point. When we were little we all vowed —'

'Jesus Christ!'

He turned and went to pour himself another drink. She'd never mentioned it because she knew it was silly. She was ashamed of it, which was something she would discover when she grew up a bit.

'You know I've got Binky,' she said, following him to where the drinks were and pouring herself some gin. 'I've told you hundreds of times how I took him everywhere. If you don't like him in the bedroom I'll put him away. I didn't know you didn't like him.'

'I didn't say that, Deborah. It's completely different, what you're saying. It's private for a start. I mean, it's your teddy-bear and you've told me how fond you were of it. That's completely different from sitting down with a crowd of idiots –'

'They're not idiots, Edwin, actually.'

'Well, they certainly don't sound like anything else. D'you mean Jeremy and Peter are going to arrive clutching teddy-bears and then sit down on the grass pretending to feed them biscuit crumbs? For God's sake, Jeremy's a medical *doctor*!'

'Actually, nobody'll sit on the grass because the grass will probably be damp. Everyone brought rugs last time. It's really because of the garden, you know. It's probably the nicest garden in South Bucks, and then there're the Ainley-Foxletons. I mean, they do so love it all.'

He'd actually been in the garden, and he'd once actually met the Ainley-Foxletons. One Saturday afternoon during his engagement to Deborah there had been tea on a raised lawn. Laburnum and broom were out, a mass of yellow everywhere. Quite pleasant old sticks the Ainley-Foxletons had been, but neither of them had mentioned a teddy-bears' picnic.

'I think she did as a matter of fact,' Deborah mildly insisted. 'I remember because I said it hadn't really been so long since the last one – eighteen months ago would it be when I took you to see them? Well, 1975 wasn't all that long before that, and she said it seemed like aeons. I remember her saying that, I remember "aeons" and thinking it just like her to come out with a word people don't use any more.'

'And you never thought to point out the famous picnic site? For hours we walked round and round that garden and yet it never occurred to you –'

'We didn't walk round and round. I'm sorry you were bored, Edwin.'

'I didn't say I was bored.'

'I know the Ainley-Foxletons can't hear properly and it's a strain, but you said you wanted to meet them –'

'I didn't say anything of the kind. You kept telling me about these people and their house and garden, but I can assure you I wasn't crying out to meet them in any way whatsoever. In fact, I rather wanted to play tennis that afternoon.'

'You didn't say so at the time.'

'Of course I didn't say so.'

'Well, then.'

'What I'm trying to get through to you is that we walked round and round that garden even though it had begun to rain. And not once did you say, "That's where we used to have our famous teddy-bears' picnic".'

'As a matter of fact I think I did. And it isn't famous. I wish you wouldn't keep on about it being famous.'

Deborah poured herself more gin and added the same amount of dry vermouth to the glass. She considered it rude of Edwin to stalk about the room just because he'd had a bad day, drinking himself and not bothering about her. If he hadn't liked the poor old Ainley-Foxletons he should have said so. If he'd wanted to play tennis that afternoon he should have said so too.

'Well, be all that as it may,' he was saying now, rather pompously in Deborah's opinion, 'I do not intend to take part in any of this nonsense.'

'But everybody's husband will, and the wives too. It's only fun, darling.'

'Oh, do stop saying it's fun. You sound like a half-wit. And something's smelling in the kitchen.'

'I don't think that's very nice, Edwin. I don't see why you should call me a half-wit.'

'Listen, I've had an extremely unpleasant day –'

'Oh, do stop about your stupid old day.'

She carried her glass to the kitchen with her and removed the chops from beneath the grill. They were fairly black, and serve him right for upsetting her. Why on earth did he have to make such a fuss, why couldn't he be like everyone else? It was something to giggle over, not take so seriously, a single Sunday afternoon when they wouldn't be doing anything anyway. She dropped a handful of noodles into the hot oil, and then a second handful.

In the sitting-room the telephone rang just as Edwin was squirting soda into another drink. 'Yes?' he said, and Angela's voice came lilting over the line, saying she didn't want to bother Debbie but the date had just been fixed: June 17th. 'Honestly, you'll split your sides, Edwin.'

'Yes, all right, I'll tell her,' he said as coldly as he could. He replaced the receiver without saying goodbye. He'd never cared for Angela, patronising kind of creature.

Deborah knew it had been Angela on the telephone and she knew she would have given Edwin the date she had arranged with Charlotte and Peter, who'd been the doubtful ones about the first date, suggested by Jeremy. Angela had said she was going to ring back with this information, but when the Chalms sat down to their chops and broccoli spears and noodles Edwin hadn't yet passed the information on.

'Christ, what are these?' he said, poking at a brown noodle with his fork and then poking at the burnt chop.

'The little things are fried noodles, which you enjoyed so much the other night. The larger thing is a pork chop, which wouldn't have got overcooked if you hadn't started an argument.'

'Oh, for God's sake!'

He pushed his chair back and stood up. He returned to the sitting-room and Deborah heard the squirting of the soda syphon. She stood up herself, followed him to the sitting-room and poured herself another gin and vermouth. Neither of them spoke. Deborah returned to the kitchen and ate her share of the broccoli spears. The sound of television came from the sitting-room. 'Listen, buster, you give this bread to the hit or don't you?' a voice demanded. 'O.K., I give the bread,' a second voice replied.

They'd had quarrels before. They'd quarrelled on their honeymoon in Greece for no reason whatsoever. They'd quarrelled because she'd once left the ignition of the car turned on, causing a flat battery. They'd quarrelled because of Enid's boring party just before Christmas. The present quarrel was just the same kind of thing, Deborah knew: Edwin would sit and sulk, she'd wash the dishes up feeling miserable, and he'd probably eat the chop and the broccoli when they were cold. She couldn't blame him for not wanting the noodles because she didn't seem to have cooked them correctly. Then she thought: what if he doesn't come to the picnic, what if he just goes on being stubborn, which he could be when he wanted to? Everyone would know. 'Where's Edwin?' they would ask, and she'd tell some lie and everyone would know it was a lie, and everyone would know they weren't getting on. Only six months had passed, everyone would say, and he wouldn't join in a bit of fun.

But to Deborah's relief that didn't happen. Later that night Edwin ate the cold pork chop, eating it from his fingers because he couldn't manage to stick a fork into it. He ate the cold broccoli spears as well, but he left the noodles. She made him tea and gave him a Danish pastry and in the morning he said he was sorry.

*

'So if we could it would be lovely,' Deborah said on her office telephone. She'd told her mother there was to be another teddy-bears' picnic, Angela and Jeremy had arranged it mainly, and the Ainley-Foxletons would love it of course, possibly the last they'd see.

'My dear, you're always welcome, as you know.' The voice of Deborah's mother came all the way from South Bucks, from the village where the Ainley-Foxletons' house and garden were, where Deborah and Angela, Jeremy, Charlotte, Harriet, Enid, Peter and Holly had been children together. The plan was that Edwin and Deborah should spend the weekend of June 17th with Deborah's parents, and Deborah's mother had even promised to lay on some tennis for Edwin on the Saturday. Deborah herself wasn't much good at tennis.

'Thanks, Mummy,' she managed to say just as Mr Harridance returned from lunch.

'No, spending the whole weekend actually,' Edwin informed his mother. 'There's this teddy-bear thing Deborah has to go to.'

'What teddy-bear thing?'

Edwin went into details, explaining how the children who'd been friends in a South Bucks village nearly twenty years ago met from time to time to have a teddy-bears' picnic because that was what they'd done then.

'But they're adults surely now,' Mrs Chalm pointed out.

'Yes, I know.'

'Well, I hope you have a lovely time, dear.'

'Delightful, I'm sure.'

'It's odd when they're adults, I'd have thought.'

Between themselves, Edwin and Deborah did not again discuss the subject of the teddy-bears' picnic. During the quarrel Edwin had felt bewildered, never quite knowing how to proceed, and he hoped that on some future occasion he would be better able to cope. It made him angry when he wasn't able to cope, and the anger still hung about him. On the other hand, six months wasn't long in a marriage which he hoped would go on for ever: the marriage hadn't had a chance to settle into the shape that suited it, any more than he and Deborah had had time to develop their own taste in furniture and decoration. It was only to be expected that there should be problems and uncertainty.

As for Deborah, she knew nothing about marriages settling into shape: she wasn't aware that rules and tacit understandings, arrangements of give and take, were what made marriage possible when the first gloss had worn off. Marriage for Deborah was the continuation of a love affair, and as yet she had few complaints. She knew that of course they had to have quarrels.

They had met at a party. Edwin had left a group of people he was listening to and had crossed to the corner where she was being bored by a man in computers. 'Hullo,' Edwin just said. All three of them were eating plates of paella.

Finding a consideration of the past pleasanter than speculation about the future, Deborah often recalled that moment: Edwin's sharp face smiling at her, the computer man discomfited, a sour taste in the paella. 'You're not Fiona's sister?' Edwin said, and when ages afterwards she'd asked him who Fiona was he confessed he'd made her up. 'I shouldn't eat much more of this stuff,' he said, taking the paella away from her. Deborah had been impressed by that: she and the computer man had been fiddling at the paella with their forks, both of them too polite to say that there was something the matter with it. 'What do you do?' Edwin said a few minutes later, which was more than the computer man had asked.

In the weeks that followed they told one another all about themselves, about their parents and the houses they'd lived in as children, the schools they'd gone to, the friends they'd made. Edwin was a daring person, he was successful, he liked to be in charge of things. Without in any way sounding boastful, he told her of episodes in his childhood, of risks taken at school. Once he'd dismantled the elderly music master's bed, causing it to collapse when the music master later lay down on it. He'd removed the carburettor from some other master's car, he'd stolen an egg-beater from an ironmonger's shop. All of them were dares, and by the end of his schooldays he had acquired the reputation of being fearless: there was nothing, people said, he wouldn't do.

It was easy for Deborah to love him, and everything he told her, self-deprecatingly couched, was clearly the truth. But Deborah in love naturally didn't wonder how this side of Edwin would seem in marriage, nor how it might develop as Edwin moved into middle age. She couldn't think of anything nicer than having him there every day, and in no way did she feel let down on their honeymoon in Greece or by the couple of false starts they made with flats before they eventually ended up in 23 The Zodiac. Edwin went to his office every day and Deborah went to hers. That he told her more about share prices than she told him about the letters she typed for Mr Harridance was because share prices were more important. It was true that she would often have quite liked to pass on details of this or that, for instance of the correspondence with Flitts, Hay and Co. concerning nearly eighteen thousand defective chair castors. The correspondence was interesting because it had continued for two years and had become vituperative. But when she mentioned it Edwin just agreeably nodded. There was also the business about Miss Royal's scratches, which everyone in the office had been conjecturing about: how on earth had a woman like Miss Royal acquired four long scratches on her face and neck between five-thirty one Monday evening and nine-thirty the following morning? 'Oh yes?' Edwin had said, and gone on to talk about the Mercantile Investment Trust.

Deborah did not recognise these telltale signs. She did not remember that when first she and Edwin exchanged information about one another's childhoods Edwin had sometimes just smiled, as if his mind had drifted away. It was only a slight disappointment that he didn't wish to hear about Flitts, Hay and Co., and Miss Royal's scratches: no one could possibly get into a state about things like that. Deborah saw little significance in the silly quarrel they'd had about the teddy-bears' picnic, which was silly itself of course. She didn't see that it had had to do with friends who were hers and not Edwin's; nor did it occur to her that when they really began to think about the decoration of 23 The Zodiac it would be Edwin who would make the decisions. They shared things, Deborah would have said: after all, in spite of the quarrel they were going to go to the teddy-bears' picnic. Edwin loved her and was kind and really rather marvellous. It was purely for her sake that he'd agreed to give up a whole weekend.

So on a warm Friday afternoon, as they drove from London in their Saab, Deborah was feeling happy. She listened while Edwin talked about a killing a man called Dupree had made by selling out his International Asphalt holding. 'James James Morrison Morrison Weatherby George Dupree,' she said.

'What on earth's that?'

'It's by A. A. Milne, the man who wrote about Pooh Bear. Poor Pooh!'

Edwin didn't say anything.

'Jeremy's is called Pooh.'

'I see.'

In the back of the car, propped up in a corner, was the blue teddy-bear called Binky which Deborah had had since she was one.

*

The rhododendrons were in bloom in the Ainley-Foxletons' garden, late that year because of the bad winter. So was the laburnum Edwin remembered, and the broom, and some yellow azaleas. 'My dear, we're so awfully glad,' old Mrs Ainley-Foxleton said, kissing him because she imagined he must be one of the children in her past. Her husband, tottering about on the raised lawn which Edwin also remembered from his previous visit, had developed the shakes. 'Darlings, Mrs Bright has ironed our tablecloth for us!' Mrs Ainley-Foxleton announced with a flourish.

She imparted this fact because Mrs Bright, the Ainley-Foxletons' charwoman, was emerging at that moment from the house, with the ironed tablecloth over one arm. She carried a tray on which there were glass jugs of orange squash and lemon squash, a jug of milk, mugs with Beatrix Potter characters on them, and two plates of sandwiches that weren't much larger than postage stamps. She made her way down stone steps from the raised lawn, crossed a more extensive lawn and disappeared into a shrubbery. While everyone remained chatting to the Ainley-Foxletons – nobody helping to lay the picnic out because that had never been part of the proceedings – Mrs Bright reappeared from the shrubbery, returned to the house and then made a second journey, her tray laden this time with cakes and biscuits.

Before lunch Edwin had sat for a long time with Deborah's father in the summerhouse, drinking. This was something Deborah's father enjoyed on Sunday mornings, permitting himself a degree of dozy inebriation which only became noticeable when two bottles of claret were consumed at lunch. Today Edwin had followed his example, twice getting to his feet to refill their glasses and during the course of lunch managing to slip out to the summerhouse for a fairly heavy tot of whisky, which mixed nicely with the claret. He could think of no other condition in which to present himself – with a teddy-bear Deborah's mother had pressed upon him – in the Ainley-Foxletons' garden. 'Rather you than me, old chap,' Deborah's father had said after lunch, subsiding into an armchair with a gurgle. At the last moment Edwin had quickly returned to the summerhouse and had helped himself to a further intake of whisky, drinking from the cap of the Teacher's bottle because the glasses had been collected up. He reckoned that when Mrs Ainley-Foxleton had kissed him he must have smelt like a distillery, and he was glad of that.

'Well, here we are,' Jeremy said in the glade where the

picnic had first taken place in 1957. He sat at the head of the tablecloth, cross-legged on a tartan rug. He had glasses and was stout. Peter at the other end of the tablecloth didn't seem to have grown much in the intervening years, but Angela had shot up like a hollyhock and in fact resembled one. Enid was dumpy, Charlotte almost beautiful; Harriet had protruding teeth, Holly was bouncy. Jeremy's wife and Peter's wife, and Charlotte's husband – a man in Shell – all entered into the spirit of the occasion. So did Angela's husband, who came from Czechoslovakia and must have found the proceedings peculiar, everyone sitting there with a teddy-bear that had a name. Angela put a record on Mrs Ainley-Foxleton's old wind-up gramophone. 'Oh, don't go down to the woods today,' a voice screeched, 'without consulting me.' Mr and Mrs Ainley-Foxleton were due to arrive at the scene later, as was the tradition. They came with chocolates apparently, and bunches of buttercups for the teddy-bears.

'Thank you, Edwin,' Deborah whispered while the music and the song continued. She wanted him to remember the quarrel they'd had about the picnic; she wanted him to know that she now truly forgave him, and appreciated that in the end he'd seen the fun of it all.

'Listen, I have to go to the lav,' Edwin said. 'Excuse me for a minute.' Nobody except Deborah seemed to notice when he ambled off because everyone was talking so, exchanging news.

*

The anger which had hung about Edwin after the quarrel had never evaporated. It was in anger that he had telephoned his mother, and further anger had smacked at him when she'd said she hoped he would have a lovely time. What she had meant was that she'd told him so: marry a pretty little thing and before you can blink you're sitting down to tea with teddy-bears. You're a fool to put up with rubbish like this was what Deborah's father had meant when he'd said rather you than me.

Edwin did not lack brains and he had always been aware of it. It was his cleverness that was still offended by what he considered to be an embarrassment, a kind of gooey awfulness in an elderly couple's garden. At school he had always hated anything to do with dressing up, he'd even felt awkward when he'd had to read poetry aloud. What Edwin admired was solidity: he liked Westminster and the City, he liked trains moving smoothly, suits and clean shirts. When he'd married Deborah he'd known – without having to be told by his mother – that she was not a clever person, but in Edwin's view a clever wife was far from necessary. He had seen a future in which children were born and educated, in which Deborah developed various cooking and housekeeping skills, in which together they gave nice dinner parties. Yet instead of that, after only six months, there was this grotesque absurdity. Getting drunk wasn't a regular occurrence with Edwin: he drank when he was angry, as he had on the night of the quarrel.

Mr Ainley-Foxleton was pottering about with his stick on the raised lawn, but Edwin took no notice of him. The old man appeared to be looking for something, his head poked forward on his scrawny neck, bespectacled eyes examining the grass. Edwin passed into the house. From behind a closed door he could hear the voices of Mrs Ainley-Foxleton and Mrs Bright, talking about buttercups. He opened another door and entered the Ainley-Foxletons' dining-room. On the sideboard there was a row of decanters.

Edwin discovered that it wasn't easy to drink from a decanter, but he managed it none the less. Anger spurted in
him all over again. It seemed incredible that he had married
a girl who hadn't properly grown up. None of them had
grown up, none of them desired to belong in the adult
world, not even the husbands and wives who hadn't been
involved in the first place. If Deborah had told him about any
of it on that Sunday afternoon when they'd visited this
house he wondered even if he would have married her.

Yet replacing the stopper of the decanter between mouth-
fuls in case anyone came in, Edwin found it impossible to
admit that he had made a mistake in marrying Deborah: he
loved her, he had never loved anyone else, and he doubted if
he would ever love anyone else in the future. Often in an
idle moment, between selling and buying in the office, he
thought of her, seeing her in her different clothes and
sometimes without any clothes at all. When he returned to
23 The Zodiac he sometimes put his arms around her and
would not let her go until he had laid her gently down on
their bed. Deborah thought the world of him, which was
something she often said.

In spite of all that it was extremely annoying that the
quarrel had caused him to feel out of his depth. He should
have been able to sort out such nonsense within a few
minutes; he deserved his mother's jibe and his father-in-
law's as well. Even though they'd only been married six
months, it was absurd that since Deborah loved him so he
hadn't been able to make her see how foolish she was being.
It was absurd to be standing here drunk.

The Ainley-Foxletons' dining-room, full of silver and
polished furniture and dim oil paintings, shifted out of
focus. The row of decanters became two rows and then one
again. The heavily carpeted floor tilted beneath him, falling

away to the left and then to the right. Deborah had let him down. She had brought him here so that he could be displayed in front of Angela and Jeremy and Charlotte, Harriet, Holly, Enid, Peter, and the husbands and the wives. She was making the point that she had only to lift her little finger, that his cleverness was nothing compared with his love for her. The anger hammered at him now, hurting him almost. He wanted to walk away, to drive the Saab back to London and when Deborah followed him to state quite categorically that if she intended to be a fool there would have to be a divorce. But some part of Edwin's anger insisted that such a course of action would be an admission of failure and defeat. It was absurd that the marriage he had chosen to make should end before it had properly begun, due to silliness.

Edwin took a last mouthful of whisky and replaced the glass stopper. He remembered another social occasion, years ago, and he was struck by certain similarities with the present one. People had given a garden party in aid of some charity or other which his mother liked to support, to which he and his brother and sister, and his father, had been dragged along. It had been an excruciatingly boring afternoon, in the middle of a heatwave. He'd had to wear his floppy cotton hat, which he hated, and an awful tan-coloured summer suit, made of cotton also. There had been hours and hours of just standing while his mother talked to people, sometimes slowly giving them recipes, which they wrote down. Edwin's brother and sister didn't seem to mind that; his father did as he was told. So Edwin had wandered off, into a house that was larger and more handsome than the Ainley-Foxletons'. He had poked about in the downstairs rooms, eaten some jam he found in the kitchen, and then gone upstairs to the bedrooms. He'd rooted around for a while, opening drawers and wardrobes, and then he'd climbed a flight of uncarpeted stairs to a loft. From here he'd made his way out on to the roof. Edwin had almost forgotten this incident and certainly never dwelt on it, but with a vividness that surprised him it now returned.

He left the dining-room. In the hall he could still hear the voices of Mrs Ainley-Foxleton and Mrs Bright. Nobody had bothered with him that day; his mother, whose favourite he had always been, was even impatient when he said he had a toothache. Nobody had noticed when he'd slipped away. But from the parapet of the roof everything had been different. The faces of the people were pale, similar dots, all gazing up at him. The colours of the women's dresses were confused among the flowers. Arms waved frantically at him; someone shouted, ordering him to come down.

On the raised lawn the old man was still examining the grass, his head still poked down towards it, his stick prodding at it. From the glade where the picnic was taking place came a brief burst of applause, as if someone had just made a speech. '. . . today's the day the teddy-bears have their picnic,' sang the screeching voice, faintly.

A breeze had cooled Edwin's sunburnt arms as he crept along the parapet. He'd sensed his mother's first realisation that it was he, and noticed his brother's and his sister's weeping. He had seen his father summoned from the car where he'd been dozing. Edwin had stretched his arms out, balancing like a tightrope performer. All the boredom, the tiresome heat, the cotton hat and suit, were easily made up for. Within minutes it had become his day.

'Well, it's certainly the weather for it,' Edwin said to the old man.

'Eh?'

'The weather's nice,' he shouted. 'It's a fine day.'

'There's fungus in this lawn, you know. Eaten up with it.'

Mr Ainley-Foxleton investigated small black patches with his stick. 'Never knew there was fungus here,' he said.

They were close to the edge of the lawn. Below them there was a rockery full of veronica and sea-pinks and saponaria. The rockery was arranged in a semicircle, around a sundial.

'Looks like fungus there too,' Edwin said, pointing at the larger lawn that stretched away beyond this rockery.

'Eh?' The old man peered over the edge, not knowing what he was looking for because he hadn't properly heard. 'Eh?' he said again, and Edwin nudged him with his elbow. The stick went flying off at an angle, the old man's head struck the edge of the sundial with a sharp, clean crack. 'Oh, don't go down to the woods today,' the voice began again, drifting through the sunshine over the scented garden. Edwin glanced quickly over the windows of the house in case there should be a face at one of them. Not that it would matter: at that distance no one could see such a slight movement of an elbow.

*

They ate banana sandwiches and egg sandwiches, and biscuits with icing on them, chocolate cake and coffee cake. The teddy-bears' snouts were pressed over the Beatrix Potter mugs, each teddy-bear addressed by name. Edwin's was called Tomkin.

'Remember the day of the thunderstorm?' Enid said, screwing up her features in a way she had – like a twitch really, Edwin considered. The day he had walked along the parapet might even have been the day of the thunderstorm, and he smiled because somehow that was amusing. Angela was smiling too, and so were Jeremy and Enid, Charlotte, Harriet and Holly, Peter and the husbands and the wives.

Deborah in particular was smiling. When Edwin glanced from face to face he was reminded of the faces that had gazed up at him from so far below, except that there'd been panic instead of smiles.

'Remember the syrup?' Angela said. 'Poor Algernon had to be given a horrid bath.'

'Wasn't it Horatio, surely?' Deborah said.

'Yes, it was Horatio,' Enid confirmed, amusingly balancing Horatio on her shoulder.

'Today's the day the teddy-bears have their picnic,' suddenly sang everyone, taking a lead from the voice on the gramophone. Edwin smiled and even began to sing himself. When they returned to Deborah's parents' house the atmosphere would be sombre. 'Poor old chap was overlooked,' he'd probably be the one to explain, 'due to all that fuss.' And in 23 The Zodiac the atmosphere would be sombre also. 'I'm afraid you should get rid of it,' he'd suggest, arguing that the blue teddy-bear would be for ever a reminder. Grown up a bit because of what had happened, Deborah would of course agree. Like everything else, marriage had to settle into shape.

Charlotte told a story of an adventure her Mikey had had when she'd taken him back to boarding-school, how a repulsive girl called Agnes Thorpe had stuck a skewer in him. Holly told of how she'd had to rescue her Percival from drowning when he'd toppled out of a motor-boat. Jeremy wound up the gramophone and the chatter jollily continued, the husbands and wives appearing to be as delighted as anyone. Harriet said how she'd only wanted to marry Peter and Peter how he'd determined to marry Deborah. 'Oh, don't go down to the woods today,' the voice began again, and then came Mrs Ainley-Foxleton's scream.

Everyone rushed, leaving the teddy-bears just anywhere

and the gramophone still playing. Edwin was the first to bend over the splayed figure of the old man. He declared that Mr Ainley-Foxleton was dead, and then took charge of the proceedings.

Being Stolen From

'I mean I'm not like I used to be.'

She had married, Norma continued, she had settled down. A young man, sitting beside her on the sofa, agreed that this was so. He was soberly dressed, jolly of manner, not quite fat. His smiling blue eyes suggested that if Norma had ever been flighty and irresponsible she no longer was, due to the influence he had brought into her life.

'I mean in a way,' Norma said, 'things have changed for you too, Mrs Lacy.'

Bridget became flustered. Ever since childhood she had been embarrassed when she found herself the centre of attention, and even though she was forty-nine now none of that had improved. She was plump and black-haired, her manner affected by her dislike of being in the limelight. It was true that things had changed for her also in the last six years, but how had Norma discovered it? Had neighbours been questioned?

'Yes, things have changed,' she said, quite cheerfully because she'd become used to the change.

Norma nodded, and so did her husband. Bridget could tell from their faces that although they might not know the details they certainly knew the truth of the matter. And the details weren't important because strangers wouldn't be interested in the countryside of Co. Cork where she and Liam had come from, or in the disappointment of their childless marriage. London had become their home, a small house in a terrace, with the *Cork Weekly Examiner* to keep them in touch. Liam had found a job in a newsagent's, the same shop he and the woman now owned between them.

'Your husband didn't seem the kind,' Norma began. 'I mean, not that I knew him.'

'No, he didn't seem like that.'

'I know what it feels like to be left, Mrs Lacy.'

'It feels like nothing now.'

She smiled again, but her cheeks had become hot because the conversation was about her. When Norma had phoned a week ago, to ask if they could have a chat, she hadn't known what to say. It would have been unpleasant simply to say no, nor was there any reason why she should take that attitude, but even so she'd been dreading their visit ever since. She'd felt cross with herself for not managing to explain that Betty could easily be upset, which was why Betty wasn't in the house that afternoon. It was the first thing she'd said to them when she'd opened the hall-door, not knowing if they were expecting to see the child or not. She'd sounded apologetic and was cross with herself for that, too.

All three of them drank tea while they talked. Bridget, who didn't make cakes because Liam hadn't liked them and she'd never since got into the way of it, had bought two kinds of biscuits and a Battenburg in Victor Value's. Alarmed at the last moment in case there wouldn't be enough and she'd be thought inhospitable, she had buttered some bread and put out a jar of apricot jam. She was glad she had because Norma's husband made quite a meal of it, taking most of the gingersnaps and folding the sliced bread into sandwiches. Norma didn't eat anything.

'I can't have another baby, Mrs Lacy. That's the point, if you get what I mean? Like after Betty I had to have an abortion and then two more, horrible they were, the last one a bit of trouble really. I mean, it left my insides like this.'

'Oh dear, I'm sorry.'

Nodding, as if in gratitude for this sympathy, Norma's husband reached for a gingersnap. He said they had a nice flat and there were other children living near by for Betty to play with. He glanced around the small living-room, which was choked with pieces of furniture and ornaments which Bridget was always resolving to weed out. In what he said, and in the way he looked, there was the implication that this room in a cramped house was an unsuitable habitat for a spirited four-year-old. There was also the implication that Bridget at forty-nine, and without a husband, belonged more naturally among the sacred pictures on the walls than she possibly could in a world of toys and children. It was Betty they had to think of, the young man's concerned expression insisted; it was Betty's well-being.

'We signed the papers at the time.' Bridget endeavoured, not successfully, to make her protest sound different from an apology. 'When a baby's adopted that's meant to be that.'

Norma's husband nodded, as if agreeing that that was a reasonable point of view also. Norma said:

'You were kindness itself to me, Mrs Lacy, you and your husband. Didn't I say so?' she added, turning to her companion, who nodded again.

The baby had been born when Norma was nineteen. There'd been an effort on her part to look after it, but within a month she'd found the task impossible. She'd been living at the time in the house across the road from the Lacys', in a bed-sitting-room. She'd had a bad reputation in the neighbourhood, even reputed to be a prostitute, which wasn't in fact true. Bridget had always nodded to her in the street, and she'd always smiled back. Remembering all that when Norma had telephoned a day or two ago, Bridget found she had retained an impression of chipped red varnish on the girl's fingernails and her shrunken whey-white face. There'd been a prettiness about her too, though, and there still was. 'I don't know what to do,' she'd said four years ago. 'I don't know why I've had this kid.' She'd said it quite out of the blue, crossing the street to where Bridget had paused for a moment on the pavement to change the shopping she was carrying from one hand to the other. 'I often see you,' Norma had added, and Bridget, who noticed that she had recently been weeping and indeed looked quite ill, had invited her in for a cup of tea. Once or twice the sound of the baby's crying had drifted across the street, and of course she'd been quite interested to watch the progress of the pregnancy. Local opinion decreed that the pregnancy was what you'd expect of this girl, but Bridget didn't easily pass judgement. As Irish people in London, there was a politeness about the Lacys, a reluctance to condemn anyone who was English since they themselves were not. 'I've been a fool about this kid,' the girl had said: the father had let her down, as simple as that. He'd seemed as steady as a rock, but one night he hadn't been in the Queen's Arms and he hadn't been there the next night either, in fact not ever again.

'I couldn't let Betty go,' Bridget said, her face becoming hot again. 'I couldn't possibly. That's quite out of the question.'

A silence hung in the living-room for a moment. The air seemed heavier and stuffier, and Bridget wanted to open a window but did not. Betty was spending the afternoon with Mrs Grounds, who was always good about having her on the rare occasions when it was necessary.

'No, it's not a question of letting her go,' the young man said. 'No one would think of it like that, Mrs Lacy.'

'We'd always like her to see you,' Norma explained. 'I mean, it stands to reason she'll have got fond of you.'

The young man again nodded, his features good-humouredly crinkled. There was no question, he repeated, of the relationship between the child and her adoptive mother being broken off. An arrangement that was suitable all round could easily be made, and any offer of babysitting would always be more than welcome. 'What's needed, Mrs Lacy, is for mother and child to be together. Now that the circumstances have altered.'

'It's two years since my husband left me.'

'I'm thinking of Norma's circumstances, Mrs Lacy.'

'I can't help wanting her,' Norma said, her lean cheeks working beneath her make-up. Her legs were crossed, the right one over the left. Her shoes, in soft pale leather, were a lot smarter than the shoes Bridget remembered from the past. So was her navy-blue shirt and her navy-blue corduroy jacket that zipped up the front. Her fingers were marked with nicotine, and Bridget knew she wanted to light a cigarette now, the way she had repeatedly done the first day she'd come to the sitting-room, six years ago.

'We made it all legal,' Bridget said, putting into different words what she had stated already. 'Everything was legal, Norma.'

'Yes, we do know that,' the young man replied, still patiently smiling, making her feel foolish. 'But there's the human side too, you see. Perhaps more important than legalities.'

He was better educated than Norma, Bridget noticed; and there was an honest niceness in his eyes when he referred to the human side. There was justice above the ordinary justice of solicitors' documents and law courts, his niceness insisted: Norma had been the victim of an unfair society and all they could do now was to see that the unfairness should not be perpetuated.

'I'm sorry,' Bridget said. 'I'm sorry I can't see it like that.'

Soon after that the visitors left, leaving behind them the feeling that they and Bridget would naturally be meeting again. She went to collect Betty from Mrs Grounds and after tea they settled down to a familiar routine: Betty's bath and then bed, a few minutes of *The Tailor of Gloucester*. The rest of the evening stretched emptily ahead, with *Dallas* on the television, and a cardigan she was knitting. She quite liked *Dallas*, J. R. in particular, the most villainous TV figure she could think of, but while she watched his villainy now the conversation she'd had with her afternoon visitors kept recurring. Betty's round face, and the black hair that curved in smoothly on either side of it, appeared in her mind, and there was also the leanness of Norma and the sincerity of the man who wanted to become Betty's step-father. The three faces went together as if they belonged, for though Betty's was differently shaped from the face of the woman who had given birth to her she had the same wide mouth and the same brown eyes.

At half past nine Miss Custle came into the house. She was an oldish woman who worked on the Underground and often had to keep odd hours, some days leaving the house shortly after dawn and on other days not until the late afternoon. 'Cup of tea, Miss Custle?' Bridget called out above the noise of the television.

'Well, thanks, Mrs Lacy,' Miss Custle replied, as she always did when this invitation came. She had a gas stove and a sink in her room and did all her cooking there, but whenever Bridget heard her coming in as late as this she offered her a cup of tea. She'd been a lodger in the house ever since the break-up of the marriage, a help in making ends meet.

'Those people came,' Bridget said, offering Miss Custle

what remained of the gingersnaps. 'You know: Norma.'

'I told you to beware of them. Upset you, did they?'

'Well, talking about Betty like that. You know, Betty didn't even have a name when we adopted her. It was we thought of Betty.'

'You told me.'

Miss Custle was a powerful, grey-haired woman in a London Transport uniform which smelt of other people's cigarettes. Earlier in her life there'd been a romance with someone else on the Underground, but without warning the man had died. Shocked by the unexpectedness of it, Miss Custle had remained on her own for the next thirty years, and was given to gloom when she recalled the time of her loss. Among her colleagues on the Underground she was known for her gruffness and her devotion to the tasks she had performed for so much of her life. The London Underground, she occasionally stated in Bridget's living-room, had become her life, a substitute for what might have been. But tonight her mood was brisk.

'When a child's adopted, Mrs Lacy, there's no way it can be reversed. As I told you last evening, dear.'

'Yes, I do know that. I said it to them.'

'Trying it on, they was.'

With that, Miss Custle rose to her feet and said good-night. She never stayed long when she looked in for a cup of tea and a biscuit because she was usually tired. Her face took on a crumpled look, matching her crumpled uniform. She would iron her uniform before her next turn of duty, taking ages over it.

'Good-night, Miss Custle,' Bridget said, observing the weary passage of her lodger across the living-room and wondering just for a moment what the man who'd died had been like. One night, a year or so ago, she had told Miss

Custle all about her own loss, not of course that it could be compared with death, although it had felt like it at the time. 'Horrible type of woman, that is,' Miss Custle had said.

Bridget cleared up the tea things and unplugged the television lead. She knew she wouldn't sleep properly: the visit of Norma and her husband had stirred everything up again, forcing her to travel backwards in time, to survey again all she had come to terms with. It was extraordinary that they'd thought she'd even consider handing Betty over to them.

In her bedroom she undressed and tidily arranged her clothes on a chair. She could hear Miss Custle moving about in her room next door, undressing also. Betty had murmured in her sleep when she'd kissed her good-night, and Bridget tried to imagine what life would be like not having Betty there to tuck up last thing, not having Betty's belongings about the house, her clothes to wash, toys to pick up. Sometimes Betty made her cross, but that was part of it too.

She lay in the darkness, her mind going back again. In the countryside of Co. Cork she had been one of a family of ten, and Liam had come from a large family also. It had astonished them when years later they had failed to have children of their own, but in no way had the disappointment impaired their marriage; and then Betty's presence had drawn them even closer together. 'I'm sorry,' Liam had said in the end, though, the greatest shock she'd ever had. 'I'm sorry, dear.'

Bridget had never seen the woman, but had imagined her: younger than she was, a Londoner, black hair like silk, predatory lips, and eyes that looked away from you. This woman and her mother had bought the newsagent's where Liam had worked for all his years in London, the manager more or less, under old Mr Vanish. The woman had been married before, an unhappy marriage according to Liam, a relationship that had left her wounded. 'Dear, it's serious,' he had said, trying to keep out of his voice a lightness that was natural in it, not realising that he was opening a wound himself. In everything he said there was the implication that the love he'd felt for Bridget, though in no way false, hadn't been touched by the same kind of excitement.

The newsagent's shop was in another neighbourhood, miles across London, but in the days of old Mr Vanish, Bridget would just occasionally take Betty on a number 9 bus. When the woman and her mother took over the business some kind of shyness prevented the continuation of this habit, and after that some kind of fear. She had been ready to forgive Liam, to live in the hope that his infatuation would be washed away by time. She pleaded, but did not make scenes. She didn't scream at him or parade his treachery, or call the woman names. None of that came easily to Bridget, and all she could wonder was what life would be like if Liam stayed with her and went on loving the woman. It wasn't hard to imagine the bitterness that would develop in him, the hatred there would be in the end, yet she had continued to plead. Six weeks later he was gone.

For a moment in the darkness she wept. It was true what she'd said to her visitors that afternoon: that she felt nothing now. It was true, yet sometimes she wept when she remembered how together they had weathered the strangeness of their emigration or when she thought of Liam now, living in mortal sin with the woman and her mother above the newsagent's, not going to Confession or Mass any more. Every month money arrived from him, which with Miss Custle's rent and what she earned herself from cleaning the Winnards' flat three times a week was enough to manage on. But Liam never came back, to see her or to see Betty, which implied the greatest change of all in him.

Memories were always difficult for her. Alone now, she too easily remembered the countryside she had grown up in, and the face of the Reverend Mother at the Presentation Convent, and Mrs Lynch's squat public house and grocery at a crossroads. Maureen Ryall had stolen her Phillips' atlas, putting ink blots over her name and substituting her own. Madge Foley had curled her hair for her. Liam had always been in the neighbouring farm, but until after they'd both left school she'd hardly noticed him. He'd asked her to go for a walk with him, and in a field that was yellow with buttercups he had taken her hand and kissed her, causing her to blush. He'd laughed at her, saying the pink in her cheeks was lovely. He was the first person she'd ever danced with, in a nameless roadside dance-hall, ten miles away.

It was then, while she was still a round-faced girl, that Bridget had first become aware of fate. It was what you had to accept, what you couldn't kick against: God's will, the Reverend Mother or Father Keogh would have said, but for Bridget it began with the kind of person you were. Out of that, the circumstances of your life emerged: Bridget's shyness and her tendency to blush, her prettiness and her modesty, were the fate which had been waiting for her before she was born, and often she felt that Liam had been waiting for her also, that they were fated to fall in love because they complemented each other so well, he so bouncy and amusing, she so fond of the shadows. In those days it would have been impossible to imagine that he would ever go off with a woman in a newsagent's.

They were married on a Saturday in June, in a year when the foxgloves were profuse. She wore a veil of Limerick lace, borrowed from her grandmother. She carried scarlet roses. Liam was handsome, dark as a Spaniard in the Church of the Holy Virgin, his blue eyes jokily darting about. She

had been glad when all of it was over, the reception in
Kelly's Hotel, the car bedecked with ribbons. They'd gone
away for three days, and soon after they'd returned they had
had to emigrate to England because the sawmills where
Liam had a job closed down. They'd been in London for
more than twenty years when the woman came into his life.

Eventually Bridget slept, and dreamed of the countryside
of her childhood. She sat on a cart beside her father, permitted to hold the reins of the horse while empty milk churns
were rattled back from the creamery at the crossroads. Liam
was suddenly there, trudging along in the dust, and her
father drew up the reins in order to give him a lift. Liam was
ten or eleven, a patch of sunburn on the back of his neck
where his hair had been cut very short. It wasn't really a
dream, because all of it had happened in the days when Liam
hadn't been important.

*

Norma's husband came on his own. 'I hope you've no
objection, Mrs Lacy,' he said, smiling in his wide-eyed way.
There was a wave in his fairish hair, she noticed, a couple of
curls hanging over his forehead. Everything about him was
agreeable.

'Well, really I don't know.' She faltered, immediately
feeling hot. 'I really think it's better if we don't go on about
it.'

'I won't keep you ten minutes, Mrs Lacy. I promise.'

She held the hall-door open and he walked into the hall.
He stepped over a Weetabix packet which Betty had thrown
down and strode away from. In the kitchen Betty was un-
packing the rest of the shopping, making a kind of singing
noise, which she often did.

'Sit down,' Bridget said in the living-room, as she would to any visitor.

'Thanks, Mrs Lacy,' he said politely.

'I won't be a minute.'

She had to see to Betty in the kitchen. There was flour among the shopping, and eggs, and other items in bags that might become perforated or would break when dropped from the kitchen table to the floor. Betty wasn't naughtier than any other child, but only a week ago, left on her own, she'd tried to make a cake.

'You go and get the Weetabix,' Bridget said, and Betty obediently marched into the hall to do so. Bridget hastily put the rest of the shopping out of reach. She took coloured pencils and a new colouring-book from a drawer and laid them out on the table. Betty didn't much care for filling already-drawn outlines with colour and generally just scrawled her name all over them: *Betty Lacy* in red, and again in blue and orange and green.

'Be a good big girl now,' Bridget said.

'Big,' Betty repeated.

In the sitting-room Norma's husband had picked up the *Cork Weekly Examiner.* As she entered, he replaced it on the pile of magazines near his armchair, saying that it appeared to be interesting.

'It's hard to know how to put this to you, Mrs Lacy.' He paused, his smile beginning to fade. Seriousness invaded his face as his eyes passed over the contents of the living-room, over the sacred pictures and the odds and ends that Bridget had been meaning to throw out. He said:

'Norma was in a bad way when I met up with her, Mrs Lacy. She'd been to the Samaritans; it was from them I heard about her. I'm employed by the council, actually. Social Services, counselling. That's my job, see.'

'Yes, I understand.'

'Norma was suffering from depression. Unhappiness, Mrs Lacy. She got in touch with the Samaritans and later she came round to us. I was able to help her. I won her confidence through the counselling I could give her. I love Norma now, Mrs Lacy.'

'Of course.'

'It doesn't often happen that way. A counsellor and a client.'

'No, I'm sure not.' She interrupted because she knew he was going to continue with that theme, to tell her more about a relationship that wasn't her business. She said that to herself. She said to herself that six years ago Norma had drifted into her life, leaving behind a child. She said to herself that the adoption of Betty had been at Norma's request. 'You're a lovely person, Mrs Lacy,' Norma had said at the time.

'I can't get to her at the moment,' Norma's husband explained. 'Ever since the other day she's hiding within herself. All the good that's been done, Mrs Lacy, all the care of our own relationship: it's going for nothing, you see.'

'I'm sorry.'

'She went to the Samaritans because she was suicidal. There was nothing left of the poor thing, Mrs Lacy. She was hardly a human person.'

'But Betty, you see – Betty has become my child.'

'I know, I know, Mrs Lacy.' He nodded earnestly, understandingly. 'The Samaritans gave Norma back her humanity, and then the council housed her. When she was making the recovery we fell in love. You understand, Mrs Lacy? Norma and I fell in love.'

'Yes, I do understand that.'

'We painted the flat out together. Saturdays we spent

buying bits of furniture, month by month, what we could afford. We made a home because a home was what Norma had never had. She never knew her parents: I don't know if you were aware of that? Norma comes of a deprived background, she had no education, not to speak of. When I first met her, I had to help her read a newspaper.' Suddenly he smiled. 'She's much better now, of course.'

Bridget felt a silence gathering, the kind there'd been several of the other afternoon. She broke it herself, speaking as calmly as she could, trying to hold her visitor's eye but not succeeding because he was glancing round the living-room again.

'I'm sorry for Norma,' she said. 'I was sorry for her at the time, that is why I took in Betty. Only my husband and I insisted that it had to be legal and through the proper channels. We were advised about that, in case there was trouble later.'

'Trouble? Who advised you, Mrs Lacy?' He blinked and frowned. His voice sounded almost dense.

'We went to a solicitor,' she said, remembering that solicitor, small and moustached, recommended by Father Gogarty. He'd been very helpful; he'd explained everything.

'Mrs Lacy, I don't want to sound rude but there are two angles we can examine this case from. There is Norma's and there is your own. You've seen the change in Norma; you must take my word for it that she could easily revert. Then consider yourself, Mrs Lacy, as another person might see you, a person like myself for instance, a case-worker if you like, an outsider.'

'I don't think of it as a case, with angles or anything else. I really don't want to go on like this. Please.'

'I know it's difficult, and I'm sorry. But when the baby has become an adolescent you could find it hard to cope, Mrs Lacy. I see a lot of that in my work, a woman on her own, no father figure in the home. I know you have a caring relationship with Betty, Mrs Lacy, but the fact can't be altered that you're alone in this house with her, day in day out. All I'm saying is that another case-worker might comment on that.'

'There's Miss Custle too.'

'I beg your pardon, Mrs Lacy?'

'There's a lodger, Miss Custle.'

'You have a lodger? Another woman on her own?'

'Yes.'

'Young, is she?'

'No, Miss Custle isn't young.'

'An elderly woman, Mrs Lacy?'

'Miss Custle still works on the Underground.'

'The Underground?'

'Yes.'

'You see, Mrs Lacy, what might be commented upon is the lack of playmates. Just yourself, and a woman who is employed on the Underground. Again, Mrs Lacy, I'm not saying there isn't caring. I'm not saying that for an instant.'

'Betty is happy. Look, I'm afraid I'd rather you didn't come here again. I have things to do now –'

'I'm sorry to offend you, Mrs Lacy.'

She had stood up, making him stand up also. He nodded and smiled at her in his patient manner, which she now realised was professional, he being a counsellor. He said again he was sorry he'd offended her.

'I just thought you'd want to hear about Norma,' he said before he left, and on the doorstep he suddenly became awkward. The smile and the niceness vanished: solemnity replaced them. 'It's like putting a person together again. If you know what I mean, Mrs Lacy.'

*

In the kitchen Betty printed her name across the stomach of a whale. She heard voices in the hall, but paid them no attention. A moment later the door banged and then her mother came into the kitchen.

'Look,' Betty said, but to her surprise her mother didn't. Her mother hugged her, whispering her name. 'You've been washing your face,' Betty said. 'It's all cold.'

★

That afternoon Bridget cleaned the Winnards' flat, taking Betty with her, as she always did. She wondered about mentioning the trouble she was having with Norma and her husband to Mrs Winnard, who might suggest something for her to say so that the matter could be ended. Mrs Winnard was pretty and bespectacled, a kind young woman, full of sympathy, but that afternoon her two obstreperous boys, twins of two and a half, were giving her quite a time so Bridget didn't say anything. She hoovered the hallway and the bathroom and the four bedrooms, looking into the kitchen from time to time, where Betty was playing with the Winnard boys' bricks. She still hadn't said anything when the time came to pack up to go, and suddenly she was glad she hadn't because quite out of the blue she found herself imagining a look on Mrs Winnard's sympathetic face which suggested that the argument of Norma and her husband could not in all humanity be just dismissed. Bridget couldn't imagine Mrs Winnard actually saying so, but her intuition about the reaction remained.

In the park, watching Betty on a slide, she worried about that. Would the same thing happen if she talked to Father Gogarty? Would an instant of hesitation be reflected in his bony grey features as he, too, considered that Norma should not be passed by? Not everyone had experienced as awful a life as Norma had. On top of that, the regret of giving away the only child you had been able to have was probably a million times worse than simply being childless.

Not really wishing to, Bridget remembered how fate had seemed to her when she was a girl: that it began with the kind of person you were. 'We're greedy,' Liam had confessed, speaking of himself and the woman. 'I suppose we're made like that, we can't help it.' The woman was greedy, he had meant, making it cosier by saying he was too.

She watched Betty on the slide. She waved at her and Betty waved back. You couldn't call Norma greedy, not in the same way. Norma made a mess of things and then looked around for other people: someone to look after a child that had been carelessly born, the Samaritans, the man she'd married. In the end Norma was lucky because she'd survived, because all the good in her had been allowed to surface. It was the man's love that had done that, his gentleness and his sincerity. You couldn't begrudge her anything. Like Liam and the woman, fate had come up trumps for her because of the person she was.

'Watch, Mummy,' Betty shouted from the top of the slide, and again Betty watched her sliding down it.

*

Eventually Bridget did speak to Mrs Winnard and to Father Gogarty because it was hard to keep the upset to herself, and because it worried her even more when she kept telling herself that she was being imaginative about what their reaction would be. Mrs Winnard said the couple's presumption was almost a matter for the police; Father Gogarty offered to go and see them, if they could easily be found. But before either Mrs Winnard or the priest spoke Bridget was certain that the brief flicker she'd been dreading had come into their faces. There had been the hesitation and the doubt and – far quicker than thought – the feeling that a child belonged more suitably with a young married couple than with a lone middle-aged woman and an ageing employee of the London Underground. In continuing to talk about it to Miss Custle herself, Bridget could swear she experienced the same intuition: beneath all Miss Custle's outrage and fury there was the same reasonable doubt.

*

The telephone rang one evening and the young man's voice said:

'Norma hasn't done anything silly. I just thought you'd like to know that, Mrs Lacy.'

'Yes, of course. I'm glad she's all right.'

'Well, she's not really all right of course. But she does take heart from your caring in the past.'

'I did what a lot of people would have done.'

'You did what was necessary, Mrs Lacy. You understood a cry for help. It's an unpleasant fact, but neither she nor Betty might be alive today if it hadn't been for you.'

'Oh, I can't believe that for an instant.'

'I think you have to, you know. There's only one small point, Mrs Lacy, if you could bear with me. I spoke to a colleague about this case – well, having a personal interest, I thought I better. You may remember I mentioned an outsider? Well, strangely enough my colleague raised an interesting question.'

'Look, I don't want to go on talking about any of this. I've told you I couldn't even begin to contemplate what you're suggesting.'

'My colleague pointed out that it isn't just Norma's circumstances which have changed, nor indeed your own.
There's a third factor in all this, my colleague pointed out:
this child is being brought up as the child of Irish parents.
Well, fair enough you may say, Mrs Lacy, until you remember that the Irish are a different kettle of fish today from
what they were ten years ago. How easy is it, you have to ask
yourself, to be a child of Irish parents today, to bear an Irish
name, to be a member of the Roman Catholic Church? That
child will have to attend a London school, for instance,
where there could easily be hostility. Increasingly we come
across this in our work, Mrs Lacy.'

'Betty is my child –'

'Of course. That's quite understood, Mrs Lacy. But what
my colleague pointed out is that sooner or later Norma is
going to worry about the Irish thing as well. What will go
through her mind is that it's not just a question of her baby
being affected by a broken marriage, but of her baby being
brought up in an atmosphere that isn't always pleasant. I'm
sorry to mention it, Mrs Lacy, but, as my colleague says, no
mother on earth would care to lie awake at night and worry
about that.'

Her hand felt hot and damp on the telephone receiver. She
imagined the young man sitting in an office, concerned and
serious, and then smiling as he tried to find a bright side.
She imagined Norma in their newly decorated flat, needing
her child because everything was different now, hoping.

'I can't go on talking to you. I'm sorry.'

She replaced the receiver, and immediately found herself
thinking about Liam. It was Liam's fault as well as hers that
Betty had been adopted and was now to be regarded as the
child of Irish parents. Liam had always firmly regarded
himself as Betty's father, even if he never came near her now.

She didn't want to go and see him. She didn't want to make the journey on a number 9 bus, she didn't want to have to see the woman's predatory lips. But even as she thought that, she could hear herself asking Mrs Grounds to have Betty for a couple of hours one afternoon. 'Hullo, Liam,' she said a few days later in the newsagent's.

She'd waited until there were no customers, and to her relief the woman wasn't there. The woman's old mother, very fat and dressed all in brown, was resting in an armchair in a little room behind the shop itself, a kind of storeroom it seemed to be, with stacks of magazines tied with string, just as they'd come off the van.

'Heavens above!' Liam said.

'Liam, could I have a word?'

The old woman appeared to be asleep. She hadn't moved when Bridget had spoken. She was wearing a hat, and seemed a bit eccentric, sleeping there among the bundles of magazines.

'Of course you could, dear. How are you, Bridget?'

'I'm fine, Liam. And yourself?'

'I'm fine too, dear.'

She told him quickly. Customers hurried in for the *Evening Standard* or *Dalton's Weekly*, children paused on their way home from school. Liam looked for rubbers and ink cartridges, Yorkie bars and tubes of fruit pastilles. Twice he said that the *New Musical Express* didn't come out till Thursday. 'Extraordinary, how some of them forget that,' he said.

He listened to her carefully, picking up the thread of what she told him after each interruption. Because once they'd known one another so well, she mentioned the intuition she felt where Father Gogarty and Mrs Winnard and Miss Custle were concerned. She watched the expressions changing on his face, and she could feel him nodding inwardly: she felt him thinking that she was the same as she'd always been, nervous where other people were concerned, too modest and unsure of herself.

'I'll never forget how pretty you looked,' he said suddenly, and for no reason that Bridget could see. 'Wasn't everything great long ago, Bridie?'

'It's Betty we have to think of, Liam. The old days are over and done with.'

'I often go back to them. I'll never forget them, dear.'

He was trying to be nice, but it seemed to Bridget that he was saying she still belonged to the time he spoke of, that she had not managed to come to terms with life as it had been since. You had to be tougher to come to terms with a world that was tough itself, you had to get over being embarrassed when you were pulled out of the background. All that hadn't mattered long ago; when Maureen Ryall had stolen her atlas she hadn't even complained. Being stolen from, she suddenly thought.

'I don't know what to say to them,' she said. 'The man keeps telephoning me.'

'Tell him to leave you alone, Bridget. Tell him he has no business bothering you.'

'I've tried saying that.'

'Tell him the thing was legally done and he hasn't a foot to stand on. Tell him he can be up for harassment.'

A child came into the shop and Liam had to look for drawing-pins. 'I'm afraid I have to shut up now,' he said when the child had gone, and as he spoke the old woman in the armchair stirred. She spoke his name. She said she'd fancy peaches for tea. 'There's a tin set aside for you, dear,' Liam said, winking at Bridget. He had raised his voice to address the old woman. He lowered it again to say goodbye.

'The best of luck with it,' he said, and Bridget knew he meant it.

'Thanks, Liam.' She tried to smile, and realised that she hadn't repeated the young man's remarks about Betty being brought up in a hostile atmosphere. She almost did so, standing at the door of the shop, imagining Liam angrily saying that the man needed putting in his place and offering to meet him. But as she walked away she knew all that was make-belief. Liam had his own life to live, peaches and a sort of mother-in-law. He couldn't be blamed for only wishing her luck.

She collected Betty from Mrs Grounds and later in the evening, when she was watching television, the telephone rang. The young man said:

'I'm sorry, Mrs Lacy, I didn't mean to bring up that thing about your nationality. It's not your fault, Mrs Lacy, and please forget I mentioned it. I'm sorry.'

'Please don't telephone me again. That's all I ask. I've given you the only answer I can.'

'I know you have, Mrs Lacy. You've been kind to listen to me, and I know you're concerned for Norma, don't think I'm not aware of that. I love Norma, Mrs Lacy, which has made me a little unprofessional in my conversations with you, but I promise we'll neither of us bother you again. It was just that she felt she'd made a terrible mistake and all the poor thing wanted was to rectify it. But as my work so often shows me, Mrs Lacy, that is hardly ever possible. Are you there, Mrs Lacy?'

'Yes, I'm here.'

'I'll never stop loving Norma, Mrs Lacy. I promise you that also. No matter what happens to her now.'

She sat alone in her living-room watching the ten o'clock news, and when she heard Miss Custle in the hall she didn't offer her a cup of tea. Instead of Betty's rattling feet on the stairs there would be Miss Custle's aged panting as she propelled her bulk to her upstairs room. Instead of Betty's wondering questions there would be Miss Custle's gloom as still she mourned her long departed lover.

The television news came to an end, an advertisement for Australian margarine began. Soon after that the programmes ceased altogether, but Bridget continued to sit in her living-room, weeping without making a noise. Several times she went upstairs and stood with the light on by Betty's bed, gazing at the child, not wiping away her tears. For Betty's well-being, and for Norma's too, in all humanity the law would be reversed. No longer would she search the faces of Father Gogarty and Mrs Winnard and Miss Custle for the signs of what they really believed. They would put that into words by saying she was good and had courage.

In the countryside of long ago her failure in marriage and motherhood might be easier to bear, but she would be a stranger there now. She belonged among her accumulated odds and ends, as Betty belonged with her mother, and Liam with the woman he loved. She would look after Miss Custle when Miss Custle retired from the Underground, as fate dictated.

Mr Tennyson

He had, romantically, a bad reputation. He had a wife and several children. His carry-on with Sarah Spence was a legend among a generation of girls, and the story was that none of it had stopped with Sarah Spence. His old red Ford Escort had been reported drawn up in quiet lay-bys; often he spent weekends away from home; Annie Green had come across him going somewhere on a train once, alone and morose in the buffet car. Nobody's parents were aware of the facts about him, nor were the other staff, nor even the boys at the school. His carry-on with Sarah Spence, and coming across him going somewhere on a train once, alone and suddenly was yours when you became fifteen and a senior, a member of 2A. For the rest of your time at Foxfield Comprehensive – for the rest of your life, preferably – you didn't breathe a word to people whose business it wasn't.

It was understandable when you looked at him that parents and staff didn't guess. It was also understandable that his activities were protected by the senior girls. He was forty years old. He had dark hair with a little grey in it, and a face that was boyish – like a French boy's, someone had once said, and the description had stuck, often to be repeated. There was a kind of ragamuffin innocence about his eyes. The cast of his lips suggested a melancholy nature and his smile, when it came, had sadness in it too. His name was Mr Tennyson. His subject was English.

Jenny, arriving one September in 2A, learnt all about him. She remembered Sarah Spence, a girl at the top of the school when she had been at the bottom, tall and beautiful. He carried on because he was unhappily married, she was informed. Consider where he lived even: trapped in a tiny gate-lodge on the Ilminster road because he couldn't afford anything better, trapped with a wife and children when he deserved freedom. Would he one day publish poetry as profound as his famous namesake's, though of course more up-to-date? Or was his talent lost for ever? One way or the other he was made for love.

It seemed to Jenny that the girls of 2A eyed one another, wondering which among them would become a successor to Sarah Spence. They eyed the older girls, of Class 1, 1A and 1B, wondering which of them was already her successor, discreetly taking her place in the red Ford Escort on dusky afternoons. He would never be coarse, you couldn't imagine coarseness in him. He'd never try anything unpleasant, he'd never in a million years fumble at you. He'd just be there, being himself, smelling faintly of fresh tobacco, the fingers of a hand perhaps brushing your arm by accident.

'Within the play,' he suggested in his soft voice, almost a whisper, 'order is represented by the royal house of Scotland. We must try and remember Shakespeare's point of view, how Shakespeare saw these things.'

They were studying *Macbeth* and *Huckleberry Finn* with him, but when he talked about Shakespeare it seemed more natural and suited to him than when he talked about Mark Twain.

'On Duncan's death,' he said, 'should the natural order continue, his son Malcolm would become king. Already Duncan has indicated – by making Malcolm Prince of Cumberland – that he considers him capable of ruling.'

Jenny had pale fair hair, the colour of ripened wheat. It fell from a divide at the centre of her head, two straight lines on either side of a thin face. Her eyes were large and of a faded blue. She was lanky, with legs which she considered to be too long but which her mother said she'd be thankful for one day.

'Disruption is everywhere, remember,' he said. 'Disruption in nature as well as in the royal house. Shakespeare insinuates a comparison between what is happening in human terms and in terms of nature. On the night of Duncan's death there is a sudden storm in which chimneys are blown off and houses shaken. Mysterious screams are heard. Horses go wild. A falcon is killed by a mousing owl.'

Listening to him, it seemed to Jenny that she could listen for ever, no matter what he said. At night, lying in bed with her eyes closed, she delighted in leisurely fantasies, of having breakfast with him and ironing his clothes, of walking beside him on a seashore or sitting beside him in his old Ford Escort. There was a particular story she repeated to herself: that she was on the promenade at Lyme Regis and that he came up to her and asked her if she'd like to go for a walk. They walked up to the cliffs and then along the cliff-path, and everything was different from Foxfield Comprehensive because they were alone together. His wife and he had been divorced, he told her, having agreed between themselves that they were incompatible. He was leaving Foxfield Comprehensive' because a play he'd written was going to be done on the radio and another one on the London stage. 'Oh, darling,' she said, daring to say it. 'Oh, Jenny,' he said.

Terms and holidays went by. Once, just before the Easter of that year, she met him with his wife, shopping in the International Stores in Ilminster. They had two of their four children with them, little boys with freckles. His wife had freckles also. She was a woman like a sack of something,

Jenny considered, with thick, unhealthy-looking legs. He was pushing a trolley full of breakfast cereals and wrapped bread, and tins. Although he didn't speak to her or even appear to see her, it was a stroke of luck to come across him in the town because he didn't often come into the village. Foxfield had only half a dozen shops and the Bow and Arrow public house even though it was enormous, a sprawling dormitory village that had had the new Comprehensive added to all the other new building in 1969. Because of the position of the Tennysons' gate-lodge it was clearly more convenient for them to shop in Ilminster.

'Hullo, Mr Tennyson,' she said in the International Stores, and he turned and looked at her. He nodded and smiled.

*

Jenny moved into 1A at the end of that school year. She wondered if he'd noticed how her breasts had become bigger during the time she'd been in 2A, and how her complexion had definitely improved. Her breasts were quite presentable now, which was a relief because she'd had a fear that they weren't going to develop at all. She wondered if he'd noticed her Green Magic eye-shadow. Everyone said it suited her, except her father, who always blew up over things like that. Once she heard one of the new kids saying she was the prettiest girl in the school. Adam Swann and Chinny Martin from 1B kept hanging about, trying to chat her up. Chinny Martin even wrote her notes.

'You're mooning,' her father said. 'You don't take a pick of notice these days.'

'Exams,' her mother hastily interjected and afterwards, when Jenny was out of the room, quite sharply reminded her husband that adolescence was a difficult time for girls. It was best not to remark on things.

'I didn't mean a criticism, Ellie,' Jenny's father protested, aggrieved.

'They take it as a criticism. Every word. They're edgy, see.'

He sighed. He was a painter and decorator, with his own business. Jenny was their only child. There'd been four miscarriages, all of which might have been boys, which naturally were what he'd wanted, with the business. He'd have to sell it one day, but it didn't matter all that much when you thought about it. Having miscarriages was worse than selling a business, more depressing really. A woman's lot was harder than a man's, he'd decided long ago.

'Broody,' his wife diagnosed. 'Just normal broody. She'll see her way through it.'

Every evening her parents sat in their clean, neat sitting-room watching television. Her mother made tea at nine o'clock because it was nice to have a cup with the News. She always called upstairs to Jenny, but Jenny never wanted to have tea or see the News. She did her homework in her bedroom, a small room that was clean and neat also, with a pebbly cream wallpaper expertly hung by her father. At half-past ten she usually went down to the kitchen and made herself some Ovaltine. She drank it at the table with the cat, Tinkle, on her lap. Her mother usually came in with the tea things to wash up, and they might chat, the conversation consisting mainly of gossip from Foxfield Comprehensive, although never of course containing a reference to Mr Tennyson. Sometimes Jenny didn't feel like chatting and wouldn't, feigning sleepiness. If she sat there long enough her father would come in to fetch himself a cup of water because he always liked to have one near him in the night.

He couldn't help glancing at her eye-shadow when he said good-night and she could see him making an effort not to mention it, having doubtless been told not to by her mother. They did their best. She liked them very much. She loved them, she supposed.

But not in the way she loved Mr Tennyson. 'Robert Tennyson,' she murmured to herself in bed. 'Oh, Robert dear.' Softly his lips were there, and the smell of fresh tobacco made her swoon, forcing her to close her eyes. 'Oh, yes,' she said. 'Oh, yes, yes.' He lifted the dress over her head. His hands were taut, charged with their shared passion. 'My love,' he said in his soft voice, almost a whisper. Every night before she went to sleep his was the face that entirely filled her mind. Had it once not been there she would have thought herself faithless. And every morning, in a ceremonial way, she conjured it up again, first thing, pride of place.

*

Coming out of Harper's the newsagent's one Saturday afternoon, she found waiting for her, not Mr Tennyson, but Chinny Martin, with his motor-cycle on its pedestal in the street. He asked her if she'd like to go for a spin into the country and offered to supply her with a crash helmet. He was wearing a crash helmet himself, a bulbous red object with a peak and a windshield that fitted over his eyes. He was also wearing heavy plastic gloves, red also, and a red windcheater. He was smiling at her, the spots on his pronounced chin more noticeable after exposure to the weather on his motor-cycle. His eyes were serious, closely fixed on hers.

She shook her head at him. There was hardly anything she'd have disliked more than a ride into the country with

Chinny Martin, her arms half round his waist, a borrowed crash helmet making her feel silly. He'd stop the motor-cycle in a suitable place and he'd suggest something like a walk to the river or to some old ruin or into a wood. He'd suggest sitting down and then he'd begin to fumble at her, and his chin would be sticking into her face, cold and unpleasant. His fingernails would be ingrained, as the fingernails of boys who owned motor-cycles always were.

'Thanks all the same,' she said.

'Come on, Jenny.'

'No, I'm busy. Honestly. I'm working at home.'

It couldn't have been pleasant, being called Chinny just because you had a jutting chin. Nicknames were horrible: there was a boy called Nut Adams and another called Wet Small and a girl called Kisses. Chinny Martin's name was Clive, but she'd never heard anyone calling him that. She felt sorry for him, standing there in his crash helmet and his special clothes. He'd probably planned it all, working it out that she'd be impressed by his gear and his motor-cycle. But of course she wasn't. *Yamaha* it said on the petrol tank of the motor-cycle, and there was a girl in a swimsuit which he had presumably stuck on to the tank himself. The girl's swimsuit was yellow and so was her hair, which was streaming out behind her, as if caught in a wind. The petrol tank was black.

'Jenny,' he said, lowering his voice so that it became almost croaky. 'Listen, Jenny –'

'Sorry.'

She began to walk away, up the village street, but he walked beside her, pushing the Yamaha.

'I love you, Jenny,' he said.

She laughed because she felt embarrassed.

'I can't bear not seeing you, Jenny.'

'Oh, well –'

'Jenny.'

They were passing the petrol-pumps, the Orchard Garage. Mr Batten was on the pavement, wiping oil from his hands with a rag. 'How's he running?' he called out to Chinny Martin, referring to the Yamaha, but Chinny Martin ignored the question.

'I think of you all the time, Jenny.'

'Oh, Clive, don't be silly.' She felt silly herself, calling him by his proper name.

'D'you like me, Jenny?'

'Of course I like you.' She smiled at him, trying to cover up the lie: she didn't particularly like him, she didn't particularly not. She just felt sorry for him, with his noticeable chin and the nickname it had given him. His father worked in the powdered milk factory. He'd do the same: you could guess that all too easily.

'Come for a ride with me, Jenny.'

'No, honestly.'

'Why not then?'

'It's better not to start anything, Clive. Look, don't write me notes.'

'Don't you like my notes?'

'I don't want to start anything.'

'There's someone else is there, Jenny? Adam Swann? Rick Hayes?'

He sounded like a character in a television serial; he sounded sloppy and stupid.

'If you knew how I feel about you,' he said, lowering his voice even more. 'I love you like anything. It's the real thing.'

'I like you too, Clive. Only not in that way,' she hastily added.

'Wouldn't you ever? Wouldn't you even try?'

'I've told you.'

'Rick Hayes's only after sex.'

'I don't like Rick Hayes.'

'Any girl with legs on her is all he wants.'

'Yes, I know.'

'I can't concentrate on things, Jenny. I think of you the entire time.'

'I'm sorry.'

'Oh God, Jenny.'

She turned into the Mace shop just to escape. She picked up a wire basket and pretended to be looking at tins of cat food. She heard the roar of the Yamaha as her admirer rode away, and it seemed all wrong that he should have gone like that, so noisily when he was so upset.

At home she thought about the incident. It didn't in the least displease her that a boy had passionately proclaimed love for her. It even made her feel quite elated. She felt pleasantly warm when she thought about it, and the feeling bewildered her. That she, so much in love with someone else, should be moved in the very least by the immature protestations of a youth from IB was a mystery. She even considered telling her mother about the incident, but in the end decided not to. 'Quite sprightly, she seems,' she heard her father murmuring.

'In every line of that sonnet,' Mr Tennyson said the following Monday afternoon, 'there is evidence of the richness that makes Shakespeare not just our own greatest writer but the world's as well.'

She listened, enthralled, physically pleasured by the utterance of each syllable. There was a tiredness about his boyish eyes, as if he hadn't slept. His wife had probably been bothering him, wanting him to do jobs around the house when he should have been writing sonnets of his own. She imagined him unable to sleep, lying there worrying about things, about his life. She imagined his wife like a grampus beside him, her mouth open, her upper lip as coarse as a man's.

'When forty winters shall besiege thy brow,' he said, 'And dig deep trenches in thy beauty's field.'

Dear Jenny, a note that morning from Chinny Martin had protested. *I just want to be with you. I just want to talk to you. Please come out with me.*

'Jenny, stay a minute,' Mr Tennyson said when the bell went. 'Your essay.'

Immediately there was tension among the girls of 1A, as if the English master had caused threads all over the classroom to become taut. Unaware, the boys proceeded as they always did, throwing books into their briefcases and sauntering into the corridor. The girls lingered over anything they could think of. Jenny approached Mr Tennyson's desk.

'It's very good,' he said, opening her essay book. 'But you're getting too fond of using three little dots at the end of a sentence. The sentence should imply the dots. It's like underlining to suggest emphasis, a bad habit also.'

One by one the girls dribbled from the classroom, leaving behind them the shreds of their reluctance. Out of all of them he had chosen her: was she to be another Sarah Spence, or just some kind of stop-gap, like other girls since Sarah Spence were rumoured to have been? But as he continued to talk about her essay – called *Belief in Ghosts* – she wondered if she'd even be a stop-gap. His fingers didn't once brush the back of her hand. His French boy's eyes didn't linger once on hers.

'I've kept you late,' he said in the end.

'That's all right, sir.'

'You will try to keep your sentences short? Your descriptions have a way of becoming too complicated.'

'I'll try, sir.'

'I really enjoyed that essay.'

He handed her the exercise book and then, without any doubt whatsoever, he smiled meaningfully into her eyes. She felt herself going hot. Her hands became clammy. She just stood there while his glance passed over her eyeshadow, over her nose and cheeks, over her mouth.

'You're very pretty,' he said.

'Thank you, sir.'

Her voice reminded her of the croak in Chinny Martin's when he'd been telling her he loved her. She tried to smile, but could not. She wanted his hand to reach out and push her gently away from him so that he could see her properly. But it didn't. He stared into her eyes again, as if endeavouring to ascertain their precise shade of blue.

'You look like a girl we had here once,' he said. 'Called Sarah Spence.'

'I remember Sarah Spence.'

'She was good at English too.'

She wanted something to happen, thunder to begin, or a torrent of rain, anything that would keep them in the classroom. She couldn't even bear the thought of walking to her desk and putting her essay book in her briefcase.

'Sarah went to Warwick University,' he said.

She nodded. She tried to smile again and this time the smile came. She said to herself that it was a brazen smile and she didn't care. She hoped it made her seem more than ever like Sarah Spence, sophisticated and able for anything. She wondered if he said to all the girls who were stop-gaps that they looked like Sarah Spence. She didn't care. His carry-on with Sarah Spence was over and done with, he didn't even see her any more. By all accounts Sarah Spence had let him down, but never in a million years would she. She would wait for him for ever, or until the divorce came through. When he was old she would look after him.

'You'd better be getting home, Jenny.'

'I don't want to, sir.'

She continued to stand there, the exercise book in her left hand. She watched while some kind of shadow passed over his face. For a moment his eyes closed.

'Why don't you want to go?' he said.

'Because I'm in love with you, sir.'

'You mustn't be, Jenny.'

'Why not?'

'You know why not.'

'What about Sarah Spence?'

'Sarah was different.'

'I don't care how many stop-gaps you've had. I don't care. I don't love you any less.'

'Stop-gaps, Jenny?'

'The ones you made do with.'

'Made do?' He was suddenly frowning at her, his face screwed up a little. 'Made do?' he said again.

'The other girls. The ones who reminded you of her.'

'There weren't any other girls.'

'You were seen, sir —'

'Only Sarah and I were seen.'

'Your car —'

'Give a dog a bad name, Jenny. There weren't any others.'

She felt iciness inside her, somewhere in her stomach. Other girls had formed an attachment for him, as she had. Other girls had probably stood on this very spot, telling him. It was that, and the reality of Sarah Spence, that had turned him into a schoolgirls' legend. Only Sarah Spence had gone with him in his old Ford Escort to quiet lay-bys, only Sarah Spence had felt his arms around her. Why shouldn't he be seen in the buffet-car of a train, alone? The weekends he'd spent away from home were probably with a sick mother.

'I'm no Casanova, Jenny.'

'I had to tell you I'm in love with you, sir. I couldn't not.'

'It's no good loving me, I'm afraid.'

'You're the nicest person I'll ever know.'

'No, I'm not, Jenny. I'm just an English teacher who took advantage of a young girl's infatuation. Shabby, people would say.'

'You're not shabby. Oh God, you're not shabby.' She heard her own voice crying out shrilly, close to tears. It astonished her. It was unbelievable that she should be so violently protesting. It was unbelievable that he should have called himself shabby.

'She had an abortion in Warwick,' he said, 'after a weekend we spent in an hotel. I let that happen, Jenny.'

'You couldn't help it.'

'Of course I could have helped it.'

Without wanting to, she imagined them in the hotel he spoke of. She imagined them having a meal, sitting opposite each other at a table, and a waiter placing plates in front of them. She imagined them in their bedroom, a grimy room with a lace curtain drawn across the lower part of the single window and a washbasin in a corner. The bedroom had featured in a film she'd seen, and Sarah Spence was even like the actress who had played the part of a shopgirl. She stood there in her underclothes just as the shopgirl had, awkwardly waiting while he smiled his love at her. 'Then let not winter's ragged hand deface,' he whispered, 'In thee thy summer, ere thou be distilled. Oh Sarah, love.' He took the underclothes from her body, as the actor in the film had, all the time whispering sonnets.

'It was messy and horrible,' he said. 'That's how it ended, Jenny.'

'I don't care how it ended. I'd go with you anywhere. I'd go to a thousand hotels.'

'No, no, Jenny.'

'I love you terribly.'

She wept, still standing there. He got down from the stool in front of his desk and came and put his arms about her, telling her to cry. He said that tears were good, not bad. He made her sit down at a desk and then he sat down beside her. His love affair with Sarah Spence sounded romantic, he said, and because of its romantic sheen girls fell in love with him. They fell in love with the unhappiness they sensed in him. He found it hard to stop them.

'I should move away from here,' he said, 'but I can't bring myself to do it. Because she'll always come back to see her family and whenever she does I can catch a glimpse of her.'

It was the same as she felt about him, like the glimpse that day in the International Stores. It was the same as Chinny Martin hanging about outside Harper's. And yet of course it wasn't the same as Chinny Martin. How could it possibly be? Chinny Martin was stupid and unprepossessing and ordinary.

'I'd be better to you,' she cried out in sudden desperation, unable to prevent herself. Clumsily she put a hand on his shoulder, and clumsily took it away again. 'I would wait for ever,' she said, sobbing, knowing she looked ugly.

He waited for her to calm down. He stood up and after a moment so did she. She walked with him from the classroom, down the corridor and out of the door that led to the car park.

'You can't just leave,' he said, 'a wife and four children. It was hard to explain that to Sarah. She hates me now.'

He unlocked the driver's door of the Ford Escort. He smiled at her. He said:

'There's no one else I can talk to about her. Except girls like you. You mustn't feel embarrassed in class, Jenny.'

He drove away, not offering her a lift, which he might have done, for their direction was the same. She didn't in the least look like Sarah Spence: he'd probably said the same thing to all the others, the infatuated girls he could talk to about the girl he loved. The little scenes in the classroom, the tears, the talk: all that brought him closer to Sarah Spence. The love of a girl he didn't care about warmed him, as Chinny Martin's love had warmed her too, even though Chinny Martin was ridiculous.

She walked across the car park, imagining him driving back to his gate-lodge with Sarah Spence alive again in his mind, loving her more than ever. 'Jenny,' the voice of Chinny Martin called out, coming from nowhere.

He was there, standing by his Yamaha, beside a car. She shook her head at him, and began to run. At home she would sit and eat in the kitchen with her parents, who wouldn't be any different. She would escape and lie on her bed in her small neat bedroom, longing to be where she'd never be now, beside him in his car, or on a train, or anywhere. 'Jenny,' the voice of Chinny Martin called out again, silly with his silly love.

Autumn Sunshine

The rectory was in County Wexford, eight miles from Enniscorthy. It was a handsome eighteenth-century house, with Virginia creeper covering three sides and a tangled garden full of buddleia and struggling japonica which had always been too much for its incumbents. It stood alone, seeming lonely even, approximately at the centre of the country parish it served. Its church – St Michael's Church of Ireland – was two miles away, in the village of Boharbawn.

For twenty-six years the Morans had lived there, not wishing to live anywhere else. Canon Moran had never been an ambitious man; his wife, Frances, had found contentment easy to attain in her lifetime. Their four girls had been born in the rectory, and had become a happy family there. They were grown up now, Frances's death was still recent: like the rectory itself, its remaining occupant was alone in the countryside. The death had occurred in the spring of the year, and the summer had somehow been bearable. The clergyman's eldest daughter had spent May and part of June at the rectory with her children. Another one had brought her family for most of August, and a third was to bring her newly married husband in the winter. At Christmas nearly all of them would gather at the rectory and some would come at Easter. But that September, as the days drew in, the season was melancholy.

Then, one Tuesday morning, Slattery brought a letter from Canon Moran's youngest daughter. There were two other letters as well, in unsealed buff envelopes which meant that they were either bills or receipts. Frail and grey-haired in his elderliness, Canon Moran had been wondering if he should give the lawn in front of the house a last cut when he heard the approach of Slattery's van. The lawn-mower was the kind that had to be pushed, and in the spring the job was always easier if the grass had been cropped close at the end of the previous summer.

'Isn't that a great bit of weather, Canon?' Slattery remarked, winding down the window of the van and passing out the three envelopes. 'We're set for a while, would you say?'

'I hope so, certainly.'

'Ah, we surely are, sir.'

The conversation continued for a few moments longer, as it did whenever Slattery came to the rectory. The postman was young and easy-going, not long the successor to old Mr O'Brien, who'd been making the round on a bicycle when the Morans first came to the rectory in 1952. Mr O'Brien used to talk about his garden; Slattery talked about fishing, and often brought a share of his catch to the rectory.

'It's a great time of year for it,' he said now, 'except for the darkness coming in.'

Canon Moran smiled and nodded; the van turned round on the gravel, dust rising behind it as it moved swiftly down the avenue to the road. Everyone said Slattery drove too fast.

He carried the letters to a wooden seat on the edge of the lawn he'd been wondering about cutting. Deirdre's handwriting hadn't changed since she'd been a child; it was round and neat, not at all a reflection of the girl she was. The blue English stamp, the Queen in profile blotched a bit by the London postmark, wasn't on its side or half upside down, as you might possibly expect with Deirdre. Of all the Moran children, she'd grown up to be the only difficult one.

She hadn't come to the funeral and hadn't written about her mother's death. She hadn't been to the rectory for three years.

'*I'm sorry,*' she wrote now. '*I couldn't stop crying actually. I've never known anyone as nice or as generous as she was. For ages I didn't even want to believe she was dead. I went on imagining her in the rectory and doing the flowers in church and shopping in Enniscorthy.*'

Deirdre was twenty-one now. He and Frances had hoped she'd go to Trinity and settle down, but although at school she'd seemed to be the cleverest of their children she'd had no desire to become a student. She'd taken the Rosslare boat to Fishguard one night, having said she was going to spend a week with her friend Maeve Coles in Cork. They hadn't known she'd gone to England until they received a picture postcard from London telling them not to worry, saying she'd found work in an egg-packing factory.

'*Well, I'm coming back for a little while now,*' she wrote, '*if you could put up with me and if you wouldn't find it too much. I'll cross over to Rosslare on the twenty-ninth, the morning crossing, and then I'll come on to Enniscorthy on the bus. I don't know what time it will be but there's a pub just by where the bus drops you so could we meet in the small bar there at six o'clock and then I won't have to lug my cases too far? I hope you won't mind going into such a place. If you can't make it, or don't want to see me, it's understandable, so if you don't turn up by half six I'll see if I can get a bus on up to Dublin. Only I need to get back to Ireland for a while.*'

It was, as he and Slattery had agreed, a lovely autumn. Gentle sunshine mellowed the old garden, casting an extra sheen of gold on leaves that were gold already. Roses that had been ebullient in June and July bloomed modestly now. Michaelmas daises were just beginning to bud. Already the crab-apples were falling, hydrangeas had a forgotten look. Canon Moran carried the letter from his daughter into the walled vegetable-garden and leaned against the side of the greenhouse, half sitting on a protruding ledge, reading the letter again. Panes of glass were broken in the greenhouse, white paint and putty needed to be renewed, but inside a vine still thrived, and was heavy now with black ripe fruit. Later that morning he would pick some and drive into Enniscorthy, to sell the grapes to Mrs Roche in Slaney Street.

'Love, Deirdre: the letter was marvellous. Beyond the rectory the fields of wheat had been harvested, and the remaining stubble had the same tinge of gold in the autumn light; the beech-trees and the chestnuts were triumphantly magnificent. But decay and rotting were only weeks away, and the letter from Deirdre was full of life. *'Love, Deirdre'* were words more beautiful than all the season's glories. He prayed as he leaned against the sunny greenhouse, thanking God for this salvation.

*

For all the years of their marriage Frances had been a help. As a younger man, Canon Moran hadn't known quite what to do. He'd been at a loss among his parishioners, hesitating in the face of this weakness or that: the pregnancy of Alice Pratt in 1954, the argument about grazing rights between Mr Willoughby and Eugene Ryan in 1960, the theft of an altar cloth from St Michael's and reports that Mrs Tobin had been seen wearing it as a skirt. Alice Pratt had been going out with a Catholic boy, one of Father Haye's flock, which made the matter more difficult than ever. Eugene Ryan was one of Father Hayes's also, and so was Mrs Tobin.

'Father Hayes and I had a chat,' Frances had said, and she'd had a chat as well with Alice Pratt's mother. A month later Alice Pratt married the Catholic boy, but to this day attended St Michael's every Sunday, the children going to Father Hayes. Mrs Tobin was given Hail Marys to say by the priest; Mr Willoughby agreed that his father had years ago granted Eugene Ryan the grazing rights. Everything, in these cases and in many others, had come out all right in the end: order emerged from the confusion that Canon Moran so disliked, and it was Frances who had always begun the process, though no one ever said in the rectory that she understood the mystery of people as well as he understood the teachings of the New Testament. She'd been a freckle-faced girl when he'd married her, pretty in her way. He was the one with the brains.

Frances had seen human frailty everywhere: it was weakness in people, she said, that made them what they were as much as strength did. And she herself had her own share of such frailty, falling short in all sorts of ways of the God's image her husband preached about. With the small amount of housekeeping money she could be allowed she was a spendthrift, and she said she was lazy. She loved clothes and often overreached herself on visits to Dublin; she sat in the sun while the rectory gathered dust and the garden became rank; it was only where people were concerned that she was practical. But for what she was her husband had loved her with unobtrusive passion for fifty years, appreciating her conversation and the help she'd given him because she could so easily sense the truth. When he'd found her dead in the garden one morning he'd felt he had lost some part of himself.

Though many months had passed since then, the trouble was that Frances hadn't yet become a ghost. Her being alive was still too recent, the shock of her death too raw. He couldn't distance himself; the past refused to be the past. Often he thought that her fingerprints were still in the rectory, and when he picked the grapes or cut the grass of the lawn it was impossible not to pause and remember other years. Autumn had been her favourite time.

*

'Of course I'd come,' he said. 'Of course, dear. Of course.'

'I haven't treated you very well.'

'It's over and done with, Deirdre.'

She smiled, and it was nice to see her smile again, although it was strange to be sitting in the back bar of a public house in Enniscorthy. He saw her looking at him, her eyes passing over his clerical collar and black clothes, and his thin quiet face. He could feel her thinking that he had aged, and putting it down to the death of the wife he'd been so fond of.

'I'm sorry I didn't write,' she said.

'You explained in your letter, Deirdre.'

'It was ages before I knew about it. That was an old address you wrote to.'

'I guessed.'

In turn he examined her. Years ago she'd had her long hair cut. It was short now, like a neat black cap on her head. And her face had lost its chubbiness; hollows where her cheeks had been made her eyes more dominant, pools of seaweed green. He remembered her child's stocky body, and the uneasy adolescence that had spoilt the family's serenity. Her voice had lost its Irish intonation.

'I'd have met you off the boat, you know.'

'I didn't want to bother you with that.'

'Oh, now, it isn't far, Deirdre.'

She drank Irish whiskey, and smoked a brand of cigarettes called Three Castles. He'd asked for a mineral himself, and the woman serving them had brought him a bottle of something that looked like water but which fizzed up when she'd poured it. A kind of lemonade he imagined it was, and didn't much care for it.

'I have grapes for Mrs Roche,' he said.

'Who's that?'

'She has a shop in Slaney Street. We always sold her the grapes. You remember?'

She didn't, and he reminded her of the vine in the greenhouse. A shop surely wouldn't be open at this hour of the evening, she said, forgetting that in a country town of course it would be. She asked if the cinema was still the same in Enniscorthy, a cement building halfway up a hill. She said she remembered bicycling home from it at night with her sisters, not being able to keep up with them. She asked after her sisters and he told her about the two marriages that had taken place since she'd left: she had in-laws she'd never met, and nephews and a niece.

They left the bar, and he drove his dusty black Vauxhall straight to the small shop he'd spoken of. She remained in the car while he carried into the shop two large chip-baskets full of grapes. Afterwards Mrs Roche came to the door with him.

'Well, is that Deirdre?' she said as Deirdre wound down the window of the car. 'I'd never know you, Deirdre.'

'She's come back for a little while,' Canon Moran explained, raising his voice a little because he was walking round the car to the driver's seat as he spoke.

'Well, isn't that grand?' said Mrs Roche.

Everyone in Enniscorthy knew Deirdre had just gone off, but it didn't matter now. Mrs Roche's husband, who was a red-cheeked man with a cap, much smaller than his wife, appeared beside her in the shop doorway. He inclined his head in greeting, and Deirdre smiled and waved at both of them. Canon Moran thought it was pleasant when she went on waving while he drove off.

In the rectory he lay wakeful that night, his mind excited by Deirdre's presence. He would have loved Frances to know, and guessed that she probably did. He fell asleep at half past two and dreamed that he and Frances were young again, that Deirdre was still a baby. The freckles on Frances's face were out in profusion, for they were sitting in the sunshine in the garden, tea things spread about them, the children playing some game among the shrubs. It was autumn then also, the last of the September heat. But because he was younger in his dream he didn't feel part of the season himself, or sense its melancholy.

*

A week went by. The time passed slowly because a lot was happening, or so it seemed. Deirdre insisted on cooking all the meals and on doing the shopping in Boharbawn's single shop or in Enniscorthy. She still smoked her endless cigarettes, but the peakiness there had been in her face when she'd first arrived wasn't quite so pronounced – or perhaps, he thought, he'd become used to it. She told him about the different jobs she'd had in London and the different places she'd lived in, because on the postcards she'd occasionally sent there hadn't been room to go into detail. In the rectory they had always hoped she'd managed to get a training of some sort, though guessing she hadn't. In fact, her jobs had been of the most rudimentary kind: as well as her spell in the egg-packing factory, there'd been a factory that made plastic earphones, a cleaning job in a hotel near Euston, and a year working for the Use-Us Office Cleansing Service. 'But you can't have liked any of that work, Deirdre?' he suggested, and she agreed she hadn't.

From the way she spoke he felt that that period of her life was over: adolescence was done with, she had steadied and taken stock. He didn't suggest to her that any of this might be so, not wishing to seem either too anxious or too pleased, but he felt she had returned to the rectory in a very different frame of mind from the one in which she'd left it. He imagined she would remain for quite a while, still taking stock, and in a sense occupying her mother's place. He thought he recognised in her a loneliness that matched his own, and he wondered if it was a feeling that their loneliness might be shared which had brought her back at this particular time. Sitting in the drawing-room while she cooked or washed up, or gathering grapes in the greenhouse while she did the shopping, he warmed delightedly to this theme. It seemed like an act of God that their circumstances should interlace this autumn. By Christmas she would know what she wanted to do with her life, and in the spring that followed she would perhaps be ready to set forth again. A year would have passed since the death of Frances.

'I have a friend,' Deirdre said when they were having a cup of coffee together in the middle of one morning. 'Someone who's been good to me.'

She had carried a tray to where he was composing next week's sermon, sitting on the wooden seat by the lawn at the front of the house. He laid aside his exercise book, and a pencil and a rubber. 'Who's that?' he inquired.

'Someone called Harold.'

He nodded, stirring sugar into his coffee.

'I want to tell you about Harold, Father. I want you to meet him.'

'Yes, of course.'

She lit a cigarette. She said, 'We have a lot in common. I mean, he's the only person . . .'

She faltered and then hesitated. She lifted her cigarette to her lips and drew on it.

He said, 'Are you fond of him, Deirdre?'

'Yes, I am.'

Another silence gathered. She smoked and drank her coffee. He added more sugar to his.

'Of course I'd like to meet him,' he said.

'Could he come to stay with us, Father? Would you mind? Would it be all right?'

'Of course I wouldn't mind. I'd be delighted.'

★

Harold was summoned, and arrived at Rosslare a few days later. In the meantime Deirdre had explained to her father that her friend was an electrician by trade and had let it fall that he was an intellectual kind of person. She borrowed the old Vauxhall and drove it to Rosslare to meet him, returning to the rectory in the early evening.

'How d'you do?' Canon Moran said, stretching out a hand in the direction of an excessively thin youth with a birthmark on his face. His dark hair was cut very short, cropped almost. He was wearing a black leather jacket.

'I'm fine,' Harold said.

'You've had a good journey?'

'Lousy, 'smatter of fact, Mr Moran.'

Harold's voice was strongly Cockney, and Canon Moran wondered if Deirdre had perhaps picked up some of her English vowel sounds from it. But then he realised that most people in London would speak like that, as people did on the television and the wireless. It was just a little surprising that Harold and Deirdre should have so much in common, as they clearly had from the affectionate way they held one another's hand. None of the other Moran girls had gone in so much for holding hands in front of the family.

He was to sit in the drawing-room, they insisted, while they made supper in the kitchen, so he picked up the *Irish Times* and did as he was bidden. Half an hour later Harold appeared and said that the meal was ready: fried eggs and sausages and bacon, and some tinned beans. Canon Moran said grace.

Having stated that Co. Wexford looked great, Harold didn't say much else. He didn't smile much, either. His afflicted face bore an edgy look, as if he'd never become wholly reconciled to his birthmark. It was like a scarlet map on his left cheek, a shape that reminded Canon Moran of the toe of Italy. Poor fellow, he thought. And yet a birthmark was so much less to bear than other afflictions there could be.

'Harold's fascinated actually,' Deirdre said, 'by Ireland.'

Her friend didn't add anything to that remark for a moment, even though Canon Moran smiled and nodded interestedly. Eventually Harold said, 'The struggle of the Irish people.'

'I didn't know a thing about Irish history,' Deirdre said. 'I mean, not anything that made sense.'

The conversation lapsed at this point, leaving Canon Moran greatly puzzled. He began to say that Irish history had always been of considerable interest to him also, that it had a good story to it, its tragedy uncomplicated. But the other two didn't appear to understand what he was talking about and so he changed the subject. It was a particularly splendid autumn, he pointed out.

'Harold doesn't go in for anything like that,' Deirdre replied.

During the days that followed Harold began to talk more, surprising Canon Moran with almost everything he said. Deirdre had been right to say he was fascinated by Ireland, and it wasn't just a tourist's fascination. Harold had read widely: he spoke of ancient battles, and of the plantations of James I and Elizabeth, of Robert Emmet and the Mitchelstown martyrs, of Pearse and De Valera. 'The struggle of the Irish people' was the expression he most regularly employed. It seemed to Canon Moran that the relationship between Harold and Deirdre had a lot to do with Harold's fascination, as though his interest in Deirdre's native land had somehow caused him to become interested in Deirdre herself.

There was something else as well. Fascinated by Ireland, Harold hated his own country. A sneer whispered through his voice when he spoke of England: a degenerate place, he called it, destroyed by class-consciousness and the unjust distribution of wealth. He described in detail the city of Nottingham, to which he appeared to have a particular aversion. He spoke of unnecessary motorways and the stupidity of bureaucracy, the stifling presence of a Royal family. 'You could keep an Indian village,' he claimed, 'on what those corgis eat. You could house five hundred homeless in Buckingham Palace.' There was brainwashing by television and the newspaper barons. No ordinary person had a chance because pap was fed to the ordinary person, a deliberate policy going back into Victorian times when education and religion had been geared to the enslavement of minds. The English people had brought it on themselves, having lost their spunk, settling instead for consumer durables. 'What better can you expect,' Harold demanded, 'after the hypocrisy of that empire the bosses ran?'

Deirdre didn't appear to find anything specious in this line of talk, which surprised her father. 'Oh, I wonder about that,' he said himself from time to time, but he said it mildly, not wishing to cause an argument, and in any case his interjections were not acknowledged. Quite a few of the criticisms Harold levelled at his own country could be levelled at Ireland also and, Canon Moran guessed, at many countries throughout the world. It was strange that the two neighbouring islands had been so picked out, although once Germany was mentioned and the point made that developments beneath the surface there were a hopeful sign, that a big upset was on the way.

'We're taking a walk,' Harold said one afternoon. 'She's going to show me Kinsella's Barn.'

Canon Moran nodded, saying to himself that he disliked Harold. It was the first time he had admitted it, but the feeling was familiar. The less generous side of his nature had always emerged when his daughters brought to the rectory the men they'd become friendly with or even proposed to marry. Emma, the eldest girl, had brought several before settling in the end for Thomas. Linda had brought only John, already engaged to him. Una had married Carley not long after the death, and Carley had not yet visited the rectory: Canon Moran had met him in Dublin, where the wedding had taken place, for in the circumstances Una had not been married from home. Carley was an older man, an importer of tea and wine, stout and flushed, certainly not someone Canon Moran would have chosen for his second-youngest daughter. But, then, he had thought the same about Emma's Thomas and about Linda's John.

Thomas was a farmer, sharing a sizeable acreage with his father in Co. Meath. He always brought to mind the sarcasm of an old schoolmaster who in Canon Moran's distant schooldays used to refer to a gang of boys at the back of the classroom as 'farmers' sons', meaning that not much could be expected of them. It was an inaccurate assumption but even now, whenever Canon Moran found himself in the company of Thomas, he couldn't help recalling it. Thomas was mostly silent, with a good-natured smile that came slowly and lingered too long. According to his father, and there was no reason to doubt the claim, he was a good judge of beef cattle.

Linda's John was the opposite. Wiry and suave, he was making his way in the Bank of Ireland, at present stationed in Waterford. He had a tiny orange-coloured moustache and was good at golf. Linda's ambition for him was that he should become the Bank of Ireland's manager in Limerick or Galway, where the insurances that went with the position were particularly lucrative. Unlike Thomas, John talked all the time, telling jokes and stories about the Bank of Ireland's customers.

'Nothing is perfect,' Frances used to say, chiding her husband for an uncharitableness he did his best to combat. He disliked being so particular about the men his daughters chose, and he was aware that other people saw them differently: Thomas would do anything for you, John was fun, the middle-aged Carley laid his success at Una's feet. But whoever the husbands of his daughters had been, Canon Moran knew he'd have felt the same. He was jealous of the husbands because ever since his daughters had been born he had loved them unstintingly. When he had prayed after

Frances's death he'd felt jealous of God, who had taken her from him.

'There's nothing much to see,' he pointed out when Harold announced that Deirdre was going to show him Kinsella's Barn. 'Just the ruin of a wall is all that's left.'

'Harold's interested, Father.'

They set off on their walk, leaving the old clergyman ashamed that he could not like Harold more. It wasn't just his griminess: there was something sinister about Harold, something furtive about the way he looked at you, peering at you cruelly out of his afflicted face, not meeting your eye. Why was he so fascinated about a country that wasn't his own? Why did he refer so often to 'Ireland's struggle' as if that struggle particularly concerned him? He hated walking, he had said, yet he'd just set out to walk six miles through woods and fields to examine a ruined wall.

Canon Moran had wondered as suspiciously about Thomas and John and Carley, privately questioning every statement they made, finding hidden motives everywhere. He'd hated the thought of his daughters being embraced or even touched, and had forced himself not to think about that. He'd prayed, ashamed of himself then, too. 'It's just a frailty in you,' Frances had said, her favourite way of cutting things down to size.

He sat for a while in the afternoon sunshine, letting all of it hang in his mind. It would be nice if they quarrelled on their walk. It would be nice if they didn't speak when they returned, if Harold simply went away. But that wouldn't happen, because they had come to the rectory with a purpose. He didn't know why he thought that, but he knew it was true: they had come for a reason, something that was all tied up with Harold's fascination and with the kind of person Harold was, with his cold eyes and his afflicted face.

In March 1798 an incident had taken place in Kinsella's
Barn, which at that time had just been a barn. Twelve men
and women, accused of harbouring insurgents, had been
tied together with ropes at the command of a Sergeant
James. They had been led through the village of
Boharbawn, the Sergeant's soldiers on horseback on either
side of the procession, the Sergeant himself bringing up the
rear. Designed as an act of education, an example to the
inhabitants of Boharbawn and the country people around,
the twelve had been herded into a barn owned by a farmer
called Kinsella and there burned to death. Kinsella, who
had played no part either in the harbouring of insurgents or
in the execution of the twelve, was afterwards murdered by
his own farm labourers.

'Sergeant James was a Nottingham man,' Harold said that
evening at supper. 'A soldier of fortune who didn't care what
he did. Did you know he acquired great wealth, Mr
Moran?'

'No, I wasn't at all aware of that,' Canon Moran replied.

'Harold found out about him,' Deirdre said.

'He used to boast he was responsible for the death of a
thousand Irish people. It was in Boharbawn he reached the
thousand. They rewarded him well for that.'

'Not much is known about Sergeant James locally. Just
the legend of Kinsella's Barn.'

'No way it's a legend.'

Deirdre nodded; Canon Moran did not say anything. They
were eating cooked ham and salad. On the table there was a
cake which Deirdre had bought in Murphy Flood's in Enniscorthy, and a pot of tea. There were several bunches of
grapes from the greenhouse, and a plate of wafer biscuits.

Harold was fond of salad cream, Canon Moran had noticed; he had a way of hitting the base of the jar with his hand, causing large dollops to spurt all over his ham. He didn't place his knife and fork together on the plate when he'd finished, but just left them anyhow. His fingernails were edged with black.

'You'd feel sick,' he was saying now, working the salad cream again. 'You'd stand there looking at that wall and you'd feel a revulsion in your stomach.'

'What I meant,' Canon Moran said, 'is that it has passed into local legend. No one doubts it took place; there's no question about that. But two centuries have almost passed.'

'And nothing has changed,' Harold interjected. 'The Irish people still share their bondage with the twelve in Kinsella's Barn.'

'Round here of course –'

'It's not round here that matters, Mr Moran. The struggle's world-wide; the sickness is everywhere actually.'

Again Deirdre nodded. She was like a zombie, her father thought. She was being used because she was an Irish girl; she was Harold's Irish connection, and in some almost frightening way she believed herself in love with him. Frances had once said they'd made a mistake with her. She had wondered if Deirdre had perhaps found all the love they'd offered her too much to bear. They were quite old when Deirdre was a child, the last expression of their own love. She was special because of that.

'At least Kinsella got his chips,' Harold pursued, his voice relentless. 'At least that's something.'

Canon Moran protested. The owner of the barn had been an innocent man, he pointed out. The barn had simply been a convenient one, large enough for the purpose, with heavy stones near it that could be piled up against the door before the conflagration. Kinsella, that day, had been miles away, ditching a field.

'It's too long ago to say where he was,' Harold retorted swiftly. 'And if he was keeping a low profile in a ditch it would have been by arrangement with the imperial forces.'

When Harold said that, there occurred in Canon Moran's mind a flash of what appeared to be the simple truth. Harold was an Englishman who had espoused a cause because it was one through which the status quo in his own country might be damaged. Similar such Englishmen, read about in newspapers, stirred in the clergyman's mind: men from Ealing and Liverpool and Wolverhampton who had changed their names to Irish names, who had even learned the Irish language, in order to ingratiate themselves with the new Irish revolutionaries. Such men dealt out death and chaos, announcing that their conscience insisted on it.

'Well, we'd better wash the dishes,' Deirdre said, and Harold rose obediently to help her.

★

The walk to Kinsella's Barn had taken place on a Saturday afternoon. The following morning Canon Moran conducted his services in St Michael's, addressing his small Protestant congregation, twelve at Holy Communion, eighteen at morning service. He had prepared a sermon about repentance, taking as his text St Luke, 15:32: '... *for this thy brother was dead, and is alive again; and was lost, and is found.*' But at the last moment he changed his mind and spoke instead of the incident in Kinsella's Barn nearly two centuries ago. He tried to make the point that one horror should not fuel another, that passing time contained its own forgiveness. Deirdre and Harold were naturally not in the

church, but they'd been present at breakfast, Harold frying
eggs on the kitchen stove, Deirdre pouring tea. He had
looked at them and tried to think of them as two young
people on holiday. He had tried to tell himself they'd come
to the rectory for a rest and for his blessing, that he should be
grateful instead of fanciful. It was for his blessing that
Emma had brought Thomas to the rectory, that Linda had
brought John. Una would bring Carley in November. 'Now,
don't be silly,' Frances would have said.

'The man Kinsella was innocent of everything,' he heard
his voice insisting in his church. 'He should never have
been murdered also.'

Harold would have delighted in the vengeance exacted on
an innocent man. Harold wanted to inflict pain, to cause
suffering and destruction. The end justified the means for
Harold, even if the end was an artificial one, a pettiness
grandly dressed up. In his sermon Canon Moran spoke of
such matters without mentioning Harold's name. He spoke
of how evil drained people of their humour and compassion,
how people pretended even to themselves. It was worse than
Frances's death, he thought as his voice continued in the
church: it was worse that Deirdre should be part of
wickedness.

He could tell that his parishioners found his sermon odd,
and he didn't blame them. He was confused, and naturally
distressed. In the rectory Deirdre and Harold would be
waiting for him. They would all sit down to Sunday lunch
while plans for atrocities filled Harold's mind, while
Deirdre loved him.

'Are you well again, Mrs Davis?' he inquired at the church
door of a woman who suffered from asthma.

'Not too bad, Canon. Not too bad, thank you.'

He spoke to all the others, inquiring about health, remarking on the beautiful autumn. They were farmers mostly and displayed a farmer's gratitude for the satisfactory season. He wondered suddenly who'd replace him among them when he retired or died. Father Hayes had had to give up a year ago. The young man, Father White, was always in a hurry.

'Goodbye so, Canon,' Mr Willoughby said, shaking hands as he always did, every Sunday. It was a long time since there'd been the trouble about Eugene Ryan's grazing rights; three years ago Mr Willoughby had been left a widower himself. 'You're managing all right, Canon?' he asked, as he also always did.

'Yes, I'm all right, thank you, Mr Willoughby.'

Someone else inquired if Deirdre was still at the rectory, and he said she was. Heads nodded, the unspoken thought being that that was nice for him, his youngest daughter at home again after all these years. There was forgiveness in several faces, forgiveness of Deirdre, who had been thoughtless to go off to an egg-packing factory. There was the feeling, also unexpressed, that the young were a bit like that.

'Goodbye,' he said in a general way. Car doors banged, engines started. In the vestry he removed his surplice and his cassock and hung them in a cupboard.

*

'We'll probably go tomorrow,' Deirdre said during lunch.

'Go?'

'We'll probably take the Dublin bus.'

'I'd like to see Dublin,' Harold said.

'And then you're returning to London?'

'We're easy about that,' Harold interjected before Deirdre

could reply. 'I'm a tradesman, Mr Moran, an electrician.'

'I know you're an electrician, Harold.'

'What I mean is, I'm on my own; I'm not answerable to the bosses. There's always a bob or two waiting in London.'

For some reason Canon Moran felt that Harold was lying. There was a quickness about the way he'd said they were easy about their plans, and it didn't seem quite to make sense, the logic of not being answerable to bosses and a bob or two always waiting for him. Harold was being evasive about their movements, hiding the fact that they would probably remain in Dublin for longer than he implied, meeting other people like himself.

'It was good of you to have us,' Deirdre said that evening, all three of them sitting around the fire in the drawing-room because the evenings had just begun to get chilly. Harold was reading a book about Che Guevara and hadn't spoken for several hours. 'We've enjoyed it, Father.'

'It's been nice having you, Deirdre.'

'I'll write to you from London.'

It was safe to say that: he knew she wouldn't because she hadn't before, until she'd wanted something. She wouldn't write to thank him for the rectory's hospitality, and that would be quite in keeping. Harold was the same kind of man as Sergeant James had been: it didn't matter that they were on different sides. Sergeant James had maybe borne an affliction also, a humped back or a withered arm. He had ravaged a country that existed then for its spoils, and his most celebrated crime was neatly at hand so that another Englishman could make matters worse by attempting to make amends. In Harold's view the trouble had always been that these acts of war and murder died beneath the weight of print in history books, and were forgotten. But history could be rewritten, and for that Kinsella's Barn was an inspiration:

Harold had journeyed to it as people make journeys to holy places.

'Yes?' Deirdre said, for while these reflections had passed through his mind he had spoken her name, wanting to ask her to tell him the truth about her friend.

He shook his head. 'I wish you could have seen your mother again,' he said instead. 'I wish she were here now.'

The faces of his three sons-in-law irrelevantly appeared in his mind: Carley's flushed cheeks, Thomas's slow good-natured smile, John's little moustache. It astonished him that he'd ever felt suspicious of their natures, for they would never let his daughters down. But Deirdre had turned her back on the rectory, and what could be expected when she came back with a man? She had never been like Emma or Linda or Una, none of whom smoked Three Castles cigarettes and wore clothes that didn't seem quite clean. It was impossible to imagine any of them becoming involved with a revolutionary, a man who wanted to commit atrocities.

'He was just a farmer, you know,' he heard himself saying. 'Kinsella.'

Surprise showed in Deirdre's face. 'It was Mother we were talking about,' she reminded him, and he could see her trying to connect her mother with a farmer who had died two hundred years ago, and not being able to. Elderliness, he could see her thinking. 'Only time he wandered,' she would probably say to her friend.

'It was good of you to come, Deirdre.'

He looked at her, far into her eyes, admitting to himself that she had always been his favourite. When the other girls were busily growing up she had still wanted to sit on his knee. She'd had a way of interrupting him no matter what he was doing, arriving beside him with a book she wanted him to read to her.

'Goodbye, Father,' she said the next morning while they waited in Enniscorthy for the Dublin bus. 'Thank you for everything.'

'Yeah, thanks a ton, Mr Moran,' Harold said.

'Goodbye, Harold. Goodbye, my dear.'

He watched them finding their seats when the bus arrived and then he drove the old Vauxhall back to Boharbawn, meeting Slattery in his postman's van and returning his salute. There was shopping he should have done, meat and potatoes, and tins of things to keep him going. But his mind was full of Harold's afflicted face and his black-rimmed fingernails, and Deirdre's hand in his. And then flames burst from the straw that had been packed around living people in Kinsella's Barn. They burned through the wood of the barn itself, revealing the writhing bodies. On his horse the man called Sergeant James laughed.

Canon Moran drove the car into the rectory's ramshackle garage, and walked around the house to the wooden seat on the front lawn. Frances should come now with two cups of coffee, appearing at the front door with the tray and then crossing the gravel and the lawn. He saw her as she had been when first they came to the rectory, when only Emma had been born; but the grey-haired Frances was somehow there as well, shadowing her youth. 'Funny little Deirdre,' she said, placing the tray on the seat between them.

It seemed to him that everything that had just happened in the rectory had to do with Frances, with meeting her for the first time when she was eighteen, with loving her and marrying her. He knew it was a trick of the autumn sunshine that again she crossed the gravel and the lawn, no more than pretence that she handed him a cup and saucer. 'Harold's just a talker,' she said. 'Not at all like Sergeant James.'

He sat for a while longer on the wooden seat, clinging to

these words, knowing they were true. Of course it was cowardice that ran through Harold, inspiring the whisper of his sneer when he spoke of the England he hated so. In the presence of a befuddled girl and an old Irish clergyman England was an easy target, and Ireland's troubles a kind of target also.

Frances laughed, and for the first time her death seemed far away, as her life did too. In the rectory the visitors had blurred her fingerprints to nothing, and had made of her a ghost that could come back. The sunshine warmed him as he sat there, the garden was less melancholy than it had been.

Sunday Drinks

There was no one else about, not even a cat on the whole extent of the common. The early morning air hadn't yet been infected by the smell of London, houses were as silent as the houses of the dead. It was half-past seven, a Sunday morning in June: on a weekday at this time voices would be calling out, figures already hurrying across the common to Barnes station; the buses would have started. On a weekday Malcolm would be lying for a last five minutes in bed, conserving his energy.

Not yet shaven, a fawn dressing-gown over striped red and blue pyjamas, he strolled on the cricket pitch, past the sight-screens and a small pavilion. He was middle-aged and balding, with glasses. Though no eccentric in other ways, he often walked on fine Sunday mornings across the common in his dressing-gown, as far as the poplars which grew in a line along one boundary.

Reaching them now, he turned and slowly made his way back to the house where he lived with Jessica, who was his wife. They'd lived there since he'd begun to be prosperous as a solicitor: an Edwardian house of pleasant brown brick, with some Virginia creeper on it, and bay trees in tubs on either side of the front door. They were a small family: quietly occupying an upstairs room, in many ways no trouble to anyone, there was Malcolm and Jessica's son.

In the kitchen Malcolm finished chapter eight of *Edwin Drood* and eventually heard the Sunday papers arrive. He went to fetch them, glanced through them, and then made coffee and toast. He took a tray and the newspapers up to his wife.

★

'I've brought you a cup of tea,' Jessica said later that morning, in their son's room. Sometimes he drank it, but often it was still there on the bedside table when she returned at lunchtime. He never carried the cup and saucer down to the kitchen himself and would apologise for that, wagging his head in irritation at his shortcomings.

He didn't reply when she spoke about the tea. He stared at her and smiled. One hand was clenched close to his bearded face, the fingernails bitten, the fingers gnawed here and there. The room smelt of his sweat because he couldn't bear to have the window open, nor indeed to have the blind up. He made his models with the electric light on, preferring that to daylight. In the room the models were everywhere: Hurricanes and Spitfires, sea-planes and Heinkel 178s, none of them finished. A month ago, on 25th May, they'd made an attempt to celebrate his twenty-fourth birthday.

She closed the door behind her. On the landing walls there was a wallpaper splashed with poppies and cornflowers, which ran down through the house. People often remarked on its pastoral freshness when Jessica opened the hall-door to them, though others sometimes blinked. The hall had had a gloomy look before, the paintwork a shade of gravy. Doors and skirting-boards were brightly white now.

'Let's not go to the Morrishes',' Malcolm suggested in the kitchen, even though he'd put on his Sunday-morning-drinks clothes.

'Of course we must,' she said, not wanting to go to the Morrishes' either. 'I won't be a minute.'

In the downstairs lavatory she applied eye-shadow. Her thin face had a shallow look if she didn't make an effort with make-up; a bit of colour suited her, she reckoned, as it did the hall. She smeared on lipstick and pressed a tissue between her lips to clear away the surplus, continuing to examine her application of eye-shadow in the mirror above the washbasin. Dark hair, greying now, curved around her face. Her deep blue eyes still managed a sparkle that spread beauty into her features, transforming her: nondescript little thing, someone once had said, catching her in a tired moment.

In the kitchen she turned on the extractor fan above the electric cooker; pork chops were cooking slowly in the oven. 'All right?' she said, and Malcolm, idling over an advertisement for photochromic lenses, nodded and stood up.

*

Their son was dreaming now: he was there, on the bank of the river. Birds with blue plumage swooped over the water; through the foliage came the strum of a guitar. All the friends there'd been were there, in different coloured sleeping-bags, lying as he was. They were happy by the river because India was where the truth was, wrapped up in gentleness and beauty. Someone said that, and everyone else agreed.

*

Anthea Chalmers was at the Morrishes', tall and elegant in green, long since divorced. She had a look of Bette Davis, eyes like soup-plates, that kind of mouth. The Livingstons were there also, and Susanna and David Maidstone, and the

Unwins. So was Mr Fulmer, a sandy-complexioned man whom people were sorry for because his wife was a stick-in-the-mud and wouldn't go to parties. June and Tom Highband were there, and the Taylor-Deeths, and Marcus Stire and his friend. There was a handful of faces that were unfamiliar to Jessica and Malcolm.

'Hullo, hullo,' their host called out, welcoming them with party joviality. The guests were passing from the sitting-room, through the French windows to the garden, all of them with glasses in their hands. The Morrishes – he pink and bluff, she pretty in a faded way – were busily making certain that these glasses contained precisely what people wanted. In the garden their French *au pair* boy was handing round bowls of nuts and shiny little biscuits from Japan. Children – the Morrishes' and others' – had congregated in a distant corner, by a tool-shed.

Jessica and Malcolm both asked for white wine, since chilled bottles of it stood there, inviting on a warm morning. They didn't say much to the Morrishes, who clearly wanted to get things going before indulging in chat. They stepped out into the garden, where a mass of flowers spectacularly bloomed and the lawns were closely shorn.

'Hi, Jessica,' Marcus Stire's friend said, a short, stout young man in a blue blazer. He'd made her black-bottom pie, he reported. He shook his head, implying disappointment with his version of the dish.

'Hullo, stranger,' Anthea Chalmers said to Malcolm.

She always seemed to pick him out. Ages ago he'd rejected the idea that a balding solicitor with glasses might possibly have some sensual attraction for her, even though all she ever talked to him about were sensual matters. She liked to get him into a corner, as she had done now, and had a way of turning interlopers away with a snakelike shift of her shoulders. She'd placed him with his back to the wall of the house, along which a creamy honeysuckle had been trained. A trellis to his right continued to support it; to his left, two old water-butts were swathed with purple clematis.

'A pig,' she said, referring to the man she'd once been married to. 'And I told him, Malcolm. I'd sooner share a bed with a farmyard pig was precisely what I said. Needless to say, he became violent.'

Jessica, having discussed the preparation of black-bottom pie with Marcus Stire's friend, smiled at the stout young man and passed on. The *au pair* boy offered her a Japanese biscuit and then a man she didn't know remarked upon the weather. Could anything be nicer, he asked her, than a drink or two on a Sunday morning in a sunny London garden? He was a man in brown suede, expensively cut to disguise a certain paunchiness. He had damp eyes and a damp-looking moustache. He had well-packed jowls, and a sun-browned head that matched the shade of his clothes. A businessman, Jessica speculated, excessively rich, a tough performer in his business world. He began to talk about a house he owned near Estepona.

*

On the surface of the tea which Jessica had earlier brought her son a skin had formed, in which a small fly now struggled. Nothing else was happening in the room. The sound of breathing could hardly be heard, the dream about birds with blue plumage had abruptly ceased. Then – in that same abrupt manner, a repetition of the suddenness that in different ways affected this boy's life – his eyes snapped open.

Through the gloom, and seeming larger than reality, the Spitfires and the Heinkels greeted his consciousness. He was in a room with aeroplanes, he told himself, and while he lay there nothing more impinged on his mind. Eventually he rose and began to dress, his youthful beard scanty and soft, quite like a bearded lady's. Tears ran into it while slowly he pulled his clothes over his white flesh.

His T-shirt was pale blue, the paler message it bore almost washed away. *Wham!* it had said, the word noisily proclaimed against lightning flashes and the hooded figures of Batman and Robin. A joke all of it had been: those years had been full of jokes, with no one wanting to grow up, with that longing to be children for ever. Tears dripped from his beard to the T-shirt now; some fell on to his jeans. He turned the electric light on and then noticed the cup of tea by his bed. He drank it, swallowing the skin and the fly that had died in it. His tears did not distress him.

*

'Well, that was it, Malcolm,' Anthea Chalmers said. 'I mean, no one enjoys a bedroom more than I do, but for God's sake!'

Her soup-plate eyes rapidly blinked, her lips were held for a moment in a little knot. The man she'd married, she yet again revealed, had not been able to give her what she'd wanted and needed. Instead, intoxicated, he would return to their house at night and roar about from room to room. Often he armed himself with a bamboo cane. 'Which he bought,' she reminded Malcolm, 'quite openly in a garden shop.'

In the honeysuckle, suburban bees paused between moments of buzzing. A white butterfly fluttered beside Malcolm's face. 'You must be awfully glad to be rid of him,' he politely said.

'One's alone, Malcolm. It isn't easy, being alone.'

She went into details about how difficult it was, and how various frustrations could be eased. She lowered her voice, she said she spoke in confidence. Sexual fantasy flooded from her, tired and seeming soiled in the bright sunshine, with the scent of the honeysuckle so close to both of them. Malcolm listened, not moving away, not trying to think of other things. It was nearly two years since Anthea Chalmers had discovered that he would always listen at a party.

In the garden the voices had become louder as more alcohol was consumed. Laughter was shriller, cigarette smoke hung about. By the tool-shed in the far distance the children, organised by a girl who was a little older than the others, played a variation of Grandmother's Footsteps.

Tom Highband, who wrote under another name a column for the *Daily Telegraph*, told a joke that caused a burst of laughter. Sandy Mr Fulmer, whom nobody knew very well, listened to the Unwins exchanging gossip with Susanna Maidstone about the school their children all attended. 'Just a little slower,' Marcus Stire's friend pleaded, writing down a recipe for prune jelly on the back of a cheque-book. Taylor-Deeth was getting drunk.

'It has its own little beach of course,' the man with the damp-looking moustache informed Jessica. You went down a flight of steps and there you were. They adored the Spaniards, he added, Joan especially did.

And then Joan, who was his wife, was there beside them, in shades of pink. She was bulky, like her husband, with a smile so widely beaming that it seemed to run off her face into her smooth grey hair. She had always had a thing about the Spanish, she agreed, the quality of Spanish life, their little churches. 'We have a maid of course,' her husband said, 'who keeps an eye on things. Old Violetta.'

Glasses were again refilled, the Morrishes together

attending to that, as was their way at their parties. She did so quietly, he with more dash. People often remarked that they were like good servants, the way they complemented one another in this way. As well, they were said to be happily married.

Glancing between the couple who were talking to her, Jessica could see that Malcolm was still trapped. The Livingstons tried to cut in on the tête-à-tête but Anthea Chalmers's shoulder sharply edged them away. Together again after their separation, the Livingstons looked miserable.

'Violetta mothers us,' the man with the damp moustache said. 'We could never manage without old Violetta.'

'Another thing is Spanish dignity,' his wife continued, and the man added that old Violetta certainly had her share of that.

'Oh yes, indeed,' his wife agreed.

Marcus Stire arrived then, lanky and malicious. The couple with the house in Spain immediately moved away, as if they didn't like the look of him. He laughed. They were embarrassed, he explained, because at another party recently they'd all of a sudden quarrelled most violently in his presence. The man had even raised an arm to strike his wife, and Marcus Stire had had to restrain him.

'You'd never think it, would you, Jessica? All that guff about cosiness in Spain when more likely that smile of hers covers a multitude of sins. What awful frauds people are!' He laughed again and then continued, his soft voice drawling, a cigarette between the rings on his fingers.

He ran through all the people in the garden. Susanna Maidstone had been seen with Taylor-Deeth in the Trat-West. The Livingstons' patched-up arrangement wouldn't of course last. The Unwins were edgy, frigidity was Anthea

Chalmers's problem. 'Suburban middle age,' he said in his drawl. 'It's like a minefield.' The Morrishes had had a ghastly upset a month ago when a girl from his office had pursued him home one night, messily spilling the beans.

Jessica looked at the Morrishes, so neatly together as they saw to people's drinks, attending now to Mr Fulmer. It seemed astonishing that they, too, weren't quite as they appeared to be. 'Oh, heavens, yes,' Marcus Stire said, guessing at this doubt in her mind.

His malice was perceptive, and he didn't much exaggerate. He had a way of detecting trouble, and of accurately piecing together the fragments that came his way. Caught off her guard, she wondered what he said to other people about Malcolm and herself. She wondered just how he saw them and then immediately struggled to regain her concentration, knowing she should not wonder that.

He was commenting now on the girl who had persuaded the other children to play her version of Grandmother's Footsteps, a bossy handful he called her. How dreadful she'd be at forty-eight, her looks three-quarters gone, famous in some other suburb as a nagging wife. Jessica smiled, as if he had related a pleasant joke. Again she made the effort to concentrate.

You had to do that: to concentrate and to listen properly, as Malcolm was listening, as she had listened herself to the talk about a house in Spain. You had to have a bouncy wallpaper all over the house, and fresh white paint instead of gravy-brown. You mustn't forget your plan to get the garden as colourful as this one; you mustn't let your mind wander. Busily you must note the damp appearance of a man's moustache and the smooth greyness of a woman's hair, and the malevolence in the eyes that were piercing into you now.

'I've written off those years, Malcolm,' Anthea Chalmers

said, and across the garden Malcolm saw that his wife had collapsed. He could tell at once, as if she'd fallen to the grass and lay there in a heap. Occasionally one or the other of them went under; impossible to anticipate which, or how it would happen.

He watched her face and saw that she was back in 1954, her pains developing a rhythm, a sweltering summer afternoon. A message had come to him in court, and when he'd returned to the house the midwife was smoking a cigarette in the hall. The midwife and the nurse had been up all night with a difficult delivery in Sheen. Afterwards, when the child had been born and everything tidied up, he'd given them a glass of whisky each.

Like an infection, all of it slipped across the garden, through the cigarette smoke and the people and the smartly casual Sunday clothes, from Jessica to Malcolm. Down their treacherous Memory Lane it dragged them, one after the other. The first day at the primary school, tears at the gate, the kindly dinner lady. The gang of four, their child and three others, at daggers drawn with other gangs. The winning of the high jump.

'Excuse me,' Malcolm said. It was worse for Jessica, he thought in a familiar way as he made his way to her. It was worse because after the birth she'd been told she must not have other babies: she blamed herself now for being obedient.

They left the party suddenly, while the children still played a version of Grandmother's Footsteps by the toolshed, and the adults drank and went on talking to one another. People who knew them guessed that their abrupt departure might somehow have to do with their son, whom no one much mentioned these days, he being a registered drug addict. The couple who had spoken to Jessica about their Spanish house spoke of it now to their hosts, who did not listen as well as she had. Anthea Chalmers tried to explain to Marcus Stire's friend, but that was hopeless. Marcus Stire again surveyed the people in the garden.

*

Anger possessed Malcolm as they walked across the common that had been peaceful in the early morning. It was less so now. Cricket would be played that afternoon and preparations were being made, the square marked, the sightscreens wheeled into position. An ice-cream van was already trading briskly. People lay on the grass, youths kicked a football.

'I'm sorry,' Jessica said. Her voice was nervous; she felt ashamed of herself.

'It isn't you, Jessica.'

'Let's have a drink on our own, shall we?'

Neither of them wishing to return immediately to their house, they went to the Red Rover and sat outside. She guessed his thoughts, as earlier he had seen hers in her face. When people wondered where all of it had gone, all that love and all those flowers, he would liked to have shown them their darkened upstairs room. The jolly Sixties and those trips to wonderland were there, he'd once cried out, with half-made aeroplanes gathering a dust. Their son had a name, which was used when they addressed him; but when they thought of him he was nameless in their minds. Years ago they'd discovered that that was the same for both of them.

'Maybe,' she said, referring to the future, trying to cheer him up.

He made a gesture, half a nod: the speculation was

impossible. And the consolation that families had always had children who were locked away and looked after wasn't a consolation in the least. They didn't have to live with a monstrous fact of nature, but with a form of accidental suicide, and that was worse.

They sat a little longer in the sunshine, both of them thinking about the house they'd left an hour or so ago. It would be as silent as if they'd never had a child, and then little noises would begin, like the noises of a ghost. The quiet descent of the stairs, the shuffling through the hall. He would be there in the kitchen, patiently sitting, when they returned. He would smile at them and during lunch a kind of conversation might develop, or it might not. A week ago he'd said, quite suddenly, that soon he intended to work in a garden somewhere, or a park. Occasionally he said things like that.

They didn't mention him as they sat there; they never did now. And it was easier for both of them to keep away from Memory Lane when they were together and alone. Instead of all that there was the gossip of Marcus Stire: Susanna Maidstone in the Trat-West, the girl from the office arriving in the Morrishes' house, the quarrel between the smiling woman and her suede-clad husband, Anthea Chalmers, lone Mr Fulmer, the Livingstons endeavouring to make a go of it. Easily, Malcolm imagined Marcus Stire's drawling tones and the sharpness of his eye, like a splinter of glass. He knew now how Jessica had been upset: a pair of shadows Marcus Stire would have called them, clinging to the periphery of life because that was where they felt safe, both of them a little destroyed.

They went on discussing the people they'd just left, wondering if some fresh drama had broken out, another explosion in the landscape of marriage that Marcus Stire had

likened to a minefield. Finishing their drinks, they agreed
that he'd certainly tell them if it had. They talked about him
for a moment, and then the subject of the party drifted away
from them and they talked of other things. Malcolm told her
what was happening in *Edwin Drood*, because it was a book
she would never read. His voice continued while they left
the Red Rover and walked across the common, back to their
house. It was odd, she reflected as she listened to it, that
companionship had developed in their middle age, when
luckier people trailed from their marriages such tales of
woe.

The Paradise Lounge

Oh her high stool by the bar the old woman was as still as a statue. Perhaps her face is expressionless, Beatrice thought, because in repose it does not betray the extent of her years. The face itself was lavishly made up, eyes and mouth, rouge softening the wrinkles, a dusting of perfumed powder. The chin was held more than a little high, at an angle that tightened the loops of flesh beneath it. Grey hair was short beneath a black cloche hat that suggested a fashion of the past, as did the tight black skirt and black velvet coat. Eighty she'd be, Beatrice deduced, or eighty-two or -three.

'We can surely enjoy ourselves,' Beatrice's friend said, interrupting her scrutiny of the old woman. 'Surely we can, Bea?'

She turned her head. The closeness of his brick-coloured flesh and of the smile in his eyes caused her lips to tremble. She appeared to smile also, but what might have been taken for pleasure was a checking of her tears.

'Yes,' she said. 'Of course.'

They were married, though not to one another. Beatrice's friend, casually dressed for a summer weekend, was in early middle age, no longer slim yet far from bulky. Beatrice was thirty-two, petite and black-haired in a blue denim dress. Sunglasses disguised her deep-rust eyes, which was how – a long time ago now – her father had described them. She had wanted to be an actress then.

'It's best,' her friend said, repeating the brief statement for what might have been the hundredth time since they had settled into his car earlier that afternoon. The affair was over, the threat to their families averted. They had come away to say goodbye.

'Yes, I know it's best,' she said, a repetition also.

At the bar the old woman slowly raised a hand to her hat and touched it delicately with her fingers. Slowly the hand descended, and then lifted her cocktail glass. Her scarlet mouth was not quite misshapen, but age had harshly scored what once had been a perfect outline, lips pressed together like a rosebud on its side. Failure, Beatrice thought as casually she observed all this: in the end the affair was a failure. She didn't even love him any more, and long ago he'd ceased to love her. It was euphemism to call it saying goodbye: they were having a dirty weekend, there was nothing left to lift it higher than that.

'I'm sorry we couldn't manage longer,' he said. 'I'm sorry about Glengarriff.'

'It doesn't matter.'

'Even so.'

She ceased to watch the old woman at the bar. She smiled at him, again disguising tears but also wanting him to know that there were no hard feelings, for why on earth should there be?

'After all, we've been to Glengarriff,' she said, a joke because on the one occasion they'd visited the place they had nearly been discovered in their deceptions. She'd used her sister as an excuse for her absences from home: for a long time now her sister had been genuinely unwell in a farmhouse in Co. Meath, a house that fortunately for Beatrice's purpose didn't have a telephone.

'I'll never forget you,' he said, his large tanned hand suddenly on one of hers, the vein throbbing in his forehead. A line of freckles ran down beside the vein, five smudges on the redbrick skin. In winter you hardly noticed them.

'Nor I you.'

'Darling old Bea,' he said, as if they were back at the beginning.

The bar was a dim, square lounge with a scattering of small tables, one of which they occupied. Ashtrays advertised Guinness, beer-mats Heineken. Sunlight touched the darkened glass in one of two windows, drawing from it a glow that was not unlike the amber gleam of whiskey. Behind the bar itself the rows of bottles, spirits upside down above their global measures, glittered pleasantly as a centre-piece, their reflections gaudy in a cluttered mirror. The floor had a patterned carpet, further patterned with cigarette burns and a diversity of stains. The Paradise Lounge the bar had been titled in a moment of hyperbole by the grandfather of the present proprietor, a sign still proclaiming as much on the door that opened from the hotel's mahogany hall. Beatrice's friend had hesitated, for the place seemed hardly promising: Keegan's Railway Hotel in a town neither of them knew. They might have driven on, but he was tired and the sun had been in his eyes. 'It's all right,' she had reassured him.

He took their glasses to the bar and had to ring a bell because the man in charge had disappeared ten minutes ago. 'Nice evening,' he said to the old woman on the barstool, and she managed to indicate agreement without moving a muscle of her carefully held head. 'We'll have the same again,' he said to the barman, who apologised for his absence, saying he'd been mending a tap.

Left on her own, Beatrice sighed a little and took off her sunglasses. There was no need for this farewell, no need to see him for the last time in his pyjamas or to sit across a table from him at dinner and at breakfast, making conversation that once had come naturally. 'A final fling,' he'd put it, and she'd thought of someone beating a cracked drum, trying to extract a sound that wasn't there any more. How could it have come to this? The Paradise Lounge of Keegan's Railway Hotel, Saturday night in a hilly provincial town, litter caught in the railings of the Christian Brothers': how *could* this be the end of what they once had had? Saying goodbye to her, he was just somebody else's husband: the lover had slipped away.

'Well, it's a terrible bloody tap we have,' the barman was saying. 'Come hell or high water, I can't get a washer into it.'

'It can be a difficult job.'

'You could come in and say that to the wife for me, sir.'

The drinks were paid for, the transaction terminated. Further gin and Martini were poured into the old woman's glass, and Beatrice watched again while like a zombie the old woman lit a cigarette.

*

Miss Doheny her name was: though beautiful once, she had never married. Every Saturday evening she met the Meldrums in the Paradise Lounge, where they spent a few hours going through the week that had passed, exchanging gossip and commenting on the world. Miss Doheny was always early and would sit up at the bar for twenty minutes on her own, having the extra couple of drinks that, for her, were always necessary. Before the Meldrums arrived she would make her way to a table in a corner, for that was where Mrs Meldrum liked to be.

It wasn't usual that other people were in the bar then. Occasionally it filled up later but at six o'clock, before her friends arrived, she nearly always had it to herself. Francis

Keegan – the hotel's inheritor, who also acted as barman – spent a lot of time out in the back somewhere, attending to this or that. It didn't matter because after their initial greeting of one another, and a few remarks about the weather, there wasn't much conversation that Miss Doheny and he had to exchange. She enjoyed sitting up at the bar on her own, glancing at the reflections in the long mirror behind the bottles, provided the reflections were never of herself. On the other hand it was a pleasant enough diversion, having visitors.

Miss Doheny, who had looked twice at Beatrice and once at her companion, guessed at their wrong-doing. Tail-ends of conversation had drifted across the lounge, no effort being made to lower voices since more often than not the old turn out to be deaf. They were people from Dublin whose relationship was not that recorded in Francis Keegan's register in the hall. Without much comment, modern life permitted their sin; the light-brown motor-car parked in front of the hotel made their self-indulgence a simple matter.

How different it had been, Miss Doheny reflected, in 1933! Correctly she estimated that that would have been the year when she herself was the age the dark-haired girl was now. In 1933 adultery and divorce and light-brown motor-cars had belonged more in America and England, read about and alien to what already was being called the Irish way of life. 'Catholic Ireland,' Father Horan used to say. 'Decent Catholic Ireland.' The term was vague and yet had meaning: the emergent nation, seeking pillars on which to build itself, had plumped for holiness and the Irish language – natural choices in the circumstances. 'A certain class of woman,' old Father Horan used to say, 'constitutes an abhorrence.' The painted women of Clancy's Picture House

– sound introduced in 1936 – were creatures who carried a terrible warning. Jezebel women, Father Horan called them, adding that the picture house should never have been permitted to exist. In his grave for a quarter of a century, he would hardly have believed his senses if he'd walked into the Paradise Lounge in Keegan's Railway Hotel to discover two adulterers, and one of his flock who had failed to heed his castigation of painted women. Yet for thirty-five years Miss Doheny had strolled through the town on Saturday evenings to this same lounge, past the statue of the 1798 rebels, down the sharp incline of Castle Street. On Sundays she covered the same ground again, on the way to and from Mass. Neither rain nor cold prevented her from making the journey to the Church of the Immaculate Conception or to the hotel, and illness did not often afflict her. That she had become more painted as the years piled up seemed to Miss Doheny to be natural in the circumstances.

In the Paradise Lounge she felt particularly at home. In spring and summer the Meldrums brought plants for her, or bunches of chives or parsley, sometimes flowers. Not because she wished to balance the gesture with one of her own but because it simply pleased her to do so she brought for them a pot of jam if she had just made some, or pieces of shortbread. At Christmas, more formally, they exchanged gifts of a different kind. At Christmas the lounge was decorated by Francis Keegan, as was the hall of the hotel and the dining-room. Once a year, in April, a dance was held in the dining-room, in connection with a local point-to-point, and it was said in the town that Francis Keegan made enough in the bar during the course of that long night to last him for the next twelve months. The hotel ticked over from April to April, the Paradise Lounge becoming quite brisk with business when an occasional function was held in the dining-room, though never achieving the abandoned spending that distinguished the night of the point-to-point. Commercial travellers sometimes stayed briefly, taking pot-luck with Mrs Keegan's cooking, which at the best of times was modest in ambition and achievement. After dinner these men would sit on one of the high stools in the Paradise Lounge, conversing with Francis Keegan and drinking bottles of stout. Mrs Keegan would sometimes put in a late appearance and sip a glass of gin and water. She was a woman of slatternly appearance, with loose grey hair and slippers. Her husband complemented her in style and manner, his purplish complexion reflecting a dedication to the wares he traded in across his bar. They were an undemanding couple, charitable in their opinions, regarded as unfortunate in the town since their union had not produced children. Because of that, Keegan's Railway Hotel was nearing the end of its days as a family concern and in a sense it was fitting that that should be so, for the railway that gave it its title had been closed in 1951.

How I envy her! Miss Doheny thought. How fortunate she is to find herself in these easy times, not condemned because she loves a man! It seemed right to Miss Doheny that a real love affair was taking place in the Paradise Lounge and that no one questioned it. Francis Keegan knew perfectly well that the couple were not man and wife, the strictures of old Father Horan were as fusty by now as neglected mice droppings. The holiness that had accompanied the birth of a nation had at last begun to shed its first tight skin: liberation, Miss Doheny said to herself, marvelling over the word.

*

They walked about the town because it was too soon for dinner. Many shops were still open, greengrocers anxious to rid themselves of cabbage that had been limp for days and could not yet again be offered for sale after the weekend, chemists and sweetshops. Kevin Ryan, Your Best for Hi-Fi, had arranged a loudspeaker in a window above his premises: Saturday night music blared forth, punk harmonies and a tenor rendering of 'Kelly the Boy from Killann'. All tastes were catered for.

The streets were narrow, the traffic congested. Women picked over the greengrocers' offerings, having waited until this hour because prices would be reduced. Newly shaved men slipped into the public houses, youths and girls loitered outside Redmond's Café and on the steps of the 1798 statue. Two dogs half-heartedly fought outside the Bank of Ireland.

The visitors to the town enquired where the castle was, and then made their way up Castle Hill. 'Opposite Castle Motors,' the child they'd asked had said, and there it was: an ivy-covered ruin, more like the remains of a cowshed. Corrugated iron sealed off an archway, its torn bill-posters advertising Calor Gas and a rock group, Duffy's Circus and Fine Gael, and the annual point-to-point that kept Keegan's Railway Hotel going. Houses had been demolished in this deserted area, concrete replacements only just begun. The graveyard of the Protestant church was unkempt; *New Premises in Wolfe Tone Street*, said a placard in the window of Castle Motors. Litter was everywhere.

'Not exactly camera fodder,' he said with his easy laugh. 'A bloody disgrace, some of these towns are.'

'The people don't notice, I suppose.'

'They should maybe wake themselves up.'

The first time he'd seen her, he'd afterwards said, he had

heard himself whispering that it was she he should have married. They'd sat together, talking over after-dinner coffee in someone else's house. He'd told her, lightly, that he was in the Irish rope business, almost making a joke of it because that was his way. A week later his car had drawn up beside her in Rathgar Road, where she'd lived since her marriage. 'I thought I recognised you,' he said, afterwards confessing that he'd looked up her husband's name in the telephone directory. 'Come in for a drink,' she invited, and of course he had. Her two children had been there, her husband had come in.

They made their way back to the town, she taking his arm as they descended the steep hill they'd climbed. A wind had gathered, cooling the evening air.

'It feels so long ago,' she said. 'The greater part of my life appears to have occurred since that day when you first came to the house.'

'I know, Bea.'

He'd seemed extraordinary and nice, and once when he'd smiled at her she'd found herself looking away. She wasn't unhappy in her marriage, only bored by the monotony of preparing food and seeing to the house and the children. She had, as well, a reluctant feeling that she wasn't appreciated, that she hadn't been properly loved for years.

'You don't regret it happened?' he said, stepping out into the street because the pavement was still crowded outside Redmond's Café.

She pitched her voice low so that he wouldn't hear her saying she wasn't sure. She didn't want to tell a lie, she wasn't certain of the truth.

He nodded, assuming her reassurance. Once, of course, he would never have let a mumbled reply slip by.

Miss Doheny had moved from the bar and was sitting at a table with the Meldrums when Beatrice and her friend returned to the Paradise Lounge after dinner. Mrs Meldrum was telling all about the visit last Sunday afternoon of her niece, Kathleen. 'Stones she's put on,' she reported, and then recalled that Kathleen's newly acquired husband had sat there for three hours hardly saying a word. Making a fortune he was, in the dry goods business, dull but good-hearted.

Miss Doheny listened. Strangely, her mind was still on the visitors who had returned to the lounge. She'd heard the girl saying that a walk about the town would be nice, and as the Meldrums had entered the lounge an hour or so ago she'd heard the man's voice in the hall and had guessed they were then on their way to the dining-room. The dinner would not have been good, for Miss Doheny had often heard complaints about the nature of Mrs Keegan's cooking. And yet the dinner, naturally, would not have mattered in the least.

Mrs Meldrum's voice continued: Kathleen's four children by her first marriage were all grown up and off her hands, she was lucky to have married so late in life into a prosperous dry goods business. Mr Meldrum inclined his head or nodded, but from time to time he would also issue a mild contradiction, setting the facts straight, regulating his wife's memory. He was a grey-haired man in a tweed jacket, very tall and thin, his face as sharp as a blade, his grey moustache well cared-for. He smoked while he drank, allowing a precise ten minutes to elapse between the end of one cigarette and the lighting of the next. Mrs Meldrum was

smaller than her companions by quite some inches, round
and plump, with glasses and a black hat.

The strangers were drinking Drambuie now, Miss Doheny noticed. The man made a joke, probably about the
food they'd eaten; the girl smiled. It was difficult to understand why it was that they were so clearly not man and wife.
There was a wistfulness in the girl's face, but the wistfulness said nothing very much. In a surprising way Miss
Doheny imagined herself crossing the lounge to where they
were. 'You're lucky, you know,' she heard herself saying.
'Honestly, you're lucky, child.' She glanced again in the
girl's direction and for a moment caught her eye. She almost
mouthed the words, but changed her mind because as much
as possible she liked to keep her face in repose.

★

Beatrice listened to her companion's efforts to cheer the
occasion up. The town and the hotel – especially the meal
they'd just consumed – combined to reflect the mood that
the end of the affair had already generated. They were here,
Beatrice informed herself again, not really to say goodbye to
one another but to commit adultery for the last time. They
would enjoy it as they always had, but the enjoyment would
not be the same as that inspired by the love there had been.
They might not have come, they might more elegantly have
said goodbye, yet their presence in a bar ridiculously named
the Paradise Lounge seemed suddenly apt. The bedroom
where acts of mechanical passion would take place had a
dingy wallpaper, its flattened pink soap already used by
someone else. Dirty weekend, Beatrice thought again,
for stripped of love all that was left was the mess of de-
ception and lies there had been, of theft and this remain-

ing, too ordinary desire. Her sister, slowly dying in the farmhouse, had been a bitter confidante and would never forgive her now. Tonight in a provincial bedroom a manufacturer of rope would have his way with her and she would have her way with him. There would be their nakedness and their mingled sweat.

'I thought that steak would walk away,' he spiritedly was continuing now. 'Being somebody's shoe-leather.'

She suddenly felt drunk, and wanted to be drunker. She held her glass toward him. 'Let's just drink,' she said.

She caught the eye of the old woman at the other table and for a moment sensed Miss Doheny's desire to communicate with her. It puzzled her that an elderly woman whom she did not know should wish to say something, yet she strongly felt that this was so. Then Miss Doheny returned her attention to what the other old woman was saying.

When they'd finished the drinks that Beatrice's companion had just fetched they moved from the table they were at and sat on two barstools, listening to Francis Keegan telling them about the annual liveliness in the hotel on the night of the April point-to-point. Mrs Keegan appeared at his side and recalled an occasion when two crates of day-old chicks, deposited in the hall of the hotel for a couple of hours, had been released by some of the wilder spirits and how old Packy O'Brien had imagined he'd caught the d.t.s when he saw them fluttering up the stairs. And there was the story – before Mrs Keegan's time, as she was swift to point out – when Jack Doyle and Movita had stayed in Keegan's, when just for the hell of it Jack Doyle had chased a honeymoon couple up Castle Hill, half naked from their bed. After several further drinks, Beatrice began to laugh. She felt much less forlorn now that the faces of Francis Keegan and his wife were beginning to float agreeably in her vision.

When she looked at the elderly trio in the corner, the only other people in the lounge, their faces floated also.

The thin old man came to the bar for more drinks and cigarettes. He nodded and smiled at Beatrice; he remarked upon the weather. 'Mr Meldrum,' said Francis Keegan by way of introduction. 'How d'you do,' Beatrice said.

Her companion yawned and appeared to be suggesting that they should go to bed. Beatrice took no notice. She pushed her glass at Francis Keegan, reaching for her hand-bag and announcing that it was her round. 'A drink for everyone,' she said, aware that when she gestured towards the Keegans and the elderly trio she almost lost her balance. She giggled. 'Definitely my round,' she slurred, giggling again.

Mrs Keegan told another story, about a commercial travel-ler called Artie Logan who had become drunk in his room and had sent down for so many trays of tea and buttered bread that every cup and saucer in the hotel had been carried up to him. 'They said to thank you,' her husband passed on, returning from the elderly trio's table. Beatrice turned her head. All three of them were looking at her, their faces still slipping about a bit. Their glasses were raised in her direc-tion. 'Good luck,' the old man called out.

It was then that Beatrice realised. She looked from face to face, making herself smile to acknowledge the good wishes she was being offered, the truth she sensed seeming to emerge from a blur of features and clothes and three raised glasses. She nodded, and saw the heads turn away again. It had remained unstated: the love that was there had never in any way been exposed. In this claustrophobic town, in this very lounge, there had been the endless lingering of a silent passion, startlingly different from the instant requiting of her own.

Through the muzziness of inebriation Beatrice glanced again across the bar. Behind her the Keegans were laughing, and the man she'd once so intensely loved was loudly laughing also. She heard the sound of the laughter strangely, as if it echoed from a distance, and she thought for a moment that it did not belong in the Paradise Lounge, that only the two old women and the old man belonged there. He was loved, and in silence he returned that love. His plump, bespectacled wife had never had reason to feel betrayed; no shame or guilt attached. In all the years a sister's dying had never been made use of. Nor had there been hasty afternoons in Rathgar Road, blinds drawn against neighbours who might guess, a bedroom set to rights before children came in from school. There hadn't been a single embrace.

Yet the love that had continued for so long would go on now until the grave: without even thinking, Beatrice knew that that was so. The old woman paraded for a purpose the remnants of her beauty, the man was elegant in his tweed. How lovely that was! Beatrice thought, still muzzily surveying the people at the table, the wife who had not been deceived quite contentedly chatting, the two who belonged together occupying their magic worlds.

How lovely that nothing had been destroyed: Beatrice wanted to tell someone that, but there was no one to tell. In Rathgar Road her children would be watching the television, their father sitting with them. Her sister would die before the year was finished. What cruelty there seemed to be, and more sharply now she recalled the afternoon bedroom set to rights and her sister's wasted face. She wanted to run away, to go backwards into time so that she might shake her head at her lover on the night they'd first met.

Miss Doheny passed through the darkened town, a familiar figure on a Saturday night. It had been the same as always, sitting there, close to him, the smoke drifting from the cigarette that lolled between his fingers. The girl by now would be close in a different way to the man who was somebody else's husband also. As in a film, their clothes would be scattered about the room that had been hired for love, their murmurs would break a silence. Tears ran through Miss Doheny's meticulous make-up, as often they did when she walked away from the Paradise Lounge on a Saturday night. It was difficult sometimes not to weep when she thought about the easy times that had come about in her lifetime, mocking the agony of her stifled love.